"This is the series for anyone looking for their next Twilight or Hunger Games. Author Lynn Mullican nails it with a fantasy novel involving classic creatures and a gripping story! Not to be missed!" —Michael S. Fields, Author of Spirits of the Darkness/The Blackwood Conspiracy

"This is a genuine pleasure to read no matter what genre you generally prefer. At times it reminded me of the '30 Days of Night' series by Steve Niles with the intricacy of vampiric story telling. Nevertheless, Lynn has also managed to balance that with a heartfelt story of a family, reminiscent of the 'Ender's Game' series by Orson Scott Card or Tobe Hooper's 'Poltergeist'. That makes the action all the more deeply impactful in that the characters are people and not just plot devices. There are elements of mystery as well with the shrouded past of the main character. I usually pride myself in being able to figure out the ending about halfway through. I must confess, with this story, I was not able to, but I had so much fun reading it that I didn't mind and when it finally came to light, I was very pleased. The surprise at the end gave me chills and made me want to read more!"—Paul Loh, Author of The Greater Number

Bad Elements: Blood for Blood

Lynn Mullican

BAD ELEMENTS: BLOOD FOR BLOOD

ISBN: 098554712X
ISBN-13: 978-0-9855471-2-7

Published by
Cryptic Bones Publishing
Phoenix, AZ 85046

PRINTED IN THE UNITED STATES OF AMERICA

DEDICATION

I'd like to thank my family, who endured the disappearance of their wife, mother, and daughter. I spent many hours locked up and hidden away so I could write my novel. Thank you for your support, your love, and your frustration during this time!

To my husband, Patrick, thank you for taking care of the family while I was busy on my book. You're a fantastic husband, father, and cook! Thank you for being there when I needed you!

To my children, Cassandra, Bridget, and Joeseph, thank you for allowing dad to take care of all of your needs and wants while I was consumed with my book. Thank you for your encouragement and your understanding!

To my mother and my stepfather, Martha and Rich, thank you for your encouragement and for being there when I needed you. You have all been an inspiration to this novel!

Also by Lynn Mullican

BAD ELEMENTS: CRYSTAL DRAGON

SACRIFICIAL BLOOD

LATE NIGHT SURVEILLANCE

"Crystal, are you okay?" Warrant asked.

He stood before me, naked, his body muscular and well-defined. His leg muscles twitched. The werewolf who had been dominant in him had disappeared.

Warrant was in his early forties. He was five foot eleven. His slightly receding brown hair was cropped short. The massive claw marks from the werewolf fight he had been in had disappeared. They left only remnants of dried blood on his skin.

He grabbed my arm. It was scratched, bruised, and bloody from tonight's events.

"I didn't hurt you, did I?" he asked. A look of concern arose on his face.

Though it was genuine, I disregarded it. My mind was on my son, Robert.

"No, you didn't," I said.

I looked away.

"Who did this?" He touched the scratches on my face.

"Nobody. I just fell."

He forced my chin up and peered into my eyes.

"Looks like you're telling the truth." He let go of my chin and sat down next to me on the motel bed. He sighed.

It was past midnight, and all I could think about was my son, Robert. I was relieved and excited that he was alive. Yet, I was frustrated and disappointed that I didn't get a chance to tell him I loved him, and how happy I was to have found him after being held captive for almost five years.

Tonight was the first night I had seen him after all that time.

I had volunteered to fight in the underground fighting circuit to assist Agent Warrant and his peers in locating a rogue vampire. In return, they would go through the state agencies and police departments to help me find my son.

But when the arena turned into a battlefield for the vampires and werewolves, I escaped with the assistance of Warrant's friend, the invisible man. We fled into the forest where we were attacked. Then, we got split up.

Robert and his friend, Deputy Torrance had been at the fight, too. When the chaos erupted, they followed us out into the woods. That was where I found my son.

Had Robert recognized me? Is that why Deputy Torrance was acting funny? Did he know I was Robert's mother?

I couldn't make up the prior five years but tomorrow was a new day. My mission was to go back to the Sheriff's office and talk to Deputy Torrance about Robert.

As I thought about my son, my thoughts switched to Warrant's friend, who had saved me from the battle at the arena. I barely had a chance to say thank you before he darted off. I had hoped to learn his name but it didn't happen.

Warrant's hand brushed against my leg, bringing my thoughts back to him.

Warrant was my other hero: biker, secret agent, and werewolf all rolled into one.

We had gotten too close, which was a mistake. He was only in town for business. Once he found and captured his suspect, he would go home.

His mistake would cost him not just my life, but his, if he wasn't careful. My mistake would break my heart. So, I savored what little time I had with him.

I was lucky to have found him by the side of the road in Flagstaff, Arizona after escaping my captors. Due to his kind nature, he picked me up and allowed me to stay with him at the motel.

"Crystal, are you okay?"

"No," I said. Tears welled up in my eyes.

"Look at me," he said, firmly. He sat up.

Our eyes met.

Too much had happened tonight. First, there was the fight. Then my prior two kidnappers, Jace and Wayne, were at the arena. I never came face-to-face with Jace, but he had pitted me in the arena against Wayne. I still can't figure out why, but that alone told me there was more to this fighting circuit than what I knew. I had already heard about the hatred between the two species, but something else was amiss.

Then I discovered my son was in the midst of the vampire/werewolf war. Why was he there?

And, Warrant. The wounds he had suffered from the battle between him and another werewolf after our escape scared the shit out of me. I thought he was going to die.

I couldn't handle it. I broke down in tears.

"Crystal?" Warrant asked. His voice was soft.

"I'm fine. Don't worry about me." I turned away.

Warrant pulled my face back around to his.

"I'm sorry about tonight. I shouldn't have let you fight." He leaned in closer. "Please forgive me."

"It's not just that," I said. "It's everything." Tears melted down my face. "It's my son, you, me…"

"I told you not to get attached to me. This isn't good. Hell, even Tristan saw it on your face out there." He pointed toward the motel door. "He knew you were getting attached. And, dammit, so did I." He sighed. Then, he stood.

My heart hurt. I refrained from letting him know it, instead I shut my mouth and stared at him.

"If he can see it, so can everybody else," he said. Tears welled up in his eyes. "It will make both of us vulnerable to anybody who wants to hurt us. Remember that."

I nodded. "Who's Tristan?"

Was he the invisible man, my savior?

"He's one of us."

"One of the snipers? Bounty hunters?" I rubbed my eyes, trying to wipe away the tears.

He nodded. "Yes, but I shouldn't be telling you this. The less you know, the better you are."

"I won't say anything, I promise." The invisible man's blue eyes were still a memory. "Does he have blue eyes?"

Warrant looked at me. "Yes, why do you ask?"

"I just noticed them," I said.

His muscles tensed. "Really, Crystal?" He stood up. "What a hell of a thing to notice while you are under attack!"

I already hurt, physically, emotionally, and mentally. I didn't need any more shit tonight. Warrant's anger over noticing something such as eye color sent me over the edge.

"You know what?" I stood up, got in his face, and stuck my finger in his chest. "You can go fuck yourself, Warrant!" I snapped. "I've had enough shit tonight! I'm done!"

"His eyes stand out because I know him from somewhere!" I turned away. "He seems familiar."

Familiar, but another piece of my life I couldn't place. Was he someone I could trust? I bit my lip.

There had been a man with blue eyes in my prison cell. I remembered his eyes vividly. Was he the same man?

"Really? If that's the case, then where do you know him from?"

Considering he could make himself invisible, I was reluctant to say anything. I glanced about. Was he in the room? And, what the hell was that about anyway?

"I'm not sure." I spun on my heels and looked at Warrant. "Does he have anything to do with the underground fighting?"

Warrant sighed. "Why do you ask?" The frustration in his voice rose.

I took a step toward him. "Does he?"

An inquisitive look crossed his face. "Not that I'm aware of. What is your concern?"

I looked away. Was Tristan the same man who had been in my cell when Wayne originally kidnapped me? Was he the man who held me down while a doctor stitched me up on the prison bed? Had he been one of the kidnappers?

If he was the same man, he had not been like my other captors. At times he was rough, and other times, he was gentle.

"Dammit, Crystal, answer the fucking question?" His voice escalated. He threw his arms out. "What is your concern?"

"I'm afraid to say anything, because I don't know what's going on." I swallowed hard.

"Warrant? Who is he? He scares me, yet I feel safe with him. I don't understand. And, who the hell was that strange wolf in the forest?" I thought about Robert. Warrant did not know that I found him. "Do you know him?"

I decided to refrain from saying too much about my son so I changed the subject.

"I recognized the Deputy, but..."

His brow rose up. "You recognized the Deputy?" He put his hands on his hips.

"Yeah, he's the one I talked to yesterday. I think I might go to the Sheriff's office and talk to him, see if he knows anything."

"Hmm…well, to answer your question, no. I don't know who the other wolf was. Tristan and the others might, but I don't. My only mission is to find the man who's creating these hybrids."

"What has Tristan been sent to do? Do you know?"

"No, we don't ask and we don't tell. We're merely sent to complete our jobs unless it requires us to converse with one another."

"Can you find out?"

He glared at me. "No. It could put us in more danger, depending on what he's been sent to do."

"You two have worked together before though, right? At least, that's what I'm sensing."

"Yes, we have." He paced the floor.

"Is he a good person?"

He peered over his shoulder at me. "Yes, he is. He saved you from me, didn't he?"

I thought about this. "Yes, he did. Do you not like him?"

"No, I do. He's a good man. He always has been."

I detected some history between the two. He wouldn't elaborate though.

"Warrant?"

"Yes?" He glanced at me.

"How does he make himself invisible?"

"Why are you so interested in Tristan?"

I sensed a bit of jealousy in his voice.

"I think anybody would be interested in knowing that. Besides, I'm just trying to figure out where I know him from."

"It's a gift. He's always been able to do that."

"But not all vampires can make themselves invisible like Tristan can. Can they?"

"No, they can't. That's one of the reasons he has this job." Warrant sat down at the table opposite me.

"Oh."

"Some snipers and bounty hunters have gifts, and that's why they get elected to the positions they're in. That's his gift."

"What's yours?"

Our eyes met again.

A thin smile crept up my face.

He maintained his intent stare. "Detaching myself from others."

My smile waned.

"Except for you. You're one of a kind." The corner of his lip curled up.

My faint smile returned. He had put distance between us when he sat at the table. I stood and crossed the carpet to kneel at his side.

"So are you. I don't want you to go." I rested my hand on his leg.

"Crystal…" He shifted in his seat, crossing his legs.

I straightened up and kissed him. My tongue slid in his mouth.

He gently, but firmly, pushed me away.

"I'm sorry, Crystal. I can't." He pressed his fingers to my lips.

"Why not?" Tears welled up in my eyes. My heart was heavy. I knew our relationship wouldn't last.

"I can't do that to you, and I can't do it to myself. I've got to sever this before it goes any further."

"One last time." I moved in closer.

He put his hand on my chest and pushed me away. "I don't want to hurt you."

With that, he left to go take a shower.

I regretted that I had slept with him. We had a brief love affair, and that was it.

After changing into my pajamas, I walked over to the window that overlooked the parking lot. I peeked through the curtains.

The forest surrounded the asphalt. A male figure stood in the foliage of the trees. I recoiled. The curtain fell back in place. My heart beat faster. Was it Tristan? Was it my son? Who was it?

Inching open the curtain, I peeked through the glass again.

Blue eyes stared back at me. Then the man disappeared into the forest.

My mouth dropped. I backed away.

The bathroom door opened. The scent of the mountain spring soap drifted my way.

"Something wrong?" Warrant asked.

I didn't look at him. As a matter of fact, I didn't answer either. My silence was the response he needed. Before I had a chance to say anything, he was at my side, peering through the curtain.

"No, nothing's wrong," I lied, turning away.

"Lying really doesn't become you," he said.

I knew it was Tristan, but I couldn't figure out why he had followed me here.

§

Robert tried to keep from waking everybody, so he snuck into the downstairs bathroom in his home. He stripped out of his clothes and stepped into the shower. The wounds he had suffered during his battle with the other werewolf had already healed. All that remained was the blood, dirt, and mud from the fight and his mother's rescue.

After almost five years since her disappearance, he had finally found her. Their reunion had left him speechless. Robert wanted to hug her, and to let her know that she was the reason he became a Deputy. But, he didn't know if she intentionally ran away from her family or if something else had happened to her. Pain had shot through his heart. The thought of her purposely leaving him and his sister behind brought tears to his eyes. Either way, he was excited and scared at the same time.

The excitement was to see her again, to introduce her to the family he had, and to reunite her with his sister, Jennifer. But, he was also scared of the thought that her desertion was intentional, that she wanted nothing to do with her family anymore. If it was deliberate, he didn't know why.

Tonight's reunion with his mother ran through his head.

Once the fights in the audience broke out, the vampires and werewolves invaded the arena. My mother's safety had been compromised. Just as I had been ready to jump in the arena to save her, an invisible creature had snatched her up and rushed her out of the arena.

Deputy Torrance and I fled the building to pursue her. Once I made it outside and out of sight, I changed into my werewolf form. Since Torrance was mortal, I didn't want to leave him behind. So, I urged Torrance to ride on my canine back. It had been the only way we could follow her together.

When I had the opportunity to take the invisible creature down without killing my mother, I lunged for him. The impact had thrown her out of the invisible creature's grip, and Torrance from my back.

I had been thankful we landed in a clearing, but it wasn't enough to keep my mom from getting hurt. She struck her head on a rock. It bled. I regretted my actions. I was mortified.

Then, Torrance approached me.

"I'm sure she's fine. I'll go check on her." Torrance's cheek was swollen, and his arms were bleeding. He turned toward my mother.

She rubbed her head and groaned. She staggered to her feet, and glanced around before turning to face Deputy Torrance and I. I was still in werewolf form. With her hand on her head, she stopped.

Despite the invisible creature being nearby, I smiled at her.

She looked at me with a confused expression.

My smile was too apparent. So, I wiped it from my face. I deliberated on changing back to my human form so I could talk to her. I didn't know what to say, and I didn't know who or where the invisible creature was, so I refrained. Torrance would have to explain who we were.

Torrance sauntered over to her. The half moon cast shadows in the darkness and faint illuminations on their faces.

"Where's your friend?" Torrance asked, looking around.

"I don't know." She glanced around.

"What's his name?"

"I don't know," she answered, backing off.

I walked over.

"Okay. Well, then, who was that invisible creature?" Torrance asked.

"I don't know."

Torrance chuckled. "Do you always let strange men take you away in the night?"

"Not if I can help it," she answered. She glanced at me. "What do you want?"

We stopped, and so did she.

"We'd just like to introduce ourselves," Torrance answered.

"I already know who you are, Deputy Torrance. Just tell me who the hell he is and get to the point," she demanded.

Before Deputy Torrance had a chance to answer, a low noise erupted nearby. A dark gray haired werewolf appeared in the distance. A belt was looped around its neck. I sensed the other werewolf. I turned and glared at the creature.

The dark gray haired werewolf bared his teeth. He snarled.

I sneered and bared my teeth at the dark gray wolf. Tension filled the air. Torrance took a couple of steps back. The other werewolf drew closer.

We bared our teeth at one another. Once the fight began, my mom disappeared into the forest.

The other wolf and I snarled and leapt at each other, colliding in mid-air before we fell to the ground. Our claws struck one another, our mouths snapping. Growls and the gnashing of teeth echoed throughout the night.

Even though Torrance knew what direction she had disappeared in, he had lost sight of her. He continued to look for her, until a blond haired vampire rushed him.

Deputy Torrance turned, his gun in hand.

The blond vampire's head snapped back. The vampire leaned backwards in a horizontal dance-like pose. It wasn't a natural look for anybody. Blood rained down upon the blond vampire, the Deputy, and the invisible creature. The rain of blood spattered the invisible man, revealing a vague human shape. His face was indiscernible. He dropped the blond vampire's headless body to the ground.

Before Deputy Torrance had a chance to fire his gun, the invisible man ripped it from his grip and threw it to the ground. The invisible man's eyes changed to a midnight blue.

Still in my wolf form, I continued to fight the other werewolf. I was ready to break free from the fight to save my friend.

"Who are you?" the Deputy asked the invisible man. His voice echoed in the clearing.

The invisible vampire didn't answer, but stared at the Deputy as he advanced toward him.

Finally, my mother appeared in the battlefield, screaming. She tried to gain the attention of the other werewolf. I was on top of him, my mouth latched onto the back of Warrant's neck.

"No! Stop it! Don't kill him!" she yelled, waving her hands in the air.

That was when the blood-splattered invisible creature ran full force at her.

She turned to run.

The invisible man snatched her up again, and flew off in the night.

Robert washed the soap through his dark hair. The incident following his fight with the other werewolf ran through his head.

My mother's foot struck soft dirt. It gave way, tossing her down the side of a ravine. She crashed to the ground and hit her head on a rock in a small creek. Water splashed her face.

Moaning, she sat up and rubbed her head. She turned. I stood there in werewolf form, behind her. Her eyes widened.

I crept forward.

Then Torrance spoke up. "We apologize. He didn't mean to hurt you."

She gazed at me, her mouth agape, as if I were the one speaking. Then Torrance walked around me. When he did, she closed her mouth.

I would have changed back to my human form but I didn't know who else may be lurking in the darkness, especially the invisible man who had been with her.

"Are you okay?" Torrance asked, nearing her. He extended his hand.

"You? What the fuck do you want with me? Why do you keep following me?" She didn't take his hand. Instead, she stood, keeping her eyes on me.

"Look, I said we're sorry. He was trying to help you, not hurt you."

She stared at us.

"Why does he want to help me? And what the fuck do you want with me?"

She started to climb the ravine, her feet sliding in the dirt. With the way she was going, she was never going to make it up alone. I motioned to Torrance to climb on my back.

Then, I came up next to her, Torrance gripping my fur.

"Allow us to help you." He extended his hand to her. "It's much easier."

I nudged her butt to help her.

"What the hell? Get away from me." She tried to shoo me away, but lost her balance instead.

She toppled over backwards. I moved in fast. She fell against my shoulder.

"Really, just allow him to help you up the side." Torrance smiled down at her, his elbows resting on his knees.

"No, thank you." She attempted the climb again.

Instead of pressuring her anymore, I crossed her path and continued up to the top.

"You are a stubborn woman."

"Yeah, well, if you led the life I did, you'd understand."

Once her head was at the top of the ravine, she slipped in the mud. She fell back down.

As she slid, I threw Torrance from my back.

"Motherfucker..." Torrance said.

I ran beneath her. By God, she was a stubborn woman. But, that was my mother.

"Hey, asshole, you didn't have to drop me. Just give me a hint next time!"

I prodded her with my head. She hesitated. Then, she climbed on my back and allowed me to take her to the top. Torrance stood there, dirt and leaves all over his backside. She slipped off of me. In the distance, I heard another battle going on. She peered back into the forest from where she had come.

"Who are those men to you?" Torrance asked.

The look on her face was unsettling. *"Nobody."*

Deputy Torrance grunted in response.

"Why? What's it to you?" she asked.

"It's nothing to me, but something to him." He motioned towards me.

Again, I deliberated about changing back to my human self. There was a battle going on in the woods, and from her continuous glances back, I presumed it may involve the bloody invisible man. This might be my one opportunity to talk to her.

"What is his problem, anyway? He keeps looking at me funny."

Torrance chuckled. *"Maybe I should have him change into his human self. Maybe then you might recognize him."*

She turned to Torrance. *"So, tell him to change. I want to see his face. I want to know who we're talking about. I know it's not Wayne."*

I was thankful she had turned. It avoided the painful visual that came with the ugly transformation. Even though I was embarrassed of standing in front of my mother naked, I needed this one opportunity to talk to her, to tell her that I never gave up looking for her. Something deep down in my heart had told me she wasn't dead.

Once I had transformed, I spoke up. *"Who's Wayne?"*

I was in my early twenties, and almost six foot. I had dark hair with dark features similar to my mom's big brown eyes and short nose. I was lean and muscular, with wide shoulders.

She turned toward me. Her mouth dropped open.

Did she recognize me?

The werewolf from earlier stepped up behind her. Then, a partially invisible man appeared. Streaks of blood across his masculine body made him vaguely discernable. The invisible man latched on to my mom and took off with her.

"No, wait!" Her voice echoed in the night. It took one second for her to disappear.

The werewolf glanced at me, then ran off.

I transformed back into my werewolf form and motioned for Torrance to climb on.

As long as I knew she was alive, then I would find her again, one way or another.

The worst part was, Robert still didn't know why she had originally left. He had to find her, get her alone, and talk to her.

Despite the night's events, he smiled. He was eager to introduce her to his wife, Rebecca, and his children, Leah, Tisa, and Katie. Most importantly, he wanted to reacquaint her with his sixteen year old sister, Jennifer. She would have her mother again, something she desperately needed.

Jennifer had anxiety and blackout issues. She couldn't remember parts of her life, which included their mother and their father. Dad disappeared when they were young. Doctors prescribed her medication and psychiatric consultations. The doctors had come to the conclusion something traumatic had happened to Jennifer, maybe even Robert. It was enough to cause Robert and Jennifer to block out parts of their life from childhood to their teenage years, including time spent with their father.

After their mother disappeared, grandma moved them. Jennifer's issues only got worse. When Robert married Rebecca, their grandmother had all but given up on Jennifer. Robert hoped Jennifer would feel better living with him, but things still weren't the same. She had been real close with mom before mom's disappearance.

Despite the loss and the move, the small city atmosphere was a good change of pace for Jennifer. Munds Park wasn't as hectic as Phoenix, so it gave her time to mourn, to become one with the surrounding forest, nature, and Robert's kids. The family decided to stay in Munds Park. With time, she got more involved in school events, and eventually got a job.

Robert rebuilt their mother's 1965 Mustang for Jennifer. He figured having mom's car would do Jennifer some good, more so on an emotional level.

Robert stepped out of the shower and grabbed a towel. As he dried himself off, something bumped against the door. He put some clean clothes on and opened the door. Jennifer leaned back against the staircase, her arms folded across her chest. Her tired brown eyes gazed up at him.

Her short dark hair was disheveled. Some of the hairsprayed pieces either stood up on end, or stuck out to the side. She looked just like mom and even stood at the same height of five foot three, except that she was twenty to thirty pounds heavier.

Jennifer's pajamas consisted of black sweatpants and an Avenged Sevenfold concert t-shirt. She picked at her t-shirt, pulling it away from her body. She rubbed her eyes.

"What are you doing up?" he asked.

"You woke me up," she said, looking him over.

"Oh, sorry. I didn't mean to."

She scratched her head. "Why are you taking a shower now?"

"I couldn't sleep, so I thought I would take one down here. I didn't want to wake Rebecca and the girls." He leaned against the door frame.

"Bullshit. You haven't been home all night." She folded her arms across her chest again. "Are you cheating on Rebecca?"

"Cute, Jennifer," he said, rolling his eyes.

"Why the hell else would you be taking a shower at three forty-five in the morning?"

He didn't need to answer to her, regardless if he had a valid excuse or not.

"Sis…?"

"Can I get in the bathroom?"

As he moved out of her way, she squeezed in and shut the door behind her. He leaned against the staircase and waited for her to come out.

When the door opened, he looked up at her.

Their eyes met.

He stuck his hands in his pockets.

She leaned against the door.

"What's up with you, anyway?" Her eyes narrowed in on him. "Have you been fucking some chick in the woods or something?"

"Watch your language, Jennifer," he said sternly.

"Why? The kids are asleep. It's just you and me." She leaned her head against the door.

"Just act like a lady, please."

She rolled her eyes. "Honestly, what's up? You got dirt and leaves all over the floor."

He glanced past her at the mess he left in the bathroom.

"I was on an investigative lead."

"Bullshit."

"Jennifer, watch…"

"No, Robert. You were not on an investigative lead, you were out fucking—oh excuse me—screwing around, weren't you?" she said with an accusatory tone.

He cocked his head.

"Just what in the hell gives you that idea?" He threw his hands up. "Does that look like I've been screwing around?" He pointed towards the bathroom. The pitch in his voice deepened. "And, how would you know the difference between cheating and an investigative lead?"

Jennifer leaned forward. "This is Munds Park. It's a small town," she said, pointing her finger toward the floor. "You couldn't have been on an investigative lead at this time. Besides, I know you weren't working yesterday. It was your day off."

He approached her.

"Jennifer, I was on a lead," he said. "Unfortunately, it was on my day off, but I was on a lead. Now, would you stop with the bullshit?"

"Robert, watch your language." The grim line on her face erupted into a faint smile. "It's nice to see you human once in awhile."

He shook his head. "You're a bitch sometimes."

"Yeah, well, you're an asshole sometimes."

They laughed at one another. Then, Jennifer stopped, her face turning serious again.

"Robert, I ran into Torrance the other day."

"Yeah?" His curiosity was aroused.

"He said you were looking for a missing woman and showed me a picture of her."

His brow rose up. "A missing woman?"

"Yeah, brunette, long hair, real pretty."

He stared at her. The Deputy in him became inquisitive.

"Did you recognize the woman?" he asked.

"No, I didn't."

He frowned.

"The picture was kind of crumpled up. It looked older, too. He didn't say who she was, but I think I may have given her a ride to a restaurant the other day."

Robert's throat tightened. "Did you get her name?"

"Yeah, it was Brandy."

"Where did you give her a ride?"

"Off Mormon Lake Road, not to far from work. She said she was going to meet someone at the restaurant on the corner. After I dropped her off, I drove around the corner and watched her…"

"What? Why?" he asked, upset that she would do such a thing.

"I…I, uh, well, she kind of looked like mom," Jennifer said. She shrugged and her eyes welled up.

He sighed. He wanted to tell her that he found their mother, but he didn't want to say anything until he could talk to mom. He didn't want to get Jennifer's hopes up and then crush them. For all he knew, mom might have deliberately vanished. Until he knew the reason why, he didn't want to say anything to Jennifer.

Since Jennifer couldn't remember much about mom, this situation could go either way. It could be the best thing that ever happened to Jennifer and Brandy. Their family had been close. After mom disappeared, Jennifer's visits to the psychiatrist increased. Robert even signed up for some counseling sessions to deal with their mother's absence.

This reunion could re-establish their relationship. Or, it may be best that Robert keep his mouth shut. It all came down to the reason why their mother had vanished.

"I guess in a way I was hoping it was mom," she said, looking down. Tears fell down her cheeks. She wiped them away.

"I miss mom." Her voice cracked. "It's like something is missing, like parts of my life have been ripped away. I remember pieces of it, mostly when I was young. But, then as I grew up, I can't remember half of it. I vaguely remember what she looks like. If I seen her on the street, I wouldn't recognize her. It's almost like that disease. Oh, what the hell do you call it?" She scratched her head.

"Alzheimer's?" he asked.

"Yeah, that's it. Do you know what I mean?"

"Yeah, I know what you mean."

Robert wrapped his arms around his sister and held her tight.

"Why can't I remember her like you do?" She clutched his shirt and smothered her face in his shoulder.

"I don't know, sis." He swallowed hard.

"You remember more of our life with her, though." She pulled away and looked at him.

"Why? Why can't I?"

The sorrow on her face broke his heart.

"I don't know. Maybe whatever trauma that's holding some of our memories back hurt you more than me? I have no clue. I'm not even sure what the hell happened to wipe out some of our memories, including those with dad."

Robert needed to talk to mom. The more time he spent consoling his sister, the more time he lost finding their mother—and the answers he desperately needed.

He grabbed Jennifer by her shoulders and looked her in the eyes.

"Listen, sis, I know this is difficult for you, and I really don't want to sound like an asshole, but this investigation is very important."

Jennifer looked up at him, her eyes red and bloodshot from crying. Her nose reminded him of Rudolph the Red-Nosed Reindeer. It was pitiful. It made him want to cry.

"Do you remember anything else?"

"Yeah, I'm sorry I followed her." A knot had formed in her throat, making it difficult to swallow.

"Don't worry about it. I just need to know what you saw."

"Okay," she nodded. "Um, yeah, some guy picked her up on a Harley and took her to a motel."

"Would you remember that Harley if you saw it again?" he asked.

"Yeah."

"And the motel…" Despite Robert being upset with Jennifer following their mother, he was excited to hear that she had found a location for mom.

"Yeah, I can drive you there…" She wiped more tears off of her cheeks.

"Good, let's go," he said.

"What? Right now? Can't it wait until tomorrow? I'm supposed to be at school in a few hours." She glanced at the wall clock.

"I don't care. I'll write you a frigging note if you need it. This is important. Get dressed," he demanded.

"Are you serious?" she asked, rolling her eyes.

"Yes, I'm serious. Get your ass in gear." With that, Robert walked into the bathroom and shut the door behind him.

"Damn you, Robert," she said.

"Get dressed," he hollered through the door.

§

Twenty minutes later, Robert drove his truck into the motel parking lot. He followed the paved road around to the back of the beige, two story motel. The woods surrounded the back of the parking lot. A car, a truck, and two Harleys were parked near the motel.

Jennifer spotted the jet black bike.

"That's it. That's the bike," she said, pointing to it.

"Did you see what room she went to?"

"No, I didn't stick around to see. I admit I'm a little weird sometimes, but I'm not a creeper."

"That's okay. I'm your brother. I can forgive you," he said, looking at the motel.

Frowning, Jennifer flipped him off.

"She's probably in one of those rooms right there because they're closest to the bike," he said. "It's a nice bike, so I'm going to say whoever owns it wants to keep an eye on it."

Jennifer glanced around the parking lot.

"He wouldn't want it to get stolen," he said.

Then, he opened the truck door.

Jennifer spun around, eyes wide. "Robert, what are you doing?"

"I'm just going to take a look," he said, casually.

"Are you nuts?" she asked. Her voice escalated. Eyes wide, she glanced at the motel, and then the parking lot.

"No, I'm just a Deputy. Hand me my gun."

She pulled his gun out of the glove box and gave it to him.

"You're crazy, Robert. People are going to think you're a creeper if you're walking around in the dark with a gun."

"Well, that's not all I'm doing," he said, checking the gun's chamber.

"What?" Jennifer stared at him.

Robert strapped his gun on his hip and straightened up.

"See those windows right there?" He pointed to a section of the motel.

"Yeah?" she asked. "Oh, no you're not!"

"Oh, yes, I am."

"Oh, that's worse! They're going to think you're a perv."

"I'm just doing my job."

"But, why?" She leaned closer to the driver's side. "Robert?"

He shut the door behind him, careful not to make much noise, and left, leaving her alone in the car.

"What the hell is going on?" she whispered.

He walked along the side of the motel, his hand resting on his gun. He neared the windows he was headed for. All he wanted to do was find her. If casually glancing in the window would take him one step further to locating her, then so be it.

He peered around the parking lot. For a fleeting moment, he met his sister's eyes. He cast one last glance back at the Harley. The incident he and Torrance had been in earlier drifted into his mind. He hoped there wouldn't be another confrontation.

But, if something did happen, at least Jennifer knew where his rifle was—strapped just below the front seat, fully loaded. Wrapped around the stock was a pouch full of additional ammo. And, next to the rifle was another pouch of ammo.

Robert had made sure she knew how to shoot a gun, and he felt some relief knowing that she could take care of herself. At the same time, he was still concerned. He despised the fact that he had to bring her here, but without her, he wouldn't have known where to find mom.

As he neared the first window, he turned his full attention back to the motel. The blinds were partially open. He stopped short of it and peered inside. A blonde woman walked into the bathroom. Nobody else was in the room with her, so he continued on to the next window. The blinds were ajar. A couple lay asleep in bed. The woman was a little bigger than mom. Robert moved on.

He glanced at the truck. Jennifer shook her head at him. He turned and peeked in through the partially closed curtain. A couple lay back-to-back in bed. Robert studied her face. It was his mother.

§

Jennifer was nervous. Even though it was cold out, she was sweating. She wiped her wet palms on her jeans, and gazed out at the driver's side view mirror. Nothing. Then she looked out at her side view mirror. Nothing. Wait! Yes, something was there. Her eyes widened. She took a deep breath and held it. She could vaguely discern a red streaked human figure yet she could see right through it.

The invisible human form came from the rear and neared the truck bed. She glanced down at the doors. They were locked. Scared, she lowered herself to the floorboard and pulled her cell phone out of her pocket. She held the phone low so that it wouldn't illuminate the inside of the truck.

Eyes wide, she glanced up. She was barely able to discern the crimson color on its body. She pressed the button to call her brother.

The invisible form moved away from the door.

She pressed the phone to her ear. "Come on, come on."

The phone rang five or six times before Robert's voicemail picked up.

"Shit." She hit the END button. She slowly rose up on knees and looked out of the window. The invisible entity advanced on her brother.

"Fuck." She pressed the REDIAL button. The phone rang one, two, three times.

Her heart beat faster. "Turn around, Robert. Turn the fuck around."

§

Robert stood with his back to the truck. He glanced at the room number, and then back at his sleeping mother. Something from his childhood drifted into his memory.

At the age of five, Robert lay in bed. His bedroom door opened, and in walked his mom. The carpeted floor masked the sound of her crossing the room. He closed his eyes and pretended to be asleep.

"Hmm, are you asleep, sweetie?" she whispered.

He didn't answer. Instead, he enjoyed her hand brushing his dark hair. She caressed his back.

"Love you, Bobby." She leaned in and placed a gentle kiss on his head.

He smiled.

His mom giggled. "I didn't think you were asleep."

His eyelids fluttered. She smiled down at him. He squeezed his eyes shut. She giggled again.

"Get some sleep, Bobby."

Wasn't that the way it was supposed to be? The mother watching her son sleep. Not the other way around.

At this point, he wasn't sure what to do. He could make up an excuse to get them out of bed so he could talk to her, but he wasn't really sure that was the answer.

He glanced back.

Jennifer jumped out of the truck.

"Robert! Behind you!"

It was too late.

Just as he turned around, the scent of blood was upon him. Something invisible threw him backwards into the motel. The impact put a dent in the wall. The invisible entity grabbed him and threw him forwards into the parking lot. Robert hit the ground, flipping twice.

"No!" Jennifer screamed.

"Fuck," he mumbled. Dizzy, he stood up. Before he had a chance to react, it was upon him again.

Jennifer came barreling at them from out of nowhere.

The invisible entity grabbed him again, and threw him up and over a truck. Robert struck the asphalt.

Her human body began the transformation into a werewolf. She cried out in pain.

Robert jumped to his feet and turned toward his sister.

Her muscles and bones enlarged, taking on the look of a canine.

"No!" Robert screamed. His mouth dropped open.

He had no idea she carried the same disease. He dreaded her becoming a werewolf. It was a horrible and life altering experience.

He turned to face the invisible entity.

In full werewolf form, Jennifer lunged at the invisible blood-streaked creature. Together, she and the invisible entity toppled over one another. The moment she pinned it to the ground, it slashed at her. She yelped. Blood dripped from her face.

Robert grabbed onto her neck fur. He wouldn't let anything happen to her. She struggled against him.

Behind them, a door opened.

The invisible entity moved toward the open door.

His mother and the man, with whom she shared a room, stood in the doorway.

Mom stared at the two of them, her mouth agape.

Jennifer reared up on her haunches, her jaws snapping at anything that moved. She didn't know how to control her aggressive alter ego.

His mother recoiled back into the room.

Robert was sure she was leery of Jennifer.

Jennifer whipped her head back and forth, snarling, trying to escape Robert's hold on her. He tightened his grip on her.

The man in the room took a step toward them.

His mother put her hand on his shoulder. "No, don't. It's…"

The blood-streaked entity grabbed Robert's mom and whisked her away into the forest.

Her screams faded into the distance.

The man in the room snapped, "Who the fuck…"

Robert ignored him. "Jennifer, we need to follow her. Just forget about him."

Jennifer snapped at Robert's arm. He narrowly dodged her mouth.

"Who are you?" the man demanded. He stared at Robert.

Robert didn't listen to him. "Jennifer, we need to go, now!"

She gazed into the forest where mom had disappeared.

Robert let go of her.

"Come on." He ran towards the forest with Jennifer in pursuit.

By the time Robert and Jennifer entered the forest, a strong wind had picked up. Robert looked back over his shoulder. Behind them, four haggard, long haired male vampires had emerged from the forest on the other side of the parking lot. They must have heard the commotion and come to feed.

Robert glanced at the motel door. It was shut but it didn't matter. Two of the vampires kicked in the motel door. The other two ran around the other side of the building after Warrant.

Robert turned. Jennifer stood next to him. He was grateful that she listened to him. It most likely saved their lives.

She peered back at the parking lot and whimpered.

"They don't look like friends, do they?"

She looked up at him.

"Did you see which direction she went in?" he asked. He looked around.

She lowered her head.

"Well, either way, we need to get out of here. Those vampires look like trouble. I can come back for my truck in a little while." He waved his hand for her to follow him. "Come on."

THE ESCAPE

After Warrant shut the motel door, he took off on foot to follow us. Once Tristan and I were out of sight, we stopped not to far from the motel. A gust of cold wind brushed against us.

We glanced back at Warrant, who had run around the back of the motel. Four male vampires slinked through the dark parking lot and up to the motel door. Two charged the door. The other two rounded the side of the motel. They jumped Warrant as he was running away.

I opened my mouth to scream. Tristan clamped it shut. Tears leaked from my eyes.

Their long fingernails slashed across Warrant's chest and throat.

Warrant's fist connected with one man's face. His jawbone expanded to form the skeletal werewolf head. He snapped at them.

They fought to gain control. One succeeded in pinning him down while the other slashed at his neck again. Blood sprayed everywhere.

A horrendous noise escaped Warrant's lips. Then, his body jerked violently beneath the vampire.

My heart lurched into my throat. I clutched at Tristan's hands to remove them from my mouth but he was much stronger than me.

"Shush," he whispered in my ear. "They'll kill you."

My eyes widened.

As Warrant's body fell limp, the long blond-haired vampire buried his fangs in Warrant's neck and fed. Once the vampire was done feeding, he kicked Warrant down the small hill behind the motel.

Warrant tumbled down, hitting his head on several rocks before coming to rest at the bottom.

Tristan kept his hand over my mouth.

The vampires scanned the area. A whistle captured their attention. It was one of the vampires who had gone to the motel room. He waved them over to the building. The vampires who had attacked Warrant left him to join the others at the motel.

Warrant lay motionless.

I couldn't swallow. The gut instinct to rip them apart overcame me. Warrant was the only friend I had.

They glanced around, as if looking for Tristan and I. I held my breath. A minute went by before they backed off and disappeared into the woods.

A couple of minutes went by before Tristan stepped out of the wooded area. He kept me behind him as we made our way down to Warrant. Blood pumped vigorously out of Warrant's neck. A large pool of blood surrounded him.

I fell to my knees beside him, my hands over my mouth. Tears overwhelmed me. I couldn't breathe. The only friend I had was dying, and I couldn't do a damn thing about it.

"No, Warrant, no." I latched on to his shirt. "You can't leave me."

I buried my face against him. Blood stained my face and chest.

Then Warrant touched me. I jumped.

"Oh, God, Warrant! Heal yourself. I know you can do it. You've done it before." I looked up at Tristan as if to get him to back me up.

Tristan said nothing. He knelt down.

Warrant weakly seized me. He unfolded my hand and then placed a small item in the middle of my palm. It was cold and hard.

"Warrant…" I looked down at my hand. It was the key to his motorcycle.

"I can't." The second I looked down at him, he was dead. "Oh, God, no." I grabbed my mouth again.

"We need to go," Tristan said.

"No, I can't. I need…"

Something rustled nearby. We glanced up at the brush. Was somebody watching us?

"We need to go, now." Tristan grabbed my arm.

Another rustle. We stood. The four male vampires were coming from the rear of us. They had circled around from the direction Tristan and I had originally run toward, the woods. Shit!

Tristan rushed me over to Warrant's Harley. The leather seat gave way beneath his weight. He grabbed my forearm, prompting me to get on the bike. I climbed on and wrapped my arms around him.

Footsteps neared the top of the hill behind the motel.

I glanced back, and then around at the woods. Where had Robert gone? He had disappeared rather quickly. I hoped he didn't run into this group of renegade vampires.

The bike roared to life. I wrapped my fists in Tristan's shirt and held on tight. I buried my face against the back of his leather jacket.

I locked my arms around his waist, nesting my hands upon his lower abdomen. The cold air and the coolness of his body lowered my body temperature. My teeth chattered. The wind dried my tears and the blood on my body.

I lay against him, wondering why Warrant's peers from the U.G.S.S. hadn't shown up. They were supposed to protect us but they had not. Only Tristan showed up to help. Why? What happened to them? Dread overwhelmed me.

As we rode, Tristan's body gradually became visible. He wore no helmet and no goggles. His dark, wavy hair was trimmed well above his neck.

I tried to get a good look at his face but it was impossible on the bike. So, I decided small conversation would be best. Since I wasn't suppose to know his name, I played stupid.

"Hey, what's your name?" I yelled.

He remained silent.

Did he even hear me?

"Hey, what's your name?" I yelled again.

"Don't worry about it!" he answered.

So, he was a bit of an asshole, too.

"Well, I figured since you're Warrant's friend, I should know your name!"

The motorcycle engine was my only answer.

"He seems to trust you with me!"

Tristan remained silent.

I sighed. "Where are you taking me?"

Again, he didn't answer. As we rode across the rocky terrain, I slid backwards on the motorcycle. I was going to fall off. My grip on him tightened.

"You might want to wrap your legs around me. We're going to go up a mountain, and I don't want to lose you!"

Good idea. I followed his advice. "You're really cold!"

"I've always been that way!"

Didn't Warrant say that, too?

"Hold on!" he yelled.

I clutched on to him.

The mountain was steep. We were not going to make it. I glanced back, afraid that the vampires would be upon us soon. But they were nowhere to be seen.

We ascended the steep, rocky mountain. I leaned forward into him. My butt slid on the seat, threatening to throw me off of the bike. I closed my eyes. The wind whistled past us. My hair whipped around my face.

Once we reached the top, the bike leveled out. Dirt and rocks flew behind us. They echoed in the night. The bike abruptly took off at high speed. We were only a few feet from the edge when something from behind grabbed me. I screamed. It tore me off of the bike.

Tristan crashed to the ground.

Dirt filled my mouth. The creature behind me growled. I froze, afraid to turn my head.

Trembling, I stared at Tristan's boots, afraid to move.

Tristan made himself invisible. The werewolf lunged at him. It crashed on top of the motorcycle.

For fear of getting attacked or falling backwards off of the top of the mountain, I lay low. I looked around for an escape route. To my left, the mountain formed a wall. I couldn't run in that direction. Then, I glanced to my right. The werewolf regained his footing. I had nowhere to go.

Just as Tristan pulled me to my feet, the werewolf turned and attacked us. Tristan pushed me to the side. I fell to the ground.

He fell over backwards with the werewolf on top of him. Branches broke off the nearby trees and brush. Tristan and the werewolf slid across the ground and over the mountain edge.

I threw my arms over my head to keep from getting struck by the falling debris as the branch whipped by.

Once Tristan and the werewolf hit the cliff bottom, a battle ensued. Growls and snarls filled the night.

I scrambled to my feet. I thought twice about looking over the edge to see if Tristan was alright but decided against it. Instead, I ran to the motorcycle.

A long wail echoed from below. Then there was silence.

I stopped, turned my head, and looked around. The silence made me nervous. Animals had a tendency to remain quiet when vampires and werewolves were around, unless of course the vampires and werewolves were too close.

Goosebumps from the cold air erupted from my skin. I glanced back at the mountain edge. It was time to get out of here.

I stepped back. My foot struck the back end of the motorcycle. I lost my balance, and over-corrected my footing. I spun completely around, and over the bike. My head bounced off of the handlebar and into a boulder. It was enough to knock me out.

FAMILY

The sun beamed through the kitchen window, casting a spotlight for the long, white curtains to dance in the cold wind. Shadows encompassed most of the room, except for the area where Robert and his family sat at the kitchen table.

"Mama, it's cold," Leah said. She rubbed her hands over her body, trying to warm up.

"Yeah, I'm freezing," Katie agreed, shivering.

"I'll take care of the window in just a second, ladies. Mama's getting the biscuits," Rebecca said.

"Mm, biscuits!" Tisa screamed.

Rebecca's black hair, braided into strands, fell in front of her face as she tossed warm biscuits into a bowl. She hummed a tune, and glided past the stove, bowl in hand. As elegant as a ballerina, she danced her tall, curvaceous, dark skinned figure over to the table.

"I'll get the window," Robert said. He turned in his seat.

Rebecca appeared in front of him. She set the bowl on the table.

"I'm already up. I'll get it," she said.

Rebecca strode over to the window and slid it shut. The curtains fell back in place. She walked over to the table and sat down with her family. Though the adults ate in silence, the children did not.

Tisa, Katie, and Leah talked amongst themselves and giggled. The girls were still dressed in their pajamas, and their dark afro hair was a mess.

Tisa, the two year-old, grabbed a biscuit and broke it in half. She went to grab the butter knife.

Rebecca snatched it before Tisa could grab it.

"I don't think so, Tisa," she said.

Rebecca buttered the biscuit.

While she tended to Tisa, the other two girls, Leah and Katie—three and four years old, respectively—kept talking.

To the right of Rebecca, Robert and Jennifer exchanged glances. When Rebecca caught them, they looked away.

Rebecca motioned with the hand holding the knife. "No, you know better."

Tisa folded her arms across her chest. She huffed. A frown had replaced the cherub smile. Her lip quivered.

Again, Robert and Jennifer looked at one another.

"Girls, stop talking and eat," Rebecca said. As she turned her head, her braids swung about.

"But, mama…" Katie said.

"Eat your food." She turned to face Robert and Jennifer. "And, what is going on with you two?" The suspicious looks between the two of them annoyed her, as if they knew something that she didn't.

Robert peered up at her. "What?"

"You know what." She turned to Jennifer. "Well?"

"What?" Jennifer's wide eyes stared at her.

It was obvious that her husband and sister-in-law were hiding something.

"Robert, what is going on?" she asked with a stern voice.

"Nothing," he answered. "Why do you ask?"

"Because something is up. I woke up a couple of times last night, and you weren't in bed. Then, I got up and found out you weren't home. And, why aren't you answering my question?"

Robert stared at her with a dumbfounded look on his face.

She turned to Jennifer. Her voice rose. "And, miss, you're in on this, and how I don't know."

Jennifer stood up. "I wish I could help you with that question but I have to go."

Rebecca stared at her. "Yeah, you do that." She slammed her hands on the table. Her utensils clanked against the plate. "You're already late for school."

"I think I know that." Jennifer faked a smile. She picked up her dishes, took them to the sink, and rinsed them off.

"I'll see you later," Jennifer said. She left the kitchen and grabbed her backpack.

Robert followed Jennifer out of the kitchen.

Rebecca remained in her seat and glared at them.

As they walked into the living room, he handed his sister a note for school. She opened the door. The fresh scent of pine slipped into the house. He turned toward Rebecca. Jennifer remained in the doorway, the door open. Her hair hung in her face. He turned back to his wife.

"Rebecca…"

Robert glanced back at Jennifer. She hadn't moved. A new scent drifted in to the house. He rushed over to the door.

Jennifer stood on the porch, staring to the left of the doorway. Her mouth hung open, and her eyes wide.

"What's going on?" Rebecca yelled from inside.

Robert blocked the entryway. He stared at the redwood porch swing where his mother lie. She was swathed in blankets, and her head was bandaged. His jaw dropped.

"Mom?"

Jennifer's mouth dropped open. She clasped her hand over her mouth.

Rebecca rushed over to him and pushed him out of the way to get outside. She turned to look at his mother.

"Oh, my God…?" She looked at him.

Robert stared down at his mom. Tears ran down his cheeks.

Was she okay? What happened to her? She didn't have a bandage on her head when he saw her last. Had she escaped the men who fought over her? Or did they bring her to him? And, if that was the case, where were they?

Rebecca brushed past him. "Brandy, can you hear me?" She gently lifted his mom's hand.

He surveyed what he could see of the property. There didn't seem to be anybody else around.

Rebecca placed her hand on his mother's forehead. She turned to him.

"She's alive."

Robert and his sister let out a sigh of relief.

"Do we need to take her to the hospital?" Jennifer asked.

"If we need to take her, we will. Let's get her in the house first so I can look her over."

§

Voices awoke me from a deep sleep. I rubbed my temple. The pain in my head throbbed. I groaned. My vision was blurry, but I made out the distinct shape of a small person.

I rubbed my eyes. My vision cleared a little bit. It was a little girl. She stood before me, staring at me. I recoiled. The last person I expected to be in my face was a child, and much less to be in somebody's living room.

"What…Where am I?" I looked at the people sitting in the chairs around the room.

The little girl was wide-eyed.

"Tisa, it's not polite to stare," the dark-colored woman said. She pulled the child into her arms.

The man who sat on the coffee table turned to look at me. My vision was still hazy.

"Do I know you from somewhere?" I asked. My temple was throbbing.

He smiled at me. "Yes, I think you do."

I rubbed my eyes again. My vision cleared a little bit more. I was staring right at my son. Oh, shit! I shot up to a sitting position. Pain rippled through my body. It stopped me from moving any more. I groaned again.

"Don't move so fast," he said. "You have a head wound. It doesn't look too bad, but you want to be careful."

I gazed up at him. He was at the fight last night. He was the fan who seemed grief stricken by what was happening.

"You're…" I began.

"Deputy," he interrupted. "I'm the Deputy you saw the other night."

"No, that was somebody else." My mind drifted to the meeting with him and the Deputy in the forest.

"You're…" My son, I thought.

Something about the way he was responding to me, told me I should say something else. I glanced at the dark-colored woman to his right, who held the child. The two other children resembled Robert, and their—mother?

My heart skipped a beat. They were my grand-children. The woman was his wife. And, the teenager was…?

The doctor handed my husband a child—a newborn girl.

Their father kissed her on the forehead and cradled her for a moment. Then he placed her in my arms.

"Look, honey, Jennifer's beautiful, just like you."

She looked up into my eyes, and I swore she smiled right at me. I smiled.

Jennifer? She was my daughter.

My heart skipped another beat. Butterflies rippled through my stomach. I was nauseous and nervous. I didn't know what to say or do.

Then, my thoughts switched back to him. What had he said? Oh, yes, he was talking about the meeting in the forest. What didn't he want them to know?

Think, Crystal, think.

"Uh, yes, I think I remember you," I said. I glanced at Jennifer. Oh, shit! She was the teenager in the Mustang. "I remember you, too."

Jennifer smiled.

"How the hell…" Rebecca began. She looked at Jennifer before turning to Robert.

"Is this a family reunion, and I'm the last one to know about it?" Rebecca asked.

"No, I, uh, gave her a ride the other day," Jennifer said. "I didn't know it was mom."

And, there it was, out in the open. It was confirmed. I was mom, and they were my children.

"You did what…?" Rebecca started. "Girl, you didn't know it was your mom and you gave her a ride. Didn't your mother ever teach you…?" Then she shut up.

We exchanged glances.

"Sorry," Rebecca said.

"Welcome home, Mom," Robert said. He opened his arms, as if unsure whether to hug me or not.

I accepted his embrace. Tears erupted from my eyes.

"It's been a long time, Mom," he said.

Jennifer sat next to him on the coffee table.

I still didn't know what to say. Instead, I held tightly onto him. Was he truly my son? Had I honestly found him after all of this time? And, how the hell did I get here?

I pulled back.

"Okay, um…" I began. I wiped tears away. "Can you just verify a couple of things for me? I would appreciate it."

"Uh, yeah, sure." A perplexed look replaced his smile. He was just as confused as I was.

He glanced at Jennifer. Tears ran down her cheeks. The corners of her lips quivered.

Pain settled in my chest. My heart ached.

Robert looked me in the eye. "What do you want to know?" he asked. His eyes brimmed up with tears.

"Um, anything, your name, your date of birth, something like that," I said.

"Okay, well, my name is Robert Drake Bouchard. I was born June twentieth, nineteen eighty-nine."

I swallowed hard. He was my son.

Robert continued, "Your name is Brandy Crystal Bouchard."

I smiled. Yes, my name was Brandy Crystal Bouchard. Now, if only I could remember more. What else did Robert know?

"What happened to your father?" I asked.

He swallowed hard. "Your husband, our father, was killed in a bar in Payson. You disappeared for five years, and I've been looking for you ever since."

My gaze shifted from one person to the other. I couldn't breathe.

"Oh, God," I said. Tears spilled down my face. I buried my face in my hands.

They were my children.

Jennifer burst out crying. "Mom, what's happened to you?"

I couldn't answer her. Instead, I tried to wipe away my tears. Jennifer wrapped her arms around me, and I clung to her.

My kidnappers never mentioned Jennifer. Why? Why did they not mention her? I wished I could remember every facet of my life but it was next to impossible.

"My God, Robert, I'm so sorry," I said.

I pulled away from my daughter, cradling her face in my hands.

"They never said anything about you. I'm so sorry," I said, kissing her on the forehead.

I hugged my children. I never wanted to let them go.

"Who didn't mention Jennifer?" Robert asked, pulling back. He was puzzled.

"Are you alright? How is your head doing?" he asked.

Rebecca gave me a bewildered look.

I didn't give a shit about my head right now. All I could think about was why my kidnapper, Wayne, had lied to me. They had never kidnapped Robert. And why did he not mention Jennifer?

Robert eyes questioned mine. I refrained from answering him, at least for now. They didn't need to know everything. Besides there were children in the room. Yes, the children, and the woman. We needed introductions.

I turned toward the woman, who in turn, looked at me. Robert and I glanced at each other. As if understanding that I didn't want to talk about it, he turned his attention to her.

Robert smiled. "Mom, this is my wife, Rebecca. Rebecca, meet my mom."

"Nice to meet you," I said, smiling.

Rebecca's lip trembled. Tears erupted. She hid her mouth behind her hand.

I could tell from the expression on her face, she thought he would never find me.

"It's nice to finally meet you, too," she said.

She moved from the recliner and over to the sofa, next to me. She wrapped her long arms around me.

I hugged her back.

"Robert never gave up hope that he would find you," Rebecca said, pulling away. "Robert and Jennifer love you very much. Your disappearance has put them through some emotional trauma, as well as I."

"Honey…" Robert started.

"No, Robert," she said, looking at him. "Your mother needs to know what you two have been through."

Rebecca and I looked at one another.

"I know it's going to be difficult for you," I said. Tears flowed down my cheeks.

"But this is also going to be difficult for me. I've been through some hard times, and honestly, I don't know what I can say or do right now to make it up to anyone."

Everyone tried to comfort me. Rebecca enclosed her hands around mine, Jennifer hugged my shoulders, and Robert touched my arm.

"Brandy…" Rebecca started.

"It's going to be okay, Mom. We're here," Jennifer said.

"Yeah, we're here," a tiny voice said.

I glanced at the little girl who stood before me.

We laughed.

The child's voice lifted my mood. I glanced up at the three girls who squeezed in next to us.

"And who are these gorgeous children?"

"These are your grand-daughters. Girls, this is your grandma, my mom," Robert said.

My God, time had passed and I had missed plenty. The lump in my throat hardened. I was so out of touch with life—so much. It hit me hard. A waterfall of tears flowed down my cheeks.

"They're gorgeous." I stared at the little one who had already lifted my spirits.

"This is Tisa. She's two," Robert said.

Tisa crawled up into her mother's lap.

I smiled and tickled her feet.

She giggled.

"Will she let me hold her?" I asked.

"Probably. She's our social butterfly," Rebecca said. She handed the child over to me.

Tisa was going to be just like her mother, in height, body stature, and resemblance, except for her eyes. Instead, she had her dad's big round eyes.

Tisa wiggled up against me and wrapped her arms around my neck.

"She's the one we have to worry about being a little too friendly with strangers," Robert said.

She was a piece of heaven.

"Hi, Tisa," I said, hugging her.

"And this is Katie." He put his arm around her. "She's three, and a little on the shy side. It usually takes her a while to get to know somebody, so please don't get offended if she's not too affectionate right off the bat."

Katie clung to her dad's leg. Remarkably, she looked identical to my son. The only difference was the caramel color of her skin.

"That's okay. We'll get to know each other," I said, smiling at her.

She returned my smile.

That little acceptance allowed me to ease her into a long-lasting relationship. So that I didn't betray her comfort zone, I caressed only her hand. She didn't move away. Instead, she laid her head upon her dad's lap.

"Yes, you will," Rebecca said.

She placed her hand upon the oldest child's shoulder.

"And this is Leah," Rebecca said. "She's four."

"Hi, Grandma," Leah said, smiling. She looked up at me, chin held high.

She was tall for her age, and had her mother's long limbs. Her shoulders were broad like her dad. She had her dad's eyes and nose, but her mother's mouth.

"Hi, Leah," I said. Again, I didn't want to betray her comfort zone, so I allowed her to come to me. As she did, Tisa ran off to play.

"Leah is our little adult, and Katie's guidance," Rebecca said.

"Hmm," she said, studying me. "You seem alright. Nice to meet you, Grandma."

We hugged each other. I couldn't help but laugh at her proper yet intellectual attitude. Four? Personality wise, I would say she was twenty-five.

"It's a pleasure to meet you too, sweetheart." The tears flowed harder.

Leah pulled away and looked me over.

"Grandma, why are you crying?" she asked.

I wiped away my tears.

"Because your grandma is very happy to see you," Robert answered. He winked at me.

The joy of being home with my family mixed with the prior night's incident, and the confusion of how I got here overwhelmed me. A breakdown was forthcoming.

"Um, can I use the restroom?" I asked. I needed a few minutes to myself so I could get my shit together.

"Of course. It's right around the corner by the staircase," Jennifer answered.

"Thanks." I followed her directions.

Once I was in the bathroom with the door shut, I stared at the mirror. Last night's events played through my head. The only thing I remembered after the invisible man went over the side of the cliff was falling.

Did the invisible man bring me here? Was he still alive? Somebody had to know who my son was, otherwise why would they bring me here. But who?

I turned on the water and splashed some of it on my face. I looked up at the mirror. Still wet, I ran my fingers through my hair, slicking it back, being careful not to remove the gauze from my head.

Was it Jace? The thought made me cringe. Jace had already reunited me with my previous kidnapper, Wayne, and the consequences surrounding it were horrifying. Goosebumps erupted on my skin.

Would he kill my loved ones? Or would he use them for bait in the fighting circuit? With Jace, anything was possible.

My family was in danger.

SECRETS

Once his mom walked into the bathroom, Jennifer and Rebecca looked at him.

"Before you start, listen to me," he said, holding up his hands. "You both know I've been looking for her for a long time and yes, I admit, I've moved us from town to town trying to find her. I'm sorry. I shouldn't have moved us around so much. But I got a lead the other day and I followed it." He turned his attention to his wife. "Rebecca, you remember how you were asking about what was going on this morning."

Rebecca nodded.

"Well, I took Jennifer to the motel where we thought mom was staying because she mentioned she gave her a ride the other day. That's why I didn't come to bed until really late. That's also why Jennifer was late for school and why she's tired. I wanted to catch my mother at the motel. I wanted confirmation that's where she was staying."

He turned to Jennifer.

"And, yes, Jennifer, that's our mother." He rubbed the top of his head, eventually brushing his hair back.

"Why didn't you tell me?" Jennifer asked. Her mouth hung open.

"I didn't want to get your hopes up if I was wrong. Like I said, I needed confirmation. I didn't want to say anything until I was sure it was her." He glanced at Rebecca.

She glared at him. "I'm happy you found her. But do you remember what I told you?"

"About?" He motioned for her to continue.

"You know. I don't think it needs to be discussed in front of Jennifer," Rebecca said.

Jennifer shot Rebecca a questioning look.

"What shouldn't be discussed in front of me? I think I deserve to know, especially if it has to do with me."

"It's not you Jennifer. It's your mother." Rebecca's eyes hardened. She turned her attention back to Robert.

"Is she the mother that you remember, Robert? Or is she a different person? Think about it. Be on guard, because she hasn't been a part of your life in almost five years. You don't know what she's been through or who she is anymore," Rebecca said, sternly.

"Rebecca, you're being…"

"What? Overprotective? Overly cautious? Paranoid?"

"Yes, paranoid," he said, staring at her. "I'm sure she's not the same. I'm sure she has been through a lot, whatever the hell happened to her, but she's still my mother and I plan on being a part of her life, regardless."

"What if she doesn't want you to be a part of her life?" She stared at him.

Jennifer's eyes widened.

Robert was taken aback. He exchanged looks with them.

"Then, I'll accept it, however hard it is. I've lived without her for this many years, I'm sure I can do it again."

"No, you haven't, Robert. You've continued to live with her in your heart, but she hasn't lived with you in her heart," Rebecca said. She pointed in the direction of the bathroom.

"She needed you to verify information. Why? Then, she said somebody didn't mention Jennifer. Who was she referring to? Do you think she's going to suddenly cast aside the life she's lived to be with you, Jennifer, me, and the kids? I highly doubt it."

Frustrated, Robert turned back to Jennifer. Tears streaked her face.

"Rebecca, I understand where you're coming from, but I'm going to attempt this relationship anyway, whether she decides to stay a part of our lives or not. She's still our mother. Do not push me any further, do you understand me?" His eyes bore into hers.

Silently, she backed off. She leaned back in the recliner and glanced over at Jennifer.

Jennifer stared wide-eyed at her.

"How do you feel, Jennifer?" Rebecca asked.

Robert looked up at his sister.

"I agree with Robert," she said. "She's our mom. I think we at least deserve to get to know her. If she doesn't want to be in our lives, then we'll learn to live without her." She wiped her tears away.

"If Mom didn't want anything to do with us, why would she be here?" She glanced back at Robert. "Right?"

"Yes, Robert, how did she get here? Who brought her here? She obviously doesn't know, or so she says." Rebecca leaned forward on her knees.

The children played on the floor with their toys.

Rebecca's grim demeanor was upsetting him, even though he was just as confused about his mother's arrival as everybody else.

"I don't know, but I will find out," he said.

"Remember what I told you, Robert," Rebecca said, pointing at him. "Bad elements have brought her to us. Nothing is ever going to be the same."

Outside, clouds formed, casting shadows through the living room window. They darkened the room, the mood, and the atmosphere.

"Robert, what is she talking about?" Jennifer asked, concerned.

"Rebecca's just being paranoid. Ignore her," he said, rolling his eyes. But, as he turned his head, he did wonder what was in store.

Rebecca was usually right about things. This time he prayed she was wrong. After the outcome of events yesterday, he didn't know what to expect.

§

I walked into the living room, my hair pulled back into a ponytail.

Robert stood. "You must be starving."

"Yes, I am."

"Tell you what, why don't you go take a shower while Rebecca and I cook you up some fresh food. Jennifer can show you your room, even take you on a tour of the second floor," he said, motioning toward his sister.

Jennifer smiled. "I'd love to."

"Then, when you get done with your shower and eating, we can take you on a tour of the rest of the house. You have some clothes up there, so they should hopefully fit. If not, let us know."

"I have clothes here?"

"Yes, you do. We kept some of your stuff, in hopes that you were still alive and came home."

Wow! I was surprised that they kept my stuff that long.

"Come on, Mom."

As Jennifer grabbed my hand, Robert and Rebecca headed to the kitchen.

Robert called out, "Take your time, you two!"

"We will!" Jennifer yelled.

She unlocked the child's gate at the foot of the staircase. The girls and I followed her up to the second floor landing where another child's gate had to be unlocked.

Once we were through the second gate, Jennifer turned to the left and proceeded down the landing that ran parallel with the stairs.

"We'll start down here and work our way back around."

"Down here, Auntie Jen?" Leah asked, running ahead.

"Yes, down there."

Leah opened the door at the end of the walkway.

I followed her inside.

"This is the office," Katie said.

I smiled.

"Well, thank you for showing it to me."

Jennifer and I glanced at each other.

"She's so serious," I said.

"Yes, she is. She acts older than her age."

We laughed.

The office was dark. Burgundy drapes hung over the two tall windows. A Native American drop rug covered the wooden floor. The room was arranged into two work areas, one for the adults, and the other for the children. A small laptop and some learning books were neatly organized on the children's desk. Only a laptop lay on the adult's desk. A printer stand stood beside it. A couple of bookcases with reference material lined the shelves.

"This is our desk," Tisa said. She ran up to it and sat down.

"And, this is our reading corner," Leah said. She plopped down on a piece of furniture that was hidden in the shadows. When she flipped on the light, it revealed a huge rustic brown corner couch.

"It's very nice, ladies," I said.

"Thank you."

The floorboards creaked beneath our feet as we exited the room.

Tisa bolted past us to the next door. It opened into a narrow bathroom. Only a toilet and a pedestal sink occupied the space. Sea life was the décor in here, from the soap dispenser to the pictures on the wall.

"This is our bathroom," Tisa said.

"Yes, it is, but they usually take their baths in Robert and Rebecca's room."

The children led the way to the next room.

"This is our room," Katie said.

I smiled.

"I helped Rebecca decorate it," Jennifer said.

Their room was large. A white crib stood in the left hand corner. Two small beds stood practically side by side against the wall opposite the crib. Above the older girls' bed was the only window. Pink curtains adorned it.

The walls were painted pink with princess memorabilia on the walls and shelves. The toy box sat along the wall next to Tisa's crib. The closet ran parallel next to the door.

"It's very cute. You two did a great job," I said.

"Thank you," Jennifer said.

The last bedroom on this side of the stairs was Robert and Rebecca's. As we entered, I glanced at the closed door opposite their room. It was the only door on the right side of the staircase.

A queen-size bed with emerald green sheets and covers occupied the room. Against the wall adjacent to the girl's room was a long maple dresser. A walk-in closet door stood ajar on the other side of the dresser. Behind the main door to the room was a second door. It was closed. Both doors, I presumed, led to the closet.

Clothes were strewn about, mostly Robert's. A tall maple dresser was opposite the bed. One window overlooked the top of the bed and the other was parallel with the bedside. Short emerald green drapes covered the windows. A green and aqua throw rug lay at the foot of the bed.

Their bathroom door was on the other side of the dresser. It was simple yet elegant in its own fashion. A dragon claw-and-ball tub stood opposite the door. The shower curtain was white with gold accents. A large mirror stood over the pedestal sink. The medicine cabinet was to the right of it. A small wooden cabinet sat between the sink and the toilet.

As we left the room, Jennifer said, "There are actually two master bedrooms in this house, theirs and yours. My bedroom is downstairs. I'll show it to you later."

She opened the door on the right side of the staircase.

"This is your room." She flipped on the light.

I stepped in to the bedroom. The floorboards creaked beneath my feet. Light burgundy drapes covered the large pane window opposite the door. A breeze carried them up into the air.

"We always open the window in here since it's unoccupied, otherwise it gets a funky smell," she said.

The headboard of a queen-size mahogany sleigh bed lay against the wall to our right. White sheets and a burgundy colored comforter covered the bed.

"Rebecca washed the blankets yesterday, so they're clean."

"Thank you."

It was inviting, but I wasn't really sure if I was going to stay or not.

I glanced around. Two rustic-looking lamps, a clock, and a statue stood atop two mahogany nightstands. I walked up to one and carefully picked up the statue.

How odd, I thought. It was a crystal dragon with inset, deep red eyes. It stared up at me.

"That was a gift from dad. Turn it over."

"Hmm..."

For the Love of My Life. You will forever be my Crystal Dragon, was etched into the bottom of the dragon.

My heart skipped a beat. Crystal Dragon? I drew in a deep breath. I couldn't swallow. I had to sit down. Otherwise I was going to pass out.

"Are you alright, Mom?"

"Yeah, yeah, I am. I just, uh..." I sat on the edge of the bed and rubbed my forehead.

Jennifer turned to the girls. "Hey girls, let's leave grandma alone?"

"But, why?" Tisa asked.

"Well, sweetie, she wants to take a shower and change her clothes. Come on, let's go."

"Alright."

"Your bathroom is right there," Jennifer said, pointing to the wall to my right.

"Okay, thank you."

"Are you going to be okay, Mom?"

"Yes, I will."

Jennifer shut the door behind her and the girls.

I drew in another deep breath. I glanced back down at the statue, as if expecting the words to disappear. They were still there.

I put the statue back in its place. Even though my thoughts remained on those words, I glanced around.

A couple of Asian serpentine dragon pictures hung above the bed. More dragons? I had to look away. I was woozy.

I stared at the long mahogany dresser and large mirror opposite me. They sat against the wall adjacent to the door. Several items sat atop the dresser.

I stood. I still couldn't get *Crystal Dragon* out of my head. Was that a nickname? Coincidence?

The silver jewelry box atop the dresser caught my attention.

I practically ran to the dresser and opened it. Several pieces of jewelry fell out of it. A heavy, silver necklace with a heart locket caught on my finger. I opened the locket. Two pictures stared back at me, one of Robert and one of Jennifer at a young age. My heart locked up. Tears welled up.

Memories from time spent with my children at the park filled my head.

My husband stood by my side, pushing Jennifer on her swing, while I pushed Robert on his.

Robert and Jennifer swung back in unison.

As they did, I smiled. I turned to say something to my husband, but his face disappeared. Then he disappeared.

My knees weakened.

§

Jennifer walked into the kitchen where Robert and Rebecca were cooking.

"I called the school for you," he said. He took a sip of his coffee.

"Oh, good. Thank you."

Rebecca flipped the bacon over in the pan.

"I told them you wouldn't be in."

"Why did you do that?" Jennifer eyed him curiously.

Rebecca pressed the bacon down with the spatula.

"I figured you'd like to spend some time with mom." He grinned and winked at her.

"Seriously?"

"Yeah, seriously." He set his coffee mug down.

"Thanks, brother," she said, hugging him. She gave him a peck on the cheek.

Robert pulled away. "Whoa, are you feeling okay?" He put his hand on her forehead.

"Yes, I'm fine."

Rebecca raised her eyebrow. Hot grease sizzled in the pan.

"What was that for?" he asked.

"Just for being my brother and looking after me." Jennifer hit him in the arm.

"I think she needs to go to the doctor," Rebecca said.

He grabbed the spatula Rebecca held, and slapped it in Jennifer's palm.

"If you're feeling so damn appreciative, then you can help with breakfast for mom. Don't get mushy with me. I don't need that shit."

§

Trinkets lay atop my dresser, one of which was a small, clear glass angel. I picked it up. An aged sticker was stuck to the bottom of it. I turned it over.

To the best Mom in the world. Love, Jen was written with a young child's handwriting. It brought tears to my eyes. I set it down.

Next, I picked up the frog candle. I flipped it over.

You're the awesomest Mom ever. Love, Bobby. It too, had been written by a young child. I smiled and set it back in its place.

Then, I moved on to the drawers. The first one contained lingerie. As I rummaged through some panties and camisoles, two photos fell to the floor. I picked them up and looked them over. The first picture was my husband. The second picture was of a different man. His eyes looked familiar. Yet, I couldn't place his face. He was probably nineteen or twenty.

I flipped them over. No names. If he meant something to me, then he should trigger a memory, but he didn't. I tossed them on the dresser.

Sighing, I turned to my right. A huge walk-in closet stood there. I stepped inside and browsed through the clothing. They were my size.

Next, I entered the bathroom opposite my bed. It had the same style tub and sink as the other master bath. The only difference was the layout and the shower curtain, which was black with gold accents. The bathtub stood to the left of the room. The toilet, small cabinet, and sink were opposite me. The medicine cabinet hung to the right of the mirror.

I opened the medicine cabinet. Inside, there was a toothbrush, toothpaste, deodorant, and brush, in their original packaging. As I shut the cabinet door, I glanced at myself in the mirror. I really did need a shower.

§

If Jace was still after me, he would probably kill my family just to get to me. It was inevitable. The only way to protect my family was to leave. I didn't want to, but I also was not going to risk my family's life. It was best to get as far away from them as possible.

As I stepped out of the shower and dried off, I glanced in the mirror. Somebody had taken care to bandage my head. But who? Was it Tristan? I thought about this while I dressed into a pair of jeans and t-shirt.

How could I leave my family? They were all so happy to see me. They had been hurt once before by my disappearance and the death of my husband. How could I hurt them again? And, the grand-kids? What the hell was I going to tell them? I regretted the choice I had to make. I lay my face in my hands and cried.

Then something struck me odd. I glanced down at the floor. The clothes I had taken off lay next to my feet. I kicked them around, then reached down and peeled them from the floor. Last night, I had been wearing pajamas, and my feet were bare when I left the motel. Now, a pair of sweatpants, a t-shirt, and wool socks hung from my hand.

Somebody had done more than care for my wounds. They had also changed my clothes. I swallowed hard. There were only two people I knew who would have helped me, Warrant or Tristan. But, as far as I knew, they were both dead. If it were Jace, what exactly were his intentions? Why would he deliver me to my family? My heart raced.

§

"It really is good to have you here. Robert and Jennifer have really missed you," Rebecca said. She smiled, but something in her eyes told me it wasn't sincere.

Then again, maybe I was being paranoid. Yet, something told me to be careful around Rebecca.

We sat at the kitchen table with Jennifer opposite me, and Robert at the head.

Rebecca set a plate down in front of me. She then took a seat.

Leah and Katie played at a toy kitchen set nearby.

"Up, up, up, up!" Tisa threw her arms open.

"She is a social butterfly," Robert said. He bit into a dry biscuit.

"Oh, yes, she is." Rebecca picked up Tisa.

Tisa struggled against her Mom.

"No! I want Grandma!" She twisted toward me.

The tears brimmed up again. I was an emotional wreck.

"Tisa, stop. She needs to eat, too." She struggled with the writhing child.

"Tisa!" Robert snapped. "That's enough!"

Her lower lip protruded. Then a high-pitch wail erupted.

"Robert, I'm telling you, I don't know what it is, but they seem to act up more when you're home. It's like they're testing me."

"She's just being a child, hon. Here, give her to me." He motioned for her to hand him Tisa.

"Actually, can I have her?" I turned to Rebecca.

"But you're eating."

"That's okay. I think I can handle her."

"Are you sure, Mom?" Robert asked.

"Uh, yeah, sorry, I'm just not used to this. Here, let me have her, please." I extended my hands to Tisa.

She accepted them and lunged for me, a toothy grin on her face. Her cheeks were still wet from the tears.

I wiped them away.

Our eyes met.

The grand-kids were guaranteed to break me.

"Listen, I've been through a lot," I said. "And, as much as I want to be a part of your lives, I'm not sure that I can."

Jennifer recoiled. "But Mom, at least give us a chance. We really want to get to know you again."

Tisa played with my hair.

Leah came up and patted me on the leg. "It's okay, we still like you."

"Thanks, sweetie." I glanced around at everyone.

My kids stared at me with tears in their eyes. Rebecca stared at me, as if she knew something the others didn't.

Katie, who stood by her mom, approached me. She laid her head on my leg.

"I still like you, too," she whispered.

"This is really difficult…"

"Why don't you eat right now, and we'll talk when you're done?" He turned his attention to the children. "And, you guys, why don't you go play? Let her eat."

"Okay," Katie muttered. She ran over to the toy kitchen set with Leah in pursuit.

Tisa climbed off of my lap and chased after her sisters.

While I ate, Robert refilled my coffee.

"I'm glad you're here. I was beginning to think we'd never see each other again," Robert said.

"Yeah, me too." I poured some creamer in my coffee.

"We heard about what happened to Dad…"

As Robert continued on about what had happened to my husband, I recollected everything in the bar that night, including my husband's death. It was obvious nobody else knew about the vampires. There had to have been some sort of a cover-up, whether it was by the vampires or the police. If the media had gotten a hold of the truth, it would have been all over the news and my children would have heard the stories. So far, it didn't sound as though they had.

When I finished eating, Rebecca picked up my plate, rinsed it off, and set it in the sink. She refilled her coffee and rejoined us at the table.

"The authorities wouldn't let anybody see him. Whoever killed him literally severed his head."

I winced. I thought about the picture upstairs.

"The police never found the person who did it." He leaned on the table. "Do you remember what the murderer looked like?"

Oh, yeah, I remember what the blonde vampire stripper looked like but they weren't going to believe me.

Instead, I replied, "No, I don't. I'm sorry. I wish I did. It was pretty traumatic."

"Do you remember anything about that night?"

"No, not really. It's just one big block."

"So, if you don't mind me asking, what happened to you? You just up and disappeared. Nobody could find you. Hell, the police even went to the cabin where you guys were supposed to be staying and found no trace of you guys ever having shown up."

"What?" I looked at him. "But we did make it up to the cabin."

I thought back to that weekend. I remembered everything about that day.

"Not according to the police."

Now I was more than ever convinced the whole night was a setup.

"We did, though. We got to the cabin, put everything away, showered, changed our clothes, got lunch, took a nap, and then went out for the night. I think we even went for a hike." I glanced back at Robert. "You're a cop, right?"

"I'm a Deputy. I saw you the other day, remember?"

The look in his eye conveyed the message to watch what I was saying around either Rebecca, Jennifer, or both of them.

"Oh, I remember. Who was the other Deputy?"

"Oh, that's Torrance. He's my partner." Robert sat upright.

I eyed him. "He's not like you though, is he?"

I was referring to Robert's alter ego, the werewolf, of which I was shocked to find out about.

He smiled at me. Winking, he said, "No, he's not. He is my partner in crime, though."

Rebecca and Jennifer exchanged looks.

"Torrance is a fine Deputy," Rebecca said. Her eyes narrowed in on Robert.

He raised an eyebrow and grinned.

"So, I'm not sure what Robert is referring to. What are you talking about?"

"Mom just caught me and Torrance out in the woods tracking an animal. That's all."

"Oh." She rolled her eyes. "Yeah, he's an avid hunter. Torrance is just learning the ropes. So, if you ever want to go hunting, he can recommend the best areas. Jennifer and I don't hunt."

I stored this in my memory.

"Well, I might have to take him up on it."

"We track around sunset sometimes, and then hang around until after dark."

"Gotcha."

I was fascinated in learning what he knew about the werewolf and vampire community. After all, he was at the fight the other night. He had to know something.

"I might be interested. You'll have to take me out sometime."

With this in mind, it might be in my best interest to get to know my family better. Maybe my son could help me in coming to terms with my own situation. But I was hesitant. I didn't want to put them in danger.

"So, what happened to you anyway? You just disappeared after dad died," he asked again.

"I really don't remember," I said. I couldn't keep avoiding the question, so I had to say something. "I suffered some amnesia so everything's been a blur."

"Oh, my God. That's horrible," Jennifer said.

"That's why I'm having some difficulty remembering everything and everybody."

Jennifer's voice rose. "You know, I've heard it said that when somebody suffers a traumatic experience, their subconscious sometimes blocks things out. That might be what happened to you."

And, maybe that was the truth.

"It's possible," I said.

"Jennifer might be on to something. People also revert to an alternate lifestyle to escape trauma," he said, raising an eyebrow. "So, what do you remember?"

My first thought drifted to my prison cell, but I had to change up my story. They didn't need to know all of the traumatic details.

Rebecca stared at me.

"Well, I woke up in somebody's house. I don't know…"

"That's not true," Rebecca snapped.

I spun around to stare at her, eyes wide. I didn't know whether to be mad or astounded by her reaction. My mouth hung open.

"Dear…!" Robert yelled.

"It's not," she said, motioning towards me. "She woke up somewhere she didn't know but it wasn't a house. As a matter of fact…"

"And how would you know?" I asked, interrupting her. The last thing I wanted to do was disrespect my son and his wife, but I sure as hell didn't appreciate her rudeness.

Then again, I was lying.

"Just tell us the truth. We are adults," she said.

I shook my head in dismay.

Robert cleared his throat. "You'll have to excuse my wife. She's…uh, hmm, how do I explain it?"

Rebecca cut him off. "Let's just tell her." She looked at me. "I'm a witch."

"Are you kidding me?" I asked. I rubbed my forehead.

Robert glanced at her.

"She's not a witch. She just has this talent." He glanced back at me. "She can tell when somebody's lying to her, knows things that normal people don't know. Oh, there's numerous shit that she's good at. So, if somebody lies to her, she knows."

Great! This was fucking fantastic!

"Really?" I asked. First, I was stuck with werewolves. Then it was vampires. Now, it was a goddamn witch.

Rebecca ignored him. "I'm a witch. It's hereditary in the women in our family, my mother, my grandmother, my great-grandmother, and so on. Once the witch hunters in Salem found out what some of my relatives were, they burned them at the stake. So, my grandmother made sure that the rest of our family learned how to control our witchery so nothing unjust would happen to us." She drew in a deep breath. "Tituba is my ancestor."

"I'm sorry to hear that," I said.

Rebecca replied, "Thanks."

"So, what would you say if I told you that I woke up in the forest with nowhere to go?"

"I would say that part of it is true, and part of it is a lie."

"Uh-huh." I sighed.

"What I see is that you woke up in a building which was located in the forest."

"Hmm." Just fucking amazing. I had been thinking about the bar which hid the underground prison cell. It had been in the forest.

"Please indulge us, Brandy. I think we can accept the truth," Rebecca said.

"What if what I told you might put you in danger?"

Everybody exchanged looks.

"We would rather you tell us, Mom," Robert said. "Especially, if it can put us in danger. I need to know so that I can protect my family."

I drew in a deep breath.

He deserved the truth.

I glanced at the kids. Leah had toy eggs in a pan. She practiced flipping the eggs. Katie had a toy pitcher and was filling cups with an invisible liquid. Tisa sat at the toy table and chairs, eating a piece of toast.

My eyes settled back on the adults.

"I'd like you to keep what I'm about to tell you to yourselves. Please, do not share it with anybody. Can you do that for me?"

They nodded.

I left out a few details as I explained everything from the beginning; primarily, the fact that Jace practically raped me, my sex life, and the names of the bounty hunters, the snipers, the werewolf, and the invisible man.

My family stared at me with a look of horror on their face.

I hadn't wanted to be a killer, and I hoped they wouldn't judge me for it.

The adults remained silent.

"If you want me to leave, I understand," I said.

The silence remained.

"Trust me, it's okay," I said, standing.

My son grabbed my hand.

"No, no, don't leave," he said. "Please, sit down."

I sat.

He swallowed hard. "Jesus, Mom," he said. "Let me get a pen and paper so we can get descriptions and put out an APB."

"No, no, I can't. I won't. They're too dangerous."

"It's all the more reason we need to get their descriptions. These guys need to be thrown in jail, Mom." His voice was stern.

"No, I refuse to give their information out."

He huffed. "Fine, I'll get it from you later though." He pointed his finger at me. "I will get it out of you."

I stared at him.

Jennifer took my hands in hers. The expression on her face was equally disturbing.

She looked up into my eyes. "I'm so sorry you had to go through that. That's horrible."

I had to look away, to avoid Jennifer's gaze.

Rebecca just sat there with her mouth open.

Robert's intense stare was unavoidable.

"How did you…or what, should I say, kept you going?" he asked. "I don't know if I could even survive an ordeal like that."

"Trust me, I thought suicide by vampire or werewolf would be easier. But then I thought about you, Robert. So, I fought back. And now that I think back, I don't remember him saying that he kidnapped you."

"Well, as you can see, I've never been kidnapped. Grandma raised Jennifer and I after you went missing. The night you and dad were attacked, Jennifer wound up in the hospital. She had a panic attack."

Then he turned to Jennifer.

"Oh, shit, that would make sense," he said. He slapped his palm off of his forehead.

"What makes sense?" Jennifer asked.

"Robert, the girls," said Rebecca, reprimanding him.

His eyes flitted from Rebecca, back to Jennifer and then me.

"Mom, do you remember anything prior to the attack?" he asked.

"No, not really," I replied. "Why?"

"Because Grandma said that I went to the hospital at the same age Jennifer did. It was also due to a panic attack. We've never really had anything traumatic happen to any of us, at least nothing that we remember. So, we never really understood why we had them."

Still unsure of where he was going with this, I motioned for him to continue.

"Grandma said that dad had some anxiety and anger issues growing up. She also said that we were all put on medication at about the same age for the same problems. It's all following a cycle. Same problems, same medications, same diagnosis, same ages."

"What are you getting at?" Jennifer asked, confused.

"Remember what happened to you the other night?"

"Yeah, that freaked me out. But, where are you going with this?" Jennifer asked. Her voice shook.

"You said that never happened before?"

"No, it hasn't. And, I don't ever want that to happen again." Her voice rose. "That shit scared the hell out of me."

Rebecca looked at him.

"Rebecca, I've got something to tell you." He turned toward her. "Mom already knows what I am. She ran into Torrance and I the other night."

Rebecca's eyes narrowed in on him.

"Only now, it's Jennifer. She has the curse, too."

"You're a werewolf too?" Rebecca threw her hands up in the air. "That figures! Now I know why I can't read you either."

"Yes," Jennifer answered. She lowered her head.

We exchanged glances.

"Don't you have to get bit to change? If so, who bit you?" Rebecca asked.

"Not always. It's also genetic," I answered.

Everybody looked at me.

"So, I've heard," I said.

"So, you're telling me that if you have sex with someone who's a werewolf, you can have werewolf babies?" Rebecca asked.

I nodded.

Rebecca rolled her eyes. Then, as if a light bulb turned on, she gazed back at her daughters.

I also looked at the children.

The girls smiled at us. It was as if they knew something we didn't.

Rebecca turned to Robert.

"No, no, it's not possible. Is it?" She glanced back at the girls. "Robert, did you know this?"

He stared at the girls.

"No, I wasn't even sure how I got it." He rubbed his chin. "Once I made the change for the first time, I knew I had a disease, one that would never go away."

"Mom, was I ever bit by something?" he asked. He looked at me.

This couldn't be happening. Could it? The bright atmosphere took an overwhelming turn to the dark side.

I stared at my grand-daughters. It became difficult to breathe.

"Mom?"

"Brandy?"

Their voices faded out.

I struggled to remember what happened before my captivity. Was their father a werewolf? Or did they get bit by someone?

"Who was our real father?" Robert asked.

§

Our conversation stirred up the memory of that fateful night.

My husband and I sat inside a country bar on the outskirts of Payson, Arizona with our friends, Abel and Ashley, on a cold rainy night. Deer, elk, and bear heads lined the walls. The wooden floors were covered in sawdust. Female strippers, dressed in only cowboy hats, thongs, and heels, danced on the stage. They gyrated against the stripper poles and the patrons.

At one point, a blonde stripper, who had already danced for our men, interfered in a conversation my husband, Chris and I were having.

The tall, sultry blonde grabbed my husband's face and turned him toward her. She climbed on to his lap. Her white cowboy hat hid her face.

My mouth dropped open. I stared at her. How rude!

I glanced at Abel. He smiled at me. I presumed he paid for a dance for Chris. Regardless, she pissed me off.

Chris was to drunk to care, much less notice I was upset over it. I let him have his dance. Besides, my bladder was full and I needed the restroom now. I rushed to the bathroom.

The restroom was full of women scrambling for the mirror. I weaved my way to the stall. As I emptied my bladder, I decided I would talk to Ashley. Maybe she would want to go to another bar, too.

Once I was done, I wound my way through the women to the sink. The ladies freshened up their make-up in the mirror but not without bumping elbows with one another. I glanced up at two of the strippers. They were gorgeous, but their skin was really pale. Behind me, some of the female patrons were getting anxious to get inside the bathroom. I hurried up. When I walked out, a scuffle broke out between the women who struggled for mirror time.

I returned to the lounge. New dancers took the stage. The strippers who had been on stage were now in the audience, including the blonde who still sat on my husband's lap.

The blonde whispered something in his ear. He grinned like the Cheshire cat. This was just pissing me off now. The stripper needed to find somebody else to play with now.

A redhead, who had been on Abel's lap, climbed off of Abel, and joined the blonde. She sat down on his other leg, and leaned against him. I sighed. Then, I glanced at Ashley's empty seat. Maybe, she was at the bar. I looked around but I didn't see her anywhere. She must have gone to the bathroom.

The music switched over on the speaker. A female voice belted out, "Let's Go Girls."

The strippers gyrated against him. My blood boiled.

I stomped up behind him and jerked his head back by his hair.

"Ow," he groaned, his eyes widening. He peered up at me, his head extended over the back of the chair.

"You surprised to see me?" I asked. I glared at the blonde.

She smiled.

I shifted my gaze to him. His Adam's apple bobbed up and down.

Yeah, I'd caught him off guard.

"Hi, honey." He brought his hands up in a questioning gesture.

"I want to go," I said, staring fiercely at him. I crossed my arms in front of my chest.

"Well, hold on, honey. Abel paid for the lap dance, so I'd hate to waste his money."

I was shocked at his attitude about the whole incident.

"Yeah, I bet." I looked up at the strippers.

The redhead stood and went back to Abel. He had no money in his hands, so I knew the lap dance wasn't paid for. The blonde didn't move.

"Hey, why don't you give the rest of the dance to my wife?"

A smirk crossed her face. She stood. He grinned.

"Cute. I'm not interested," I said.

She walked around the chair and came toward me.

I put my hand up as a warning to back off. "Look, bitch, I'm not interested. So, go away."

I started to walk around her when she stepped in my path. Her dark eyes gleamed with delight. I glanced around the bar. Other patrons were watching us, as if we were the show. I glanced down at my husband. He continued to lie with his head back, smiling at us.

"Are you enjoying this, asshole?" I asked him.

I peered over at Abel. He sat drunk and motionless in his chair. He had that same stupid look on his face. I shook my head. The redhead had her face buried in his neck. I gazed at the empty seat where Ashley had sat. Was she in the bathroom? I hoped she was alright.

We needed to get out of here.

"Babe, let's go," I said, turning my attention back to Chris.

The blonde was on his lap again, her face buried in his shoulder.

"Look, bitch, get off him."

I walked around to the front of him, which was the back of her, and jerked her hair. She didn't flinch. Her head remained tight to his neck.

What the hell?

I grabbed her by her hair again and pulled back. Flesh ripped from his neck. Blood gushed from his mouth. A gurgle escaped his lips. She turned and hissed. Blood covered her face. It flowed down her chest. Her eyes were dark. My gaze shifted to my husband. Blood poured down his neck and chest. Muscles and skin were shredded and torn away.

§

"Mom!" Robert yelled. "Who was our father?"

"I don't know," I said. I shook my head. It was the most honest answer I could give them for now.

"Was he a werewolf?"

I looked up at them.

They stared at me.

I thought about that. If he was a werewolf, why didn't he sense the strippers were vampires? Why didn't he transform into his alter ego? Why didn't he defend himself? With his heightened senses, shouldn't he have detected the vampire's aggressive nature?

I presumed he was human since he didn't act on his paranormal intuition. Yet, there was no guarantee he wasn't a werewolf.

"I'm not sure," I answered.

"Robert, get your birth certificates," Rebecca instructed.

"What do you want those for? That's not going to prove if my dad is a werewolf or not," he said.

"No, it won't. But, if we can track down who he is, we might be able to find out *what* he is."

Robert sighed and lowered his eyes.

"Fine, then I'll get them," Rebecca said.

The moment she stood, Robert spoke up. "They're not there."

She glared at him. "What do you mean, they're not there?"

"Exactly what I said."

"So where are they? I'll get them."

"Rebecca, sit down. You're not going to find them in the house."

Rebecca sat down. Her eyes met his. "Where are they?"

He frowned. "Remember when the house was broke into?"

"Yes?"

"And I told you that nothing was taken?"

"Yeah…?" Her eyes were hard and cold.

"Well, I was wrong. I found out a couple of days ago that our birth certificates are missing. I presume that whoever broke in took them."

"And you didn't tell me?" Rebecca asked.

"I've been busy. I was going to tell you but I didn't get around to it. Sorry, hon."

Rebecca shook her head.

"I've already requested copies of yours and the girls," he said.

"And what about yours and Jennifer's?" Rebecca asked.

"I still need to request them."

"Who the hell would steal birth certificates?" Jennifer asked.

"Identity theft," Robert answered.

"Or maybe whoever broke in knows that you and Brandy are related," Rebecca suggested.

"But who would know that?" Jennifer asked.

"I don't know," I replied, looking around.

An alarm system on the wall caught my attention. Since nothing was said about the alarm going off during the robbery, I presumed Robert had the system installed after the incident happened.

"Well, obviously someone knows because they brought you here," Robert said.

Jennifer chimed in, "That can't be just coincidence."

"Right." I stared out the window. Tristan came to mind.

The others followed my gaze.

"What is it?" Robert asked.

"I was just thinking about last night," I responded.

"What about it?"

"Warrant's friend Tristan tried to help me last night. He's the only person I can think of that would bring me here."

Everybody looked at me.

"So, where is he? Can you ask him?"

I lowered my eyes. "No, I can't. I don't know where he is."

Robert prodded. "Do you have his phone number? Maybe you can call him, or better yet, maybe we can drive by his place?"

"No, I can't. I'm sorry, Robert." I looked up at him and sighed. "I don't know where he lives or what his phone number is."

I shouldn't be here, especially after last night. If the werewolf that attacked us knew where I was, he might be watching. I may have dug my family's graves.

I buried my face in my hands.

"Are you alright, Mom?" Jennifer asked.

"I should go. It's quite possible you are all in danger."

I stood.

"No, Mom." He grabbed my arm. "Wait…"

Jennifer interrupted him. "You should stay here with us."

"Whether you leave or not, I can guarantee somebody already knows you're here. If you leave, they may decide to come after us anyway. Not that I want to put you in any more danger; but if you're here, that's still more protection for you, Rebecca, Jennifer, and the kids. Rebecca can help with some protection, but she's not the fighter that you are. If it comes down to fighting, we may need you."

I still wasn't convinced.

"Maybe…" Before I could finish my sentence, Robert stood.

He placed his hand on the back of my shoulder. "Good, then it's settled. And I'm not going to take no for an answer."

I turned to the kids. Fear settled deep inside. "Rebecca, are you sure you're okay with this? I don't want to…"

"Shush. It's already done."

"Since that's settled, and now that you're finished with breakfast, let's finish giving you the grand tour."

I glanced down at my plate. It was empty. I barely remembered eating, much less finishing, all of my food.

Robert waved me over.

We joined him at the kitchen entry way.

"Since you've already seen the living room, and the bathroom here, we'll move on," he said.

We walked past the bathroom to the first room in the hallway under the stairwell.

"This is the den. I really don't let the kids in here, because we refer to this as the quiet room." He winked at me. "Like I ever really get any quiet in here anyway, but we do try to keep it to a minimum." He chuckled.

The décor was old-style. The walls were deep wood. Pillars in the corners gave the room an old rustic look. Bookcases lined several of the walls. One large window centered the wall and overlooked the backyard. A large, rustic carpet with several shades of brown lay in the middle. Wicker chairs were set up randomly throughout. A 1940's style burgundy colored couch sat just inside the rug. Two wicker chairs sat opposite it.

The thick floor-length curtains were a deep mahogany. A chandelier hung above the couch and chairs.

"We have all kinds of books in here, so you might find something you like."

I smiled. "I'll have to browse through them later."

He shut the door behind us. We headed down the hallway to the second room.

"This is Jenn…"

"Uh, it's not clean," Jennifer interrupted. "I'll show it to her later."

"Okay, well, then on we go," he said. "Down here, we have the laundry room."

The door to the laundry room stood open. Not even halfway down the hall, I was blinded by the sun and the white walls.

"Wow! That's bright." I rubbed my eyes.

"Sorry about that. I've actually been meaning to get in here and paint it a different color. Rebecca complains about it all of the time."

The wooden flooring was the only different color in the room. All of the cleaning products were stocked up on the shelves above the washer and dryer.

Robert turned to the door opposite us.

"This door opens into the side yard. And this…?" He reached across to the wall to my left. His fingers latched onto an inset handle. "Opens into the kitchen."

"Oh, I didn't even notice that."

He opened the door.

I poked my head inside the kitchen. "That's pretty cool."

"Rebecca really liked that."

Rebecca nodded.

"And we're going to head back out the way we came."

He shut the door and led us down the hallway, through the living room, and to the left, toward the back of the house.

A small entryway took us into a back room where there were several pieces of exercise equipment, including an elliptical machine, weight machines, and free weights. A large mirror encompassed the wall in front of the workout machines.

Behind the weight machines, against the farthest wall, stood a small beige couch. Crayons and coloring books sat on it.

"This is our exercise room. It's not very large, but it's accommodating," he said. "Behind you is the door to the garage."

I glanced back at the door which was to the right of the room.

"Then of course, we have the backyard."

Robert opened the door to the big grassy yard. A swing set and slide had been built for the kids and a bench for the adults. A birdbath was positioned to the left of the bench. Several trees stood in the yard. An eight foot block fence surrounded their yard.

"I just recently put that fence up. We had an issue with a mountain lion coming into the backyard."

"Oh, that's not good," I said. "Do you think it will keep him out?"

"Well, we haven't seen him back here since. Oh, and by the way, the kids are not allowed to go outside without us."

"Got it."

He and Rebecca sat down on the bench.

"Have a seat, Mom."

There was just enough room for one more person, so I parked myself next to them.

A breeze pushed the swings to and fro.

"Thanks for letting me stay here. I honestly didn't expect you to."

"Don't worry about it. You're my mom," he said, smiling. He wrapped his left arm around my shoulders. "Listen, Rebecca and I were talking. We really want you to stay as long as you can. I know you said it might be difficult for you, but we think it's for the best. Her intuition gets the best of her sometimes, so we want to apologize."

I was sure he meant witchery, not intuition. Either way, it didn't matter. It was something I would have to get used to.

"Yes, I'm really sorry for earlier," she said.

"That's alright. It's not like you really know me. I'm just worried about what might happen from here on out."

"Yeah, well, from what it sounds like, they may come after you. I'd like to think not, but knowing how criminals act, they don't just go away. We have to come to terms with the possibility of an assault on our home." He had an intense stare. "I'll do what I can to find out about this guy, Jace. Also, I'll see if I can get a sketch artist to come up here and draw something up from your description of him."

"That's a good idea," I said.

Rebecca nodded. "Good idea."

"I would like to show you something else, Mom." Robert stood up with Rebecca. He held her hand. "Come on."

I followed them through the house and into the garage.

He flipped on the light.

Everything in the garage was neatly organized on shelves and cabinets. A small rowboat hung above the vehicles. Life jackets were stacked inside of it. A blue 2005 Toyota Four Runner and silver 2010 Sequoia occupied the garage.

Robert walked up to a bench, reached into a tin can, and pulled out a set of keys.

"Catch," he said.

I caught the keys.

"What's this for?"

"The Four Runner's a backup vehicle. I keep everything up on it. It's in great condition. It has a few dents here and there but nothing major. We keep the keys in the can, but since you're here, I'm going to suggest you hang onto them. There's a spare house key on there, too."

"I can't…," I couldn't take his vehicle.

"It'll get you around, so don't fret over it."

"But…."

He held up his hand. "Stop. I want you to have the keys. If anything happens, you got the Four Runner. She'll get you anywhere you need to go. She's got a full tank of gas. Oil, spark plugs, and filters have all been changed. Besides, it belonged to you and dad anyway. It's yours."

The keys dangled off of my fingers. I stared at the vehicle. It was mine?

"As soon as we get the chance we'll put it in your name so you can have it back. I'd give you back your other car, but I kind of fixed it up for Jennifer and gave it to her. I'd hate to take it back from her."

"Oh, God no, I wouldn't allow that anyway."

"I tried to give her the Four Runner, but she wouldn't take it. She wanted your Mustang."

"Yeah, she told me you fixed it up for her." I hugged my son. "You've been a good brother to her, and that means a lot to me. Thank you so much for taking care of her."

He held on to me. "Anytime, Mom. I love you."

Those three words melted my heart. "I love you, too." Tears welled up.

He cried. "God, I missed you."

Rebecca slipped out of the garage.

Tears streamed down my face.

We held each other for what seemed like hours.

Finally, he pulled away. His nose was red and stuffy.

"Sorry," he said.

"That's alright. I think we both needed that." My nose was stuffy, too. I wiped away my tears.

He smiled. "I'm just really glad to have you back. I want the girls to get to know their grandma. I wish dad were here, so they could get to know him, too. But that's not going to happen."

"I'm sorry. And thank you." I leaned back against the car.

"And I want you all to live together in the home you grew up in. I'm actually surprised you haven't said anything."

"I grew up here?" I looked around.

"Yeah, I didn't say anything because I was hoping you might recognize it, or it might trigger some memories, or something. You lived here when you were a kid. This was grandma and grandpa's house."

I stared at him, dumbfounded. How could I not recognize my home? This was getting absurd.

He shook his head. "Damn, mom, you really are fucked in the head."

I laughed. Tears spilled down my cheeks.

"Sorry, Mom. This is just crazy."

"That's alright. You're right. I am fucked in the head."

Fucked in the head? Wasn't that the truth? I rubbed my eyes with the heels of my palm.

"After dad's death, grandma moved into town to raise us. She actually wanted to raise us here, but didn't want to take us away from our friends and school. The room you're in use to be grandma and grandpa's. After her death, she left the house to us."

"How did she die?"

"Emphysema. She lasted awhile, but then it finally took its toll on her. She passed away a few months ago. I figured that if you came back, you should have her room." He frowned. "Sorry you have to find out this way."

"It's not your fault."

It felt good to laugh and enjoy life with him. I just hoped it wouldn't be short-lived.

"By the way, those girls are adorable."

"Yes, they are. But I'm biased. They can be a handful sometimes, especially Tisa. She's a wildcat, and the other two, don't let them fool you. Leah and Katie might be quiet sometimes, but they are sneaky."

"Yeah, I bet."

"How about we go inside and see what everybody is doing? I'm sure everybody wants to know what you're up to and what your plans are."

As I followed him, I thought about what he had said. That was a good question. What were my plans?

Once we were in the living room, I sat on the floor with my back to the couch. The girls plopped down next to me, crowding me. I laughed. Tisa struggled to find a comfortable position up against me.

"What are you guys doing?" Robert sat down on the floor. "Give her some space. She just got here." He pulled Tisa on to his lap.

"That's alright." I cradled Katie's cheeks in my hand. "They just want to see me."

Katie giggled.

"Yeah, Daddy," Leah said. Her cheeks were rosy red.

"Yeah, Daddy," I said.

Leah and I giggled.

"So, do you know what you're going to do now?" he asked. He leaned against the foot of the chair Rebecca sat in.

"I really don't know." I shook my head. "I need to get my paperwork and identification first. After that, I'm not sure what I'm going to do."

Jennifer perked up. "You know what you should do?"

"What?"

"You should open your own Kenpo dojo. That is if you remember your techniques and stuff. If not, we can always try to locate your old instructor. Robert can probably find him for you," Jennifer said.

Visions of fighting swirled in my head. I tried to push it away.

"I'll think about it. Besides, even if I wanted to do that, it's going to cost money, and that's going to take time." My eyes narrowed in on her. "What did you call that? Kenpo?"

Jennifer became excited. "Yeah, Chinese Kenpo. I think you might have some books in the den on it. And some sparring gear."

Robert interrupted her. "Yeah, the sparring gear is around here somewhere. But I'm not sure if Mom really wants to think about that right now. She needs a break. You know what I mean?"

Jennifer frowned. "Sorry, Mom. I just thought it might be something you would be interested in."

I smiled. "That's alright. I appreciate the thought, but Robert is right. I do need a break. You do have a great idea, though. And it is something to think about, but not now. Thank you, hon."

Jennifer smiled. Her cheeks puffed out.

"We'll get your birth certificate, driver's license, and all that stuff requested ASAP," Robert said.

"Thank you," I said.

Rebecca turned to Robert. "Don't you have your mom's birth certificate?"

"All of that paperwork was together, babe. It was all stolen."

§

Over the next couple of weeks, I rummaged through my stuff in hopes something else would trigger my memory. Nothing.

As the girls slept, Rebecca and I stood in my room.

"I thought you should see this. I discovered it while I was cleaning in here," Rebecca said. She removed a framed photo from the wall.

The small space revealed a small hanging wrought iron handle. Rebecca tugged on it. A hidden door popped open. The dust around the door frame billowed out.

My mouth dropped open. Two hidden doors in the house. Hmm…

"Now, be careful Brandy. Some of the flooring hasn't been completed. I'm presuming they were going to make this room bigger but never finished it."

The door opened into a large room. It was dusty and smelled of dirt. The floor was missing several wooden slats.

I followed her in.

"If you look down, you can see the ceiling over the living room. They just didn't complete the floor itself, like maybe this was an add-on."

"Looks like it," I agreed.

We inched across the room to the window that overlooked the front yard. Three intricate intertwining red roses were etched into both glass panes. The vines wrapped around each other, forming a bouquet. Butterflies rested on the tip of one of the rose petals.

"This is a nice view," I said.

"Yes, it is. You can see pretty far, too."

We peered out across the grassy plain where the pine trees in the forest formed almost a perfect boundary for the property. Colorful flowers were in full bloom. They formed a nice frame around the patio. It was an amazing view. Why hide it?

I looked back over my shoulder. The door remained open.

"I wonder why he put a hidden door on it."

"I don't know. But he did that downstairs with the laundry room and the kitchen, too. Did you see that?"

"Yes, I did." I turned my attention back to the window. "This is gorgeous."

"I think so, too. That's one of the reasons why I wanted to show it to you. That and I wanted to know if you knew anything about it."

"I wish I did."

She studied me.

After a minute, she said, "If you want, maybe we can have Robert and his friends finish it for you. They built the swing set for the kids. So, they are good with a hammer. Plus, with the addition, your room takes up half of the living area up here, anyway. We might as well have Robert put in a mini kitchen, if you'd like."

She stood up.

"It's a thought," I said. "I wonder why he was building hidden doors?"

§

Later that afternoon, as Rebecca, Jennifer, and I sat on the bench in the backyard, Robert walked outside with a rubber ball in his hand.

He grinned.

"What was that grin for?" Rebecca asked. "You look like you're up to something."

"Nothing much. Just going to play ball with my girls."

Leah walked up to him.

"Right, Leah?"

"Right," she answered. She snagged the ball and ran off.

"Hey, give me that back!"

Leah ran around the swing set, the ball in hand.

Robert chased after her.

Tisa and Katie ran around Robert and joined their sister, who threw the ball to them. Katie caught it.

Robert switched direction and chased after her.

Katie threw the ball to Tisa, who caught it.

"Alright, you little stinkers, I'm going to get you," he said, laughing.

Tisa bolted past him, taunting him.

"Hey, what the…" He sped up.

Then, she sped up.

Our mouths dropped open.

She was running faster than him.

Leah and Katie joined her. The three girls bolted past us.

Robert stopped. "What the…?"

The kids ran full circles around us. They became a blur. Their bodies turned into rays of light as they whizzed past us.

Jennifer sprang up and looked at me, eyes wide. "Mom, what's wrong with them?"

"I don't know." I stared in awe.

There was no way in hell a child or even an adult could run that fast.

Then, Leah came to a stop. She threw the ball, and caught him off guard. It struck him hard enough in the forehead to knock him to the ground. He stared at her, stunned.

"Oh, my God, Robert!" Jennifer screamed. "Are you alright?"

"Catch me now, Daddy!" She giggled.

The girls turned back into a flash of light. They zoomed around the swing set.

We exchanged looks.

"You're funny, honey," Rebecca said.

He looked at us. A large, purple knot was already forming on his forehead.

"Yeah, yeah. I'll be fine." Robert sat up.

Rebecca's mouth dropped open. She rushed to his side. "I thought you had a rubber ball?"

"I did," he said.

The girls stopped.

"I'm sorry, Daddy," Leah said. "I didn't mean to hurt you."

Leah wrapped her arms around him.

"That's alright, honey." He hugged her back. "But where did you learn to run that fast?"

They climbed on to their dad.

"From you, Daddy," she said. "I watched you from my window when you were outside."

He and I exchanged looks. Our eyes widened.

"Babe?" Rebecca stared at him.

Tisa climbed up her mother.

"What is it?" Rebecca asked him.

He did not answer. Instead, he stood. Katie and Leah remained wrapped around his torso.

"Answer her question, Robert," Jennifer said.

"I already answered it," he said, gruffly. He let go of his children, his arms close by, ready to catch them if they let go. But they did not.

"They're going to fall and hurt themselves. Hold onto them," Rebecca demanded. Her eyes were wide with fear and curiosity.

"No, they're not."

"Yes, they are."

"No, they're not." Robert held his arms out wider. "Because they're too much like me. They have no fear. It's the anxiety that..."

Jennifer interrupted. "The anxiety that gets their heart to beating, pushing their adrenaline hard through their body, so hard it almost feels like it's going to pump its way out of their chest."

Everybody turned to look at her.

Her eyes were wide.

"Robert, you're right. It's not an anger problem I have," Jennifer said. "It's the creature inside that wants to get out. It's the anxiety, the fear, the anger, and the jealousy–any emotion that pushes me to my limits that tests the wolf in me. The medication only helped to keep my emotions in check. Whether I take the pills or not, I can still feel it deep down inside, twisting my body around..."

The sky darkened. Heavy clouds rolled in.

Robert cut her off. "We need to have that talk now, the talk we never finished. Come on, Jennifer. It won't take that long."

He grabbed his sister's arm and took her inside, leaving Rebecca and I alone with the kids. I was thankful the children had calmed down.

"Do you think they'll change?" I asked.

"I don't know." She sat down and buried her face in her hands.

Leah rested her hand on her mom's shoulder. "Are you okay, Mommy?"

Rebecca looked up at her. "Yes, I'm fine honey. Leah, have you ever seen your father do anything weird?"

"What do you mean, Mommy?"

Rebecca lowered her head.

"Well, like, has he ever..."

She looked at me for assistance on how to broach the subject.

"Has your daddy ever looked different than he does now?" I asked. I glanced at Rebecca.

She smiled.

"Yeah, has he ever looked different, kind of like a dog?" Rebecca asked.

Leah nodded. "Yeah, when he gets mad."

"This isn't working." Rebecca hung her head.

"Leah, come here, sweetie." I held my arms out.

She jumped in my lap.

"I know this sounds funny, but I really need you to think and not make up any stories. Alright?"

"Okay."

"I know daddy, actually a lot of people, look funny when they get mad. But does your daddy ever grow, like, a lot of hair all over his body?"

The girls giggled.

I laughed. "I know, it sounds silly. But, tell me, have you ever seen him do anything weird like that?"

She shook her head.

I smiled. "We'll keep that question our little secret, okay?"

"Okay," she said. She tried to keep a straight face, but couldn't. Her lips parted into a smile.

I hugged her tight. Maybe it was a good thing I was here. We might not have learned each other's secrets and been able to talk things out.

Rain poured down on us.

"Shit!" I yelled.

The kids shrieked.

§

Once I was upstairs, I stripped out of my wet clothes and grabbed a towel. As I dried off, a noise caught my attention.

I wrapped the towel around me and peeked out at the bedroom window. Tree branches scraped against the glass. A heavy sigh escaped my lips.

I approached the window from the side to avoid walking in front of it. As I grabbed the curtain, I noticed a figure in the near distance. It clung to a tree branch.

My breath caught in my throat. I remained motionless behind the drapes, hoping to remain inconspicuous to any potential observer. I closed and reopened my eyes, hoping it was a figment of my imagination.

Another figure appeared at the edge of our property. It hunkered down within the tree branches. If these creatures had been the bounty hunters or the snipers, they would have made themselves invisible. Instead, they remained out in the open.

I slipped out from behind the curtain, dressed, and slid inside the hidden room. Carefully and quietly, I moved to the front window.

Streaks of lightning lit up the sky. Rain pelted against the house. More figures appeared. They never came any closer than our property line.

I tried to distinguish a face, but they were too far away and it was too dark. I wondered if they were Jace and his men. If not, who were they and what did they want?

Thunder boomed overhead, followed by a crack of lightning.

I ducked below the window ledge, hoping that they hadn't seen me. Robert needed to know someone was watching the house.

As I ran out of the room, branches screeched across the window.

Halfway down the stairs, I slowed down.

Everybody was in the kitchen, getting ready for dinner.

Then Robert came around the corner.

"I was just coming to get you. Dinner's ready."

"Thanks."

I glanced at the front door.

It was unlocked. But did that matter? If the watchers outside were vampires or werewolves, a lock on a door wasn't going to stop them.

"Are you okay?" he asked.

"Yeah," I said.

Outside, the wind picked up.

I stared at the door.

"You sure? Because you seem nervous or something." He glanced back at the door.

Our eyes met.

Without another word, I motioned for him to follow me. I didn't want to scare the family, especially the kids.

"I'll be right back," he said.

"Alright," Jennifer yelled from the kitchen.

He followed me into the hidden area of my room. "What's going on?"

"Keep low, Robert. I don't want them to see you," I whispered.

He hunkered down next to me. "Who?"

"I don't know who they are."

Robert and I peered over the window ledge out into the forest beyond.

"Right there..." I pointed to where the figures had been standing. But, they had disappeared.

"Who?" He raised his hands up in confusion. "Where?"

"They were right there. I just saw them. Men, women, I don't know. I couldn't see their faces."

He studied the area where I was pointing. "Are you sure?"

"I'm positive."

"Were they vampires? Werewolves?"

"I don't know. It's too far to tell.," I said. My voice shook. I trembled. "Robert, I don't know if I should be here."

"Don't even think about it, Mom. We'll fight this together."

I looked into his eyes. "I'm worried about the children."

"I know you are, but we'll be fine."

Screams pierced the air. Something shattered.

§

Rebecca stood at the kitchen counter, pouring the girls drinks.

The wind chimes rattled outside the kitchen window.

"Rebecca, would you mind pouring me a drink, too?" Jennifer asked. She pushed the girls' chairs into the table.

"Sure. Do you have a glass?"

"No, I don't."

As Rebecca grabbed a glass out of the cabinet, a pale face with red eyes appeared in the window. She screamed.

He snarled, revealing ragged sharp teeth. His hair was knotted up and disheveled. His claw-like fingernails struck the window pane.

She jumped. Her arm struck the bowl and the cups on the counter. The bowl fell onto the floor and shattered. Grated cheese and milk spilled everywhere.

Jennifer and the girls peered up at Rebecca from the kitchen table.

The vampire turned his attention to them. Tisa and Leah ran for their mother. Tisa clamored for her mother to pick her up. Katie screeched. She threw a fork at the window. Robert and Crystal ran down the stairs.

Rebecca gazed back at the window. The vampire disappeared.

"Is everybody alright?" Robert asked, eyes wide. He started towards his kids but Jennifer and his mom beat him to it.

"Come here, girls," they said, kneeling down. The girls ran to them.

Tisa locked her arms around Jennifer's neck and cried on her shoulder.

"It's okay, sweetie," Jennifer said, kissing her on the cheek. She held Tisa in her arms and rubbed her back.

Crystal sat on the floor, hugging Katie and Leah. They melted into her lap and cried on her shoulders. She smoothed their hair back and wiped tears from their eyes.

"Everything is alright," she said to them.

He turned his attention to Rebecca.

"What the hell happened?" he asked.

"Are you alright?" Robert hugged his wife. He glanced back at the girls.

"Yes," she answered.

"Girls, are you alright?" he asked.

"We're fine," Jennifer answered. She pressed Tisa tightly against her chest.

"What happened?" he asked. He turned his attention back to Rebecca.

Rebecca motioned toward the window. "There was a man outside, right there!"

"What?" Robert headed for the front door.

"Robert, no!" she screamed. She grabbed his arm.

But that didn't stop Robert.

"Stop!"

After he had taken another step, he stopped. "You're right…"

Relief washed over her.

Then, Robert went for the closet door under the staircase. He opened the closet door and grabbed his 44 Magnum.

The family backed off except for Rebecca.

"I need this first. Silver bullets will stop whoever or whatever is out there," he said. He checked the chamber. It was loaded.

Rebecca's eyes widened in horror. "You could get hurt."

Robert glanced back at her. "I'll be fine."

"You're going to get killed!"

Before she could say any more, he exited into the night and shut the door behind him.

§

Robert considered transforming into his werewolf form, but decided otherwise. If somebody was still out here, he preferred that they underestimate him.

He surveyed his surroundings. No one. With gun still in hand, he walked around the side of the house. The door lock clicked behind him. That would be Rebecca.

The safety of his family was priority. So, strict instructions had been set if there were signs of danger. Regardless of her outburst, she was following his orders.

Robert rounded the side of the house. No sign of the stranger. He moved toward the front when the side door opened.

Jennifer stared at him. "Let me go with you."

"Get back in the house."

"I'm…."

"Get back in the house!" Robert snapped.

Huffing, she shut the door and locked it.

He walked around to the other side of the house. Again, nothing. He peered off in to the direction his mother had seen the figures. No one was there.

He went to the front door and knocked. "Open the door."

"What's the code?" Rebecca asked.

He pressed his mouth against the crack between the door and the door frame.

"Honey bunches of pie," he said.

She opened the door. "Well?"

"Nothing. There was nobody out there."

She locked the door behind him.

"Did you lock up the house?" he asked.

Jennifer walked up behind Rebecca. "Yes, we did."

"There was somebody out there," Rebecca said. "I saw him. He was at the window. I think he was a vampire. His eyes were red."

"I can attest to that," Jennifer said.

He glanced at his mother. She said nothing.

"I believe you. Come on, let's eat. I'm sure the kids are hungry," he said. He tucked the gun into the waistband of his pants.

Tisa ran up to him, her cheeks wet from her tears.

He picked her up.

"I really wish you wouldn't stuff the gun in your pants," Rebecca said, nervously.

He glared at her. "Would you stop nitpicking? That's all you do lately. Can you do something besides bitch?"

Her eyes widened.

"What!" He threw one arm up in surrender.

"The language…"

He stomped into the kitchen.

"Hey, baby girl, daddy's not going to let anything happen to you guys, got that?" He hugged Tisa tight and kissed her on the forehead.

Tisa wiped her arm across her nose. "Yes, Daddy."

His other two daughters ran up and hugged him.

"And the same goes for you two," he said, looking down at them.

He sat Tisa in a chair at the dining room table, and kissed Leah and Katie. He sat down opposite his mother and began scooping mashed potatoes on to his plate.

Rebecca maintained her silence.

Tired of her constant bitching, he stabbed his food and shoveled it into his mouth. He went at the steak again, but drove his fork into the plate.

A chip of porcelain broke off. It flew back into his face.

"God…crap," he snapped.

Frowning, Rebecca stood. She had worry lines in her forehead. She touched his shoulder.

Robert drew in a deep breath and glanced up at her through the corner of his eye.

She slid her arms around his neck. Then she leaned her cheek against his face.

"I'm sorry, honey. I love you," she said.

He set the fork down.

"I love you too." He enclosed his hands around hers.

"I'm sorry I've been such a witch." She giggled.

Robert looked up at her.

"I always knew you were," he said, laughing.

She smacked him on the side of the head.

Robert laughed. Then he glanced back at the kitchen window. Still nothing.

This was going to be a long night.

Robert pulled his cell phone out of his pocket.

He dialed the Sheriff's office while she sat down.

"Hi, it's Robert. I'm not going to make it in. I have an issue here at the house. Yes. No, they didn't break in this time, but somebody's playing games and I'm about to put a stop to it. Okay, thank you. I will. See you tomorrow."

He shut the phone and threw it on the table.

AT LONG LAST

The next morning, I awoke to a knock on my bedroom door. I rolled over and stared at it.

"Come in!" I rubbed my eyes.

The door creaked open. Rebecca stood in the doorway.

She was out of focus. Again, I rubbed my eyes.

"Are you okay?" she asked.

"Yeah, why do you ask?" I groaned.

"I'm asking because it's one-thirty in the afternoon. You've been sleeping all morning, and I was worried about you."

"Oh, shit." It wasn't like I had anything to do, but I was sleeping half of the day away. It was time that I could spend with the kids.

I sat up. My shirt hung to the side, half exposing my breast. I straightened it out.

"Sorry," I said.

"No problem. I really didn't want to wake you."

"Thanks. I'm fine, though."

"The girls and I are meeting up with a friend of mine for a couple of hours. We'll be back in a little bit."

"Alright. Have fun," I said. Drats! She was leaving with the kids. Oh, well. I would find something to do.

She shut the door.

I fell back on the mattress. Robert and I had been up most of the night watching for anything suspicious. I hoped tonight was not going to be a repeat of last night. I got little to no sleep.

After I showered, dressed, and ate, I would go for my daily run. Besides, maybe I could find some physical evidence as to who might be watching us at night, whether it was Jace or somebody else. If I did find something, then maybe Robert could follow up on it.

Nobody was home, so I locked the door.

The sun was bright, and the air chilly. I walked through the front yard to where I had seen the watchers, keeping an eye open for anything out of the ordinary. As I approached the property line, I slowed down. No one was here, at least nobody that I could see.

I stepped into the forest. Birds chirped above me. A squirrel scurried up a tree. The movement of forest life was a good sign. It meant that no vampires or werewolves were around for they had a tendency to scare off the wildlife. I gazed up at the trees where I had seen the watchers. There were no scratches or marks on them. I lowered my gaze to the ground and looked around. No debris had been left behind.

Since nothing had been found, I decided to go on my daily run. I took once last glance around the area, swept my hair back, and ran along the path through the forest. It was the same route we had taken to the park many times before. It would be a quick jaunt since I didn't want to be out past dark. Considering the watchers were only seen after dark, I presumed they wouldn't be out until then.

Once in awhile I would take a break and look around. I wanted to make sure nobody was following me after the incident last night.

After a bit, I stopped for another break. A squirrel emerged from the brush and darted out in front of me.

I jumped. Again, I glanced around. Nobody. Just me and my overzealous mind. I drew in a deep breath and ran on.

The chill from the wind picked up and blew my hair across my face. My lips were parched. I took a swig from my water bottle. I tucked the bottle under my arm, took out my lip balm, and rubbed it on.

It wasn't much longer before I came upon a pasture to the right. The stench of manure wafted up my nose.

"Damn, that smells."

A ranch was on the other side of the pasture. A few cows grazed on the tall grass. White clouds rolled in overhead.

I hurried to get away from the stench.

By the time I arrived at the park, I decided to get to know the area for safety concerns. I traveled past it and into the forest beyond.

As I ran, dark clouds emerged. The sun lowered behind the mountain. It had to be close to five or five-thirty because of the position of the sun. So, I decided to head back. I sure as hell didn't want to get caught out here after dark.

Something moved in the trees.

I halted. The woods were thick with brush and dead broken trees. A flash of brown caught my eye. Was it the large mountain lion Robert had mentioned? I swallowed hard.

No other motion.

I was afraid to move. So, I waited for about ten minutes with my eyes open and my fists up. I waited for something to attack. Eventually, I lowered my hands. Thunder reverberated through the woods. Rain sprinkled down. So I zipped up my jacket and headed home. Everybody was probably home by now. I quickened my pace.

As I neared the park, the wind picked up. The chill penetrated my bones.

Bushes lined the path that I ran on. A large tree loomed overhead. The sun peeked over the top of the mountain. The swings swung to and fro. Branches whipped the air. The fresh scent of pine, moisture, and the nearby foliage filled my nostrils.

I peered back at the winding path. No one was there. Yet, I sensed a presence. My hair stood on end. I glanced at the park, the swing sets, the slide, the plastic tunnels, the monkey bars, and the thick shrubbery. Anything or anybody could be hiding behind them. I glanced at the chain link fence that separated the park and the woods. If a wild animal was blood thirsty or hungry enough, it wouldn't take much for him to leap over the fence.

I glanced behind me.

Red sun rays lit the top of the mountain on fire. Dark clouds drifted over the sun, casting a burnt orange glow on a small section of the pavement. Then, a figure stepped out of the shadows.

He was approximately six foot, medium built, rough looking with short, dark, wavy hair that was messed up from the wind. Black sunglasses covered his eyes. His goatee was closely trimmed, his sideburns medium length and thin. He wore jeans, a black button-up shirt, a black leather jacket, and black leather boots.

I preferred not to fight, but if I had to, I would. Instead, I ducked off the path and fled toward the park's public bathroom. My hair whipped around my face, obstructing my view.

His footsteps pounded the pavement behind me. He was getting closer.

As I ran, the exterior light on the bathroom facility blew out. The wind spun the sparks back into my face, just below the eye.

Despite the pain, I ran past the building and into the meadow to the left of the park. The rain fell harder.

"I don't want to hurt you," he said.

Then, he touched my back. I spun around to fight him. My foot slipped in the mud. I lost my balance. He caught me before I hit the ground.

He repeated, "I don't want to hurt you."

I was tired from running. "Then why are you following me?"

"I've been watching you."

I stared at him, unsure of where he was going with this. Something about him seemed familiar. Oddly, I felt protected within his embrace.

I pulled away from him. "I'm sorry, but I don't know who you are or what you want. Please, just let me go. And leave my family alone," I pleaded.

The rain and wind pelted us. My hair clung to my face. I was cold and my limbs were going rigid.

"Tell the others to leave us alone, too," I said.

"I can protect you and your family from the others," he whispered.

Where the hell did I know him from? I originally thought he was one of the strangers who had been watching my home. But now I was not so sure.

"Please, trust me. I know you don't understand, but I can help you. I'm the only one who can protect all of you," he said. The man pulled his glasses off. Hypnotic blue eyes stared back at me.

I gazed up at him, eyes wide. My mouth dropped open.

"Tristan?"

"Yes." He smiled.

Relief washed over me. I threw my arms around him.

"Oh, my God. I was worried. What happened to you?" I asked, pulling back. I looked him over.

He was unscathed.

"Eh, a little scuffle but nothing to worry about. I'm fine," he said. He looked around. "We should really get you home. You're cold. And, I'm sure your family is worried about you."

"Yes, I'm sure they are," I said. I rubbed my arms.

"You know, I can get you home quicker. Better than walking in the rain and catching a death of a cold."

I laughed. "Very true. If you would be so kind, I would appreciate it."

§

Once we arrived at my house, I took his hand in mine. I wasn't sure how Robert was going to react to me bringing this man home. It was inevitable that Tristan would be spending time with the family to watch over us. That troubled me as well, especially with the kids. After all, he was a vampire. But he was one of the few I trusted.

"Thank you for everything, Tristan. I really do appreciate it."

I meant that with sincere respect. From here, I didn't know what to expect. I pulled my hand back.

He gripped it firmly. "You're welcome, Brandy."

I smiled.

We walked up the brick stone among the lilies.

The moment I stepped onto the patio, Robert threw the front door open. The screen door bounced off the side of the house. Robert stared at me, eyes wide.

"You know, we really need to fix that," I said.

"You're concerned about that damn door, and we've been worried sick about you." He did a double take when he saw Tristan.

"I'm sorry, Robert," I said.

Robert looked at Tristan.

"Hi Robert, I'm Tristan." He offered his hand to my son.

Robert sniffed the air before shaking his hand. His eyes narrowed in on the stranger.

"We ran into each other at the park," Tristan said.

Smiling, I winked at Robert.

"I thought it was best to walk her home since it was raining. Sorry I didn't get her home sooner." Tristan smiled.

"Hi, no, that's okay. I, uh, didn't know she was with anybody," Robert said. "Won't you come in?"

"Yes, please," I asked.

Robert opened the door wider.

Tristan and I stepped into the foyer. He helped me take my jacket off.

"Let me get you some towels." Robert shut the door, and then disappeared into the hallway.

In the light, Tristan's facial features were rough. He looked like somebody that should have been behind bars. I was surprised my son wasn't reading him the riot act, unless he had seen something in Tristan's eyes that I hadn't. They were his softest feature.

"Your son is very protective of you."

"Yeah, well, he knows what I've been through. Most of it anyway. He doesn't need to know everything."

"I understand."

Robert reappeared behind me. "Will you stay for dinner?"

I grimaced. I hoped he hadn't heard everything I had said.

Tristan and I each took a towel.

"Yes, will you?" I already knew what he was going to say.

"Yes, I will. Thank you."

I handed our jackets to Robert. Except for the rough exterior, my son could have easily passed for Tristan's son. They had the same build and physique.

"Do you have some clothes that might fit him? He might catch a death of a cold in these," I said with a smirk.

Tristan caught it, too. He grinned.

Robert looked him over. "I'm sure I do."

We'd almost gotten our shoes off by the time the kids came running around the corner. Their faces brightened up.

"Grandma!" they yelled.

"Hi, girls!"

They hugged me.

"Oh, girls, you're going to get all wet." I crouched down and gave them kisses. "Why don't you three go see your mama?"

They ran in to the kitchen.

"Hi Mom," Jennifer said. She stood in the entryway of the dining area with a big smile. She glanced at Tristan.

"Who is he?"

"I'm Tristan." Tristan shook her hand.

"Jennifer. Nice to meet you," she said with a devilish grin.

We exchanged glances.

"Is Rebecca in the kitchen?" I asked.

"Yes, and dinner is almost done. So why don't you two go change your clothes, and get ready for dinner?" she said. Jennifer disappeared into the kitchen.

Robert appeared with some dry clothes. "Here you go. Hopefully they'll fit you, and we can put yours in the dryer. If not, let me know and I'll see what else I can find."

Robert handed a neat stack to Tristan. Then, he brushed past me, heading towards the kitchen.

"Sorry. My kids are, uh…um, a little protective," I apologized.

"That's alright. They're just worried about their mother. And it doesn't matter how old you are, or how old they are, they're still going to worry about you. Be thankful." He smiled.

"Thank you. Um, the first door on your right is the bathroom." I pointed toward the restroom. "You can change in there. Just leave your clothes on the counter, and I'll put them in the dryer for you."

We went our separate ways. Once I was in my bathroom, I finished drying off. As I changed my clothes, I thought about Tristan and where he would sleep if he stayed the night. Only two rooms, other than the living room, were available. I wasn't sure if Robert wanted Tristan sleeping alone in any part of the house.

The only room that was dark enough for him to sleep was mine, if he slept at all. He was a vampire. He would be awake all night. Very awkward! Yes, he would definitely need to sleep in my room.

Besides, he didn't need to make any noise in the middle of the night. Robert might come out of his bedroom with a gun, thinking it was an intruder, and shoot him. Not good. Hell, who knows, Robert might interrogate him. Shit! He was probably interrogating him now.

I darted out of my room, fumbled with the child's gates, and damn near fell on my face when Tristan rounded the corner.

"Whoa! You alright there?" he asked.

I spun around.

He had just come out of the bathroom.

"Uh, yeah."

"You know, you could get yourself hurt running down the stairs like that."

"I was just hurrying," I said. "I'm hungry, what about you?"

"I could probably eat a bite or two," he said, grinning.

I thought about his remark. Vampires didn't eat, at least not people food. Oh, Christ, this was going to be fun.

"Uh, I didn't think about that," I whispered.

He patted my shoulder.

"That's okay. We'll make it through."

Rebecca and Jennifer finished setting the dinner table when we walked in.

Rebecca looked at him and straightened up. She had a curious look in her eye.

Jennifer sat down and grinned at me.

The girls chattered away as they climbed into their seats.

Then, Rebecca and Robert sat down toward the head of the table.

I sat across from Jennifer with Tristan at my side.

Tristan glanced at Leah, who sat next to him.

She gave him a flirtatious smile.

A big smile crossed his face.

I smiled, drawing in a deep breath. I hoped for a peaceful dinner with no sign of attack.

Tristan leaned over. "And what's your name?"

"She's Leah." Rebecca stabbed a steak on the platter with her fork.

"Mama, I was going to tell him my name," Leah said.

Robert gave Rebecca a dirty look, telling her to back down.

"Mama's sorry, isn't she?" he said.

Rebecca looked at her daughter. "I'm sorry, honey. Yes, you can tell him your name. Mama's just being overprotective." She kept her eye on Tristan.

Tristan was courteous enough to smile at her.

"I'm Leah," she said. She had a gleam in her eye. "And, these are my sisters. That's Tisa next to my mommy and this is Katie, next to me."

"Hello, ladies." Tristan gazed up at Robert and Rebecca. "You have beautiful daughters. They look just like their mother."

Rebecca blushed. She exchanged glances with her husband, and then Tristan.

"Well, thank you," she said, sweeping back her hair.

I smiled. He knew how to turn on the charm. Already, he was growing on Rebecca. That was quite a feat.

Jennifer snuck a peek at Rebecca. Her eyes lit up, and a devilish grin appeared.

Rebecca's voice lowered. "There's steak here, potatoes, salad, and bread. Help yourself. There's plenty."

Yes, she was flattered by his charm.

"Ah, thank you. I'm not real hungry, but I might take a steak."

Even though we offered him to choose first, he did not. He waited for the rest of us to pick ours. Then, he picked his piece, the rawest on the platter. Blood pooled around the meat.

"Robert, that one is really rare. I thought you got it done."

"Sorry, I can cook that one more for you. I don't want you to eat it if you don't like it raw." Robert took a bite of his steak. It was also undercooked and very bloody. He glanced up at Tristan.

"No, I'm good. Thank you."

Jennifer and I finished getting our food. We kept our eye on the men.

"Ew, that's really nasty," Leah said. "It's…"

Rebecca interrupted Leah. "That's not nice. You watch your manners and apologize."

She pointed her fork at Leah. Leah looked up at her daddy.

"Sorry, Daddy." Her little lips upturned.

Pouting, she looked at Tristan. "Sorry…Tristan."

"That's alright. Apology accepted," he said, winking at her.

She smiled, and then dug into her food.

"They are adorable, Robert," he said.

"Thank you." Robert took a bite out of his biscuit.

"So, how do you know Mom?" Jennifer asked. She took a sip from her glass.

Tristan and I glanced at her.

I considered this carefully. "Uh…well, you know how I told you everything that happened?"

"Yeah?" She took a bite of her salad.

"Well, Tristan is the one who saved me when my friend Warrant was attacked. He…"

Tristan studied me.

"He's the one who got me away from the motel and took me to safety."

"I'm the one who brought her here," he said.

Everybody looked at him.

"Relax, I have connections," he said, holding up his hands. "I wanted to make sure she was safe, so I had somebody do some research for me. Warrant said he thought you had family here, so we decided to try to help you. We didn't say anything, just in case we couldn't find your family. I do hope everybody's happy."

"Well, then, I guess I owe you some gratitude." Robert's eyes softened. "Thank you. I've been looking all over for her."

"Yes, thank you, Tristan. I didn't know," I said.

"Well, you wouldn't have known. I've been working a lot and, well, things just happened to crisscross and I was able to figure it out."

I stuck a piece of steak in my mouth.

"What do you do for a living?" Robert asked.

I glanced up at Robert.

"I'm in law enforcement."

"Oh, nice." Robert straightened up. "Which agency?"

I chewed my food faster so that I could swallow it and help answer questions.

"I'm sorry. I'd like to answer that question but my position doesn't allow me to divulge that information." Tristan took a bite of his steak.

"Secret service, eh? Gotcha, I understand." Robert grinned.

Tristan smiled.

"You don't look like Secret Service," Robert said. But I guess that's the whole point. Don't worry. Your secret is safe with us."

Robert turned his attention back to his food.

A drop of blood from the meat sat on Tristan's lips.

Our eyes met.

Tristan winked at me. He licked the crimson liquid from his lip.

Was he flirting with me?

My heart skipped a beat. I turned away.

Jennifer caught our interaction, and she winked, too.

I shoveled more food in my mouth.

Please, not in front of my kids, especially Jennifer. She seemed to be the only one who caught it, and apparently found it rather amusing.

I peeked up at her.

She giggled.

Tristan turned his attention back to Robert.

I mouthed the words, *stop it.*

She mouthed the word, *no.*

It was time to call it quits at the table.

I pushed my chair back. "Well, I'm done. That was great. Thank you for dinner. Son, you made a fantastic steak."

I picked up my half-eaten plate and walked into the kitchen with it. I was worried Tristan and Robert were getting a little too close for comfort.

Before I knew it, the girls wanted down and everybody was full. Jennifer, Rebecca, and I stood in the kitchen, washing the plates.

"So, where's his car, Mom?" Jennifer asked.

"I don't know. He must have parked it somewhere. We decided to take a walk," I lied.

Rebecca rolled her eyes. "Really? It's raining pretty hard out there. Who takes a walk in the rain?"

"We did." I didn't lie.

"What I meant, is what type of person walks in the rain?"

"Us." Again I didn't lie.

Rebecca's eyes narrowed in on me. She gazed out the window.

"Is he going to stay the night, Mom?" Jennifer asked. "I think he needs to. He shouldn't be walking out there."

It was obvious my daughter hadn't become accustomed to her young wolf's senses yet. Once she did get used to them, she would know what he was. Right now, she saw a knight in shining armor trying to woo her mom.

"Yeah, is he going to stay the night?" Rebecca asked, sternly. She raised her eyebrows.

I got the hint. It was apparent she suspected he was one of the creatures who had been watching our house.

"He's not one of them, Rebecca."

"Not one of whom?" Jennifer asked.

I'm sure Rebecca's witch senses were on high alert.

Jennifer wasn't stupid, either. Her mind just happened to be elsewhere.

"Nothing," we said at the same time.

Jennifer gave us a funny look and turned away to gather the empty dishes that were still on the table.

Tristan stood before Jennifer, a few dinner plates in hand.

Jennifer stopped short of running into him.

"Oh, you didn't have to do that. Let me take those," she said.

"It's no problem," he replied.

He moved to the side to go around her.

With dishes still in hand, his attention was on Rebecca. She was busy putting empty plates in the sink.

That was until Jennifer cut him off. "You like my mom, don't you?" She put her hands on the plates in his hand.

I gasped.

"Yes, I do." He studied her. "She's a wonderful and beautiful woman, just like you. Do me a favor, Jennifer?"

"What's that?"

"Listen to your mom. She's a good person, and she knows what's right. She only wants the best for you," he whispered.

"I will."

"Good. You can have your plates then!" He handed her the plates.

As Robert tried to get Katie out of her seat, she struggled to get out of his hands.

Tristan walked up to them.

"No, Daddy, no," she screamed.

"Katie, I'm trying to get you down." He shook his finger at her. "Now will you stop?"

"I want him to get me down." She pointed her finger at Tristan.

"You don't even know him. Why do you want him to get you down?" Robert asked.

"I want to see," she moaned.

"I don't know what you're talking about, so you're out of luck."

He set her down on the floor. She flailed about.

Katie, Leah, and Tisa ran around the table. Their speed accelerated beyond the velocity of any mortal human.

Tristan studied them. He put his hands down and caught Katie.

"You're fast. Where did you learn to run that fast?"

"My daddy."

Robert and Tristan exchanged glances.

Tristan turned back to her. "Is your daddy that fast?"

"He's really fast." She threw her hands out in a wild gesture.

"So, what is it you wanted to *see*?" His eyes widened.

"You," she said, pointing at him.

"Why me?" he asked, his voice child-like. He picked her up, so that her bottom sat on his forearm.

"You're different." She cocked her head.

"Yeah, how?"

"You're not like mommy, or daddy, or auntie Jen, or grandma, or my sisters."

"How am I different though?"

She squished his cheeks with her hands and peered into his eyes. "You're…"

Rebecca whisked her daughter out of his hands.

"It's bath time. Sorry, Tristan, another time," she said. Her voice shook and her hands trembled. "Come on, girls."

I stared after them. What exactly did Katie want to see?

NIGHT

Everybody had gone to bed, except for Tristan and me. While he went outside to check out the property, I glanced around my bedroom. My curtains were not thick enough to block the sunlight from shining through and killing him in the daytime, so I located a thick blanket to hang over my window.

I would need his help hanging it. So, until he got back, I changed into my pink pajama short set.

Thirty minutes passed. The rain beat harder against the window. I was getting more concerned about Tristan. Why was it taking him so long?

As I peered out of the window, a soft click came from the doorway.

I stared back at the door. It was closed. The room was empty. Something about it set me off. But why? There was nothing there.

I gazed out of the window.

Then, something shifted.

I spun around.

The room was still empty, but the bathroom door stood ajar. It was dark inside.

I approached the door, slipped my hand inside, and flipped on the light switch. No one stood inside. Yet, Tristan's wet clothes lay in the tub instead of my towel. What the hell…?

"Tristan…?" I spun around.

Still, no one. An invisible being touched my shoulder.

My heart beat jumped. I started to scream.

"Shush." Tristan's invisible hand covered my mouth. "You're going to wake your family."

The bastard. My heart was racing.

"You scared the shit out of me."

"Sorry about that." Tristan's face became visible. "I wasn't trying to scare you. I just wanted to dry off and get dressed real quick."

He tossed the towel on the mattress.

My gaze drifted to the bed. His dry clothes and pajama pants lay on the end of the bed. Wait? He still wasn't dressed. My eyes fell on his pale, lean, and nude body. Oh, shit!

I pulled away. Then I tripped over my own feet.

Tristan caught me. His muscles tightened.

This was awkward.

"You really should watch your step."

"And, maybe you should remain visible so I can see when you're getting dressed."

Wait, that didn't sound right.

He raised an eyebrow.

"What…" I said.

His lips met mine. His kiss was cool, gentle, and inviting.

Our kiss surmounted into something warm and passionate. It overwhelmed my senses.

I embraced him and all of his desire.

His hold on me tightened. His kiss trailed down my neck.

It elicited an innate desire to bed him. I melted in his arms.

He picked me up and laid me down upon the bed. His lips moved over every inch of my neck and throat.

A sharp tooth grazed my skin.

Memories of Jace filled my head. Oh, no, please no. Fear settled deep inside.

My eyes flew open. "Tristan?"

"Hmm." His voice was muffled against my neck.

"You're not going to bite me, are you? I don't want…"

He pulled away. "No, not intentionally, anyway."

Again, he kissed me.

I squirmed.

Not intentionally? What did he mean by that?

His lips found my neck again.

"What did you mean by that?"

He found the soft spot behind my ear.

I moaned.

"Just what I said," he whispered.

"Well, you wouldn't have said that for the hell of it, right?" I whispered.

He turned my face to his. "You're ruining the moment."

"I'm sorry, I just…"

Sighing, he pulled away.

"You just let me know when you're ready. I'll wait," he said, standing.

Dammit, Crystal. How could you? You want him just as much as he wants you. Let it go. He's not Jace.

Frustrated, I bit my lip. I propped myself up on my elbows.

Tristan put on his pajama bottoms.

"Hey."

He said nothing. Instead, he grabbed the blanket and walked over to the window.

Dammit, I wished I hadn't said anything. I followed him.

"I'm sorry."

He avoided eye contact.

"Look at me, please?"

"That's okay. I said I'll wait. I don't want to force you into anything you don't want to do."

"It's not that I don't want to. It's just that somebody hurt me, and I'm a little leery…" I really didn't want to talk about it, so I shut up.

Silence followed.

His eyes questioned mine.

I bit my tongue. My mind raced back to the night Jace practically raped me. Though Jace had forced himself on me, there had been a hypnotic trance that coerced me into it. I honestly couldn't tell Tristan if Jace raped me or not, for I eventually welcomed his advances. Regardless, it was still rape.

"What's on your mind?" He lowered the blanket.

"Nothing," I answered.

"Bullshit, you're lying," he said, pointing at me.

Should I tell him? I looked away.

"What is it?"

I had his full attention. I swept my hair back, and gazed up at him.

"Well, I…" I couldn't look at him.

He stepped in front of me.

"What happened? And, tell me the truth?"

I took a deep breath. What did I have to lose by telling him the truth? I told him everything that happened that night.

"When I find this man, I will destroy him," he said, his eyes intent on mine. They were red and filled with anger. His fangs protruded over his lips.

I was surprised by his over zealous anger toward Jace.

"Tristan…" I took a step toward him and grasped his arm.

Our eyes met.

He bit his lip hard enough to draw blood.

I gasped.

Then, his eyes softened. "I would never hurt you." He dropped the blanket, took me into his arms, and consoled me.

"What I said earlier about not intentionally biting you, I said because when we hit our climax we have an extremely difficult time controlling our urges." He caressed my cheek. "I would do everything within my willpower to not change you, and not to bite you."

My breath caught in my throat.

He placed his cool hands on my cheeks.

I took his hand in mine.

"Tristan, come lie with me. I don't want to think about him right now."

I walked backwards, pulling him along with me. The back of my knees found the bed. I toppled back on to the mattress. It was closer than I expected.

Tristan fell with me, but caught himself with his hands braced against the bed.

"I thought you wanted to wait," he whispered.

"Yeah, well, I don't want to spend the night with an angry vampire, either."

He grinned. His red eyes turned back to their original, captivating blue.

Visions of a blue-eyed man flooded into my head, the same man who washed my hair in prison. My eyes had been almost swollen shut, making it difficult to get a good look at him.

Tristan's mouth overpowered mine.

He was the same man who held me down while my shoulder was being stitched up in prison. I had not seen his face that day, but I distinctly remembered his voice and his scent.

His hands explored my body. I relinquished myself to him.

The blue-eyed man was the cop who arrested me outside of the bar the night my husband was murdered. I had an overwhelming recollection of his face. That man was Tristan.

No, it couldn't be. Could it?

I was finally able to connect some of my past together. My eyes fluttered open.

"Tristan?" I whispered, beneath his lips.

"Yes."

"I thought you said you were in law enforcement." I stared up at the ceiling, afraid to look down and meet his eyes.

"I am," he mumbled.

His lips were on that sweet spot again.

"Then why the hell did you kidnap me and put me in that horrible place?"

He froze.

"Why did you leave me there? I thought you were a good person."

He pulled back.

"You tricked me."

Our eyes met.

"Crystal...Brandy, it was for your protection."

I was right.

"We knew you were going to be safer there than being out on your own."

"Who's we?" I asked, pushing him off of me. I rolled on to my side to face him.

"The U.G.S.S. The Underground Secret Service," he said, propping his elbow up on the bed. He lay his chin on his hand.

"I don't understand what I have to do with the U.G.S.S., and why they would protect me. What connections do I have with them?"

He sighed. "The U.G.S.S. was after your husband Chris, the night the two of you went to the bar and he got killed. He got pretty far in debt gambling on the underground fighting circuit. He couldn't make the payments so they sent somebody to take him out."

My mouth dropped open. I thought about the stripper that killed him. Was she an agent? And, if so, why would the U.G.S.S. be interested in gambling debts?

"I guess I'm still confused." I scratched my head.

"The U.G.S.S. regulates the circuit. Any and all gambling affairs go through them at some point. You know how it is with government, they have to have their hands in everything, which includes making money off the winners, the losers, and the *fighters*," he said, stressing the last word.

I nodded. My brow furrowed in.

"They'll take anything they want, especially mortals who know how to fight."

I sat up and stared at him. "Like me?" I asked.

"Yes, we had to keep you safe from the U.G.S.S. Director. If he sees something he likes, he takes it."

I swallowed hard. I didn't like where this was going.

"If the director had the chance, he would have captured you that night and held you prisoner. After your fight with the stripper, all eyes were on you, but thankfully, somebody made the call to remove you from the bar."

"Was it you?" I asked.

He rubbed his chin. "No, another agent made that decision. That person preferred to remain anonymous. I just received the message to get you out of there. Whoever that agent is has a vested interest in you, though. He didn't want to see you get hurt." He looked away.

"And, believe it or not, you were better off in your cell than out in the open. Your piece of shit husband was willing to give your life up in exchange for his."

I cringed.

"That's exactly what his intentions were at that bar. The Director was going to be there that night."

It was a good thing Chris was dead, and that I didn't remember anything about him. Otherwise, I would kill him myself.

I lay back down, my head upon his chest. He had no heartbeat.

"You're better off without him, anyway." Tristan ran his fingers through my hair. "What triggered your memory?"

"I don't know, your eyes maybe." I looked up at him. "Do you remember when you told Warrant he was getting to close to me?"

He nodded.

"I think you're doing the same."

"Maybe."

I missed Warrant. But I kept my mouth shut. My attachment to Tristan was growing. Maybe it was the need to be comforted or feel loved.

I sighed. Sadness overwhelmed me. Tristan must have detected it for he gazed down upon me.

"Though I can't survive in the daytime, I can make it up to you. I can show you some beautiful things at night, if you'd like."

"I'd like that." I smiled.

"Good. When it stops raining, I'll take you out in the woods. It's absolutely gorgeous," he said, closing his eyes.

He stretched out his arms, his taut muscles flexing and moving beneath his pale flesh.

My eyes lingered on his muscular arms. Then my gaze trailed down his body. The waist band of his pants hung lower than his hips, revealing a thin line of hair which disappeared beneath the material.

I wanted to reach out and touch him, to allow my fingers to slip inside his pants.

Oh, I was getting myself worked up. Not that he wouldn't mind. Did I really want to come across as an easy woman? No, I didn't.

But I couldn't help it. The thought of kissing his chest and licking his nipples popped into my head.

Stop it! I was not going to get any sleep. What the hell was I going to do, sit here and stare at his masculine body all night?

I shook my head as if it would get rid of the naughty thoughts.

Tristan glanced down at me.

"Are you alright?" he asked. His voice was low and seductive.

It was obvious we wanted each other.

I closed my eyes and ignored him.

"Brandy?"

I tried to think about something else that would draw my attention away from him. I drew in a deep breath.

"It's hard not to think about, isn't it?" he whispered.

"What are you talking about?" I played stupid.

"You're thinking about making love to me."

My eyelids fluttered open. How the hell could he know?

"Well, then I'll think about something specific. Tell me, what am I thinking about now?"

Pleasuring him just popped into my head. Shit! Please tell me, he couldn't read my thoughts.

He chuckled. "Some I can, at least if they have to do with me?"

Egads! He knew what I was thinking this whole time.

"You're kissing my chest, moving down my stomach."

I closed my eyes.

"You're pulling my pants down, ready to…"

"That's good enough," I said, opening my eyes.

Tristan lowered his face down to mine, his eyes intense.

"It's your turn," he whispered.

Yes, it was my turn to seduce him. Only now, there was no going back.

I lunged for him, eager for his insatiable desire. Our mouths intertwined, our hunger ravenous. I climbed atop him, my mouth seeking every inch of his flesh, from his lips to his ear.

Tristan moaned. He pressed me harder against him and rolled me onto my back. He rocked his hips against mine. His manhood strained against his pants.

"Oh, yes," I whispered. Oh, how I wanted him inside me.

He tore my shirt open. Buttons flew off. He lowered his face to my breast, licking and sucking on my nipples.

I arched my back, pushing my breasts up into his face.

He wrapped his hands around my hips, his fingers inching over the waistband of my shorts. He gazed up at me, as if seeking my final approval.

"Take me now." I curled my hands over his, urging him to remove my shorts and panties. He slid off my clothing.

Smiling, Tristan looked me over.

I sat up, grabbed his pants, and pulled them down.

His manhood sprung free.

I grinned and peered up into his eyes. They were soft, but hard, unrelenting yet sensitive. I rested my hands on his shoulders and sat on his lap, positioning myself over him.

He grabbed my hips and pulled me down atop him. He slid deep inside.

"Oh, Tristan," I moaned. I gave it all to him.

We moved in perfect rhythm, gratifying our hunger and desire. Multiple waves of pleasure overtook me. Then, he rolled me on to my back, and plunged deep inside, driving me to my ultimate climax.

He buried his face in my neck, his fangs grazing my skin. A thin line of blood leaked from the wound. His tongue flicked over it. Then, an animalistic sound escaped his lips.

TRUTH

Once Brandy was asleep, Tristan slipped quietly out of her bedroom. He glanced at the closed doors on the second floor. It was dark and quiet. Yet, he sensed something was amiss. Silently, he leapt over the second floor balcony. The moment his feet hit the first floor, he spun around.

Robert emerged from the darkness of the hallway.

"I want to know who you are and what you've done to my wife," Robert said. He looked Tristan over.

"For starters, I've done nothing to your wife. And, secondly, if I told you who I was, then I'd have to kill you." A sly smirk crossed Tristan's face.

Robert stood still. He studied Tristan.

"Your wife is a special woman, you should treasure her," Tristan said. "Trust her premonitions, trust her thoughts, and do not doubt her. She knows more than you think she knows."

"I know she does." Robert nodded. "I try to avoid confrontation with her. She can be a dangerous woman," he said, glancing up at the ceiling.

"And you can be a dangerous man. Maybe that's why you two fit. She knows the spell to rid the pain of your lovemaking when your alter ego comes through. And when you do hurt her, you can heal her, make the wounds go away quicker. Is that not true?" Tristan raised his eyebrow. He knew what Rebecca was.

Robert took a couple of steps. Then he gazed back at Tristan.

"Yes, that's true." Robert crossed his arms. "She called your name as if she were making love to you tonight. I can only presume she was feeling my mother's pleasure and pain? She's only ever felt the children's emotions."

Tristan stared past Robert at the shut door of the den. He turned his full attention back to Robert again.

"Her magic sides with the strongest female of the clan," Tristan said. "Even though you're her husband, her clan is her children. You are her alpha. Jennifer has not fit into that clan yet, but she will when she becomes stronger. Brandy is the strongest of the females here, including your wife. She'll need to protect her mind with a spell, that way she won't link up with Brandy anymore."

Robert sighed. "Hmm." He shoved his hands in his pockets.

"I'm going to take the risk of you having to kill me and I'm going to ask, who are you? What is it you want and why?"

Tristan cocked his head. Then, he became invisible.

The door behind Robert opened. He turned and stared at Jennifer, who stood in the doorway, rubbing her eyes.

"Robert?" she mumbled.

"Sorry. Did I wake you?"

"Yeah. Who are you talking to?" Jennifer looked around.

"Nobody. I was just talking to myself. Sorry, I couldn't sleep. I was headed into the den. Go back to bed."

"Okay," she said. Jennifer glanced around again. She walked into her room, shaking her head. The door closed behind her.

Robert looked for Tristan. The den. Tristan had been eyeing the door. Robert turned and opened it.

Tristan sat kicked back in a wicker chair, his legs crossed.

Robert walked in and shut the door behind him.

He stared at Tristan. "How the hell did you do that?"

"It's a gift. Something I was born with."

Robert sat down in the wicker chair opposite Tristan. "A gift?"

"Yes, like something your daughter has. Not you, or your sister, but Katie. The others don't have it, but she does," he said, pointing toward the ceiling. "See, you and your sister were born with a curse, along with your children. Katie, on the other hand, has a gift. Now, I know we don't know each other, but promise me something."

Robert eyed Tristan.

"Let Katie learn her gift. Teach her, help her. She has a gift to see beyond what we see. She needs to experience it so she can expand upon her knowledge. I'm not exactly sure what she sees yet, but it's something. Something beyond what we know."

Robert leaned forward on his knees. "Yeah...yeah, I'll do that. She's my daughter. Of course, I'm doing to help her, but how, if I don't know what it is?"

"She'll let you know. Now, your sister, on the other hand, she has much to learn. She is a young wolf, with no knowledge on how to use or control her alter ego. Had she been experienced, she would have known I was there with you in the hallway."

"I'm working with her on it."

"Keep doing that," Tristan said, tapping his fingers on the chair arm. "She needs you to help her. She has much to learn, but once she does, she will be a strong and powerful creature that no one can stop. Her anger gets the best of her. The medicines helped to keep it under control, but now that she's stopped taking them, she's going to have outbursts. Be prepared."

"And how do you know all this?" Robert asked.

Tristan leaned forward in his chair. He propped his elbows on his knees and gazed up at Robert.

"Whatever I tell you stays in this room. I'm not at liberty to discuss details of my job, but from one law enforcement agent to another, I know you're not going to back off."

"That's right, I'm not. So you might as well give it up, Tristan."

They grinned at one another.

"Brandy told you about Warrant, I presume."

"Yes, but I'm still not sure who he was. A boyfriend? Friend, maybe? She never gave me details."

"Good, she did what she was supposed to do."

"What's that?"

"Trust no one and regardless of whom she was talking to—family, friend or whomever—do not tell anyone who we are."

Robert's eyebrows narrowed. "I don't understand. Was Warrant a law enforcement officer, too?"

"Something like that. Warrant was sent to find a man—a vampire—who is experimenting with immoral and unethical practices. We believe that your mom was supposed to be a part of that experiment. With her knowledge and master of the martial arts, we believe he was going to use her to delve further into his experimentation. Warrant was sent to find that vampire. I, on the other hand, was sent to find and protect your mother."

Robert straightened up. His eyes widened.

Tristan continued. "My secondary mission is to kill that vampire."

Robert held his hand up. "Wait a minute. Why would you kill the vampire? Why wouldn't Warrant kill him?"

"Because I was originally sent to find and protect your mother. Warrant was tracking him. If we found him, then we would kill him.

But, we have yet to find him. We know what he looks like and we've been running searches on him, but so far they've been unsuccessful."

"Well, so much for your law enforcement agency."

"I don't work for the law enforcement agencies as you know them, Robert. I work for The Underground Secret Service," Tristan said, firmly.

"I guess I still don't understand."

"Warrant and I are both snipers, only he works for the werewolf community and I work for the vampire community. Because we're both loners, and not in with a clan, we've dedicated our lives and our services to assisting each other's community in locating the unethical and immoral work of criminals. Believe it or not, we can work together. Those of us who have learned to control our instincts and bury the past."

"Interesting. I knew there were some unethical practices, but I've never heard of the Underground Secret Service."

"We also have the bounty hunters who are sent to capture and bring the criminals back for prosecution and extermination."

"Okay, then, why weren't the bounty hunters sent instead of snipers? Why not prosecution?"

"With prosecution, a jury is selected to determine guilt or innocence, just as in your world. We don't need to prove either in this instance. We already know he's guilty of the crimes. We already have evidence. He's already killed three of our agents."

Robert perked up. "Wow! So, there's like a war going on that we don't know about?"

"That's right."

Robert rubbed his chin. "It sounds like this is something that's being hidden from the mortals."

Tristan nodded. "That's correct. We don't want humans to know about this. Much like your government, we would prefer to contain it before we have to notify the human government."

"But, if it came down to it, would you contact our government?"

"Yes we would, but it also depends on the circumstances. In the meantime, we need to concentrate on catching this vampire. He needs to die before he kills more innocent people. He's an extremely dangerous man."

"On that note, I have another question. Why are his deeds criminal as compared to how you survive?"

Tristan continued. "J.T. medically transforms humans, vampires, and werewolves into hybrids such as a werewolf-vampire hybrid. We have reason to believe he wanted to use your mother in his experimentation. She just happened to be in the wrong place at the wrong time under the wrong circumstances."

"Interesting."

"Your father had been betting in the fighting circuit for a while and then got in over his head. He owed the owner a lot of money."

"The owner of…?"

"The Southwest Regional fighting circuit," Tristan answered. "He started with the bookies. The bookies stopped lending him money. So then your father went to the owner of the regional circuit, Dominic Fanucci. Dominic let him bet a few times and your father was able to pay him back. The last time he bet, he couldn't pay Dominic back. That put your parents lives on the line."

Robert's eyes widened. "I never knew that."

"Well, you were a child. You wouldn't know that," Tristan said. "Fortunately for you and Jennifer, Dominic was a family man. He wouldn't go after the children, only the parents. The night your parents went out was a setup. Your father was slated to be killed, but because Fanucci had seen your mother fight in martial arts competitions before, he wanted her alive, under his command."

"Let me guess, he's a vampire or a werewolf?" Robert leaned in closer.

"Yes, he's a vampire. But, trust me when I say this." Tristan pointed his finger at Robert. "You'd better be glad that a wolf stepped in to not only save her, but capture her alive. That was better punishment for Fanucci than anything. Brandy was going to bring him the money that your father lost. Instead, he lost it when she remained undefeated for the next four and a half years. He lost a lot of money and a lot of pride. Towards the end, he wanted to kill her. He didn't like being made a fool."

Robert scratched his head. "Holy shit. That's a lot to take in."

"Sorry you have to learn everything this way. Your mom wouldn't like it."

"Thanks." Robert frowned.

Tristan leaned forward. "And, as for the creatures that watch your house, I'm not sure who hired them. It could be either Fanucci or J.T. Both have the motive to kill her."

"How would Fanucci or J.T. know about my family, though?"

Tristan didn't answer. One of the two men had to have hired the creatures to watch the house. He didn't believe it was coincidence.

"Tristan?"

"In order for them to find your family, either J.T. or Fanucci would have to have a connection in the mortal world. Logically speaking, Fanucci does, but I'm not so sure he hired the creatures. If that's not the case, then there's a security breach within the U.G.S.S."

Robert's jaw tightened.

Tristan mulled it over.

Robert was also silent. He rubbed his chin again.

"Would you do a favor for me, Robert?"

"What's that?"

"Would you run a picture of J.T. through your work for me?"

Robert looked up at him. "Yes, of course."

"Maybe you can access something in the mortal world that we can't. Anything helps."

"I'll see what I can find on him," Robert said, nodding.

"Thanks, I appreciate it. I'll get you a photo." Tristan leaned back. "I'm still concerned, though."

"What about?"

"That our only way to find J.T. is going to be through the circuit. He's playing God with these hybrids he's making, and he's killed some of our agents. I think we'll find him in the circuit."

"So, why are you concerned about that?"

When Tristan didn't immediately answer, Robert's eyes widened. "Ah, shit–mom?"

"Yes."

Robert hung his head. "She's going to have to fight again, isn't she?"

"Probably."

"Will he show up to watch her?"

"I'm sure he will."

"And what about Fanucci?"

"If she fights, I'm sure Fanucci will be around, too."

"Shit." Robert rubbed his forehead. "I don't want mom in this situation. She just got out of it."

"Neither do I. But we have to worry about Fanucci, J.T., and these hybrids that J.T. is creating. I have another concern there."

"And that is?" Robert peered up at Tristan.

"What I need to tell you, we have to talk to Brandy about. And I don't think she's going to like it."

THE DIFFERENCE BETWEEN LIFE AND DEATH

The next few days spun into the next couple of weeks as Tristan stayed with us. My family accepted him for who and what he was. I was still surprised that Tristan had told my family so much after all the secrets in the beginning. Robert worried over what could happen when he wasn't home to defend us. So, he was glad to have another protector around the house, especially another man. When Robert wasn't home in the evening, Tristan was there.

Despite the fact that I was a ruthless competitor, four and a half years undefeated, I wasn't getting much credit from the household. I was taking most everything sitting down. Robert was the head of the household here, and I didn't want to overstep my boundaries with him.

I hadn't seen our regular visitors since the first evening Tristan was here, but I knew they were lurking in the forest. Robert and Tristan hunted close to home should anything happen.

One evening, Tristan, Robert, and I were relaxing in the living room eating cheesecake and chatting. My eyelids were growing heavy.

"Well, I think I'm going to go to bed. I'm tired," I said.

"Night, Mom. Get some rest."

"I will. Thanks, Robert." I smiled.

Tristan stood. "If you don't mind, I'm going to stay down here and chat with Robert some more."

"No, that's fine."

"Good night," Tristan said.

"Good night," I said.

I took my plate to the kitchen sink, rinsed it off, and then walked upstairs.

Tristan and Robert laughed about something.

I opened the door to my room. Then, Robert said something.

"When are you going to talk to her?" Robert asked.

I halted at the door, and listened in on their conversation.

"I will. I just haven't been able to bring it up," Tristan answered.

"Well, you need to say something soon."

"Shush, she's listening," Tristan whispered.

Silence. Then, the subject matter changed.

I waited for the conversation to switch back to whatever Robert was referring to, but it didn't. So, I closed the door and went to bed.

After that, I tried to listen in on their conversations over the next few days. When Tristan and Robert figured out I was listening, they changed the subject to hunting, killing, or some other macabre matter that I had no interest in.

No matter how hard I tried to listen in, it didn't work. That didn't discourage me, though. I would find out one way or another.

I stared out of the window from my darkened bedroom. The trees swayed with the breeze. The moon cast its reflection inside my room where I stood near the foot of the bed.

A soft click came from the door. I inhaled deeply. The fresh scent of pine, musk, and blood entered the room. Tristan was back from his hunting trip.

The door shut. Then, he touched me, his hand sliding down the sheer black negligee I wore. Earlier that night, I found the negligee laid out on my bed. A single red rose lay on it. The rose now rested on the nightstand.

The scent of blood was strong. I wrinkled my nose and remained where I was, with my back to him.

Tristan had gone too long without feeding. He had a voracious appetite when he left the house so I presume he went after big game tonight. The stench was becoming unbearable.

"Tristan, can you shower?"

He spun me around, his body invisible.

"Oh…"

The blood from his prey stained his chin and lower lip.

He swept my hair out of my face and kissed me. His tongue ravenously lashed out, into my mouth. The taste of blood was still on him. At first, I resisted because I didn't want blood on me nor did I want to taste it.

But, as our passion grew, I relinquished my body to his. I was getting use to his agenda when he returned from hunting, which was the desire to make love. But tonight it was different.

Tristan revealed his human form.

I pushed away.

He pulled me back into him, his mouth pressing hard against mine. He pushed the black straps of my negligee aside, so they draped below my shoulders. The negligee slipped, barely exposing my breasts.

He slid his hands around my hips and pulled me in tighter, molding me against him. His manhood hardened.

The coolness of his bare chest sent chills through the sheer material. My nipples hardened. I wrapped one leg around his hip.

He curled his hands around my legs and hoisted me up around his waist.

I hurried to remove the negligee.

He had a different look in his eyes tonight. They were not soft like they had been when we made love. Instead, he had a hunger, a passionate insatiable need.

Embracing me, he lowered me to the bed, his hands moving to mine. He forced them above my head, and pinned them down. His tongue slid across my nipples.

I wanted to touch him, and to pleasure him, but his grip tightened. I struggled against his hold on me.

"Oh, fuck me, please," I moaned.

He grinned. Slowly, he pressed his hips into me, his manhood pushing hard, deep inside.

I gasped. The momentum of his thrusts became more forceful, and harder.

I moaned. Oh, yes. I liked this animalistic side of him. It was eager and dominant, forceful yet sensual and erotic.

Taking my nipple in his mouth, he sucked, and nibbled on it. The graze of his teeth intensified my desire to touch and hold him.

"Oh, Tristan." I closed my eyes, and arched my back.

He pulled me up and atop him, draping me backwards so he could continue to tantalize my pink rosebuds. He sat beneath me, pulsating deep inside. The sheets lay crumpled around our hips.

The bed disappeared from beneath my body.

Tristan levitated us above the bed, anchoring me around him. The sensation of making love in air, weightless and free, without holding onto anything was enticing.

Our rhythm escalated. It forced me to pull myself back up again. I enveloped him.

He shifted. The sheet hung around us. It flowed, caressing my skin with every thrust.

"Oh, Crystal," he moaned. His voice was throaty.

He cradled my head. Our rhythm moved faster, harder, pushing us to our climax.

I arched my back. My head rolled back. A piercing pain stung my neck. Even in a state of climax, the pain shot through me. It sent waves of shock and convulsions throughout my body.

My limbs went numb, my eyelids fluttered, and my chest rose. I gasped for air.

His fangs remained intact in my neck.

The pain intensified. Blood trickled from the wound and on to the white sheets below me. I hung nearly upside down, almost lifeless, his body still molded to mine. I shivered from the cold. My eyes rolled backwards, my eyelids closing.

§

As Jennifer opened the front door the next morning, the chill from the wind struck her hard. She shivered. She pulled her brown fleece jacket in tighter and zipped it. The sun glared into her eyes, blinding her. She tossed her backpack onto her other shoulder and put a hand up to block the glare. She shut the door and turned to leave. That's when she saw the bloody man on the porch.

Jennifer screamed.

The front door flew open.

Rebecca stood in the doorway. "What the hell is…? Oh, shit."

She clamped a hand over her mouth and peeked back at the door. The girls were still in the house. Thank God. She didn't need them seeing this.

The bloody man didn't move.

Was he dead? Jennifer took a step toward him. Her heart pounded in her chest.

"We need to…um, take the girls upstairs." Rebecca approached the man.

"What! And leave you alone down here with him?"

They exchanged looks.

"Has he moved?" Rebecca asked. She peered down at the man.

"No, he hasn't." Jennifer gazed down at him.

He was in his mid-forties. His brown, receding hair was short, and his facial hair was unshaven.

Jennifer figured he was around five foot ten. He was well-toned and dressed in only jeans and a t-shirt. He had no shoes or socks on.

In this cold of weather, he should have had a jacket on too, but he didn't.

Jennifer peered at the outskirt of their property where the forest lie. She sensed no other presence.

Jennifer turned her attention back to him, and then the patio. His clothes were shredded as if something had attacked him. Lacerations, claw marks, and bruises covered his body. No blood stained the patio. How had he wound up here without getting some blood on it?

"Take the girls to their room, now," Rebecca said. "Then, come help me get him inside. And bring the first aid kit. We're going to need it."

§

Jennifer climbed the stairs to awaken her mother, so that she could assist Rebecca. As she ascended them, she wondered why her mother had not been awakened by everybody's screams. Hell, they could have woken the dead.

So, why did they not wake her mother?

She rapped on her mother's bedroom door, and waited. Her mother did not answer.

She knocked harder and yelled through the bedroom door. "Mom! Rebecca needs you. Can you come help her?"

When Tristan was over, her mother would stay up late to spend time with him, which meant she would sleep in later. But something seemed wrong.

Cautiously, Jennifer cracked the door open. She was wary that Tristan may be laying naked beside her mom, so she kept her distance at first.

"Mom?"

Before the blankets had been put over the window, the room had been much brighter. But now, shadows and darkness lingered, providing a much different atmosphere than before. Where it had once been homely and warm, it was now cold and uninviting.

Fortunately, only her mother lay in bed, so Jennifer slipped inside the room and shut the door. She glanced around, half expecting Tristan to emerge from the shadows like some old horror movie. She knew better, though. It was daylight. Tristan wouldn't come out.

But, once the sun went down, he would be up, and like a guard dog, he would make his rounds around the house and property to make sure everything was secure and intact.

It was nice having him around, although he did make her nervous occasionally, primarily with her nieces. She didn't trust anybody she didn't know with her nieces. But mom had conviction in him, and Jennifer had faith in her mom's decision making.

Plus, he was smitten with her mom. The way he treated her revealed a softer side of him. It seemed genuine. For now, they would accept him, but if he revealed his dark side to them, her and Robert would kick his ass.

"Wake up!" Could anybody be that deep of a sleeper? How many times did she have to call out?

Her mom lay on her stomach, spread out on the bed. The blankets were wrapped around her body, her back exposed, and her face buried in the mattress.

Jennifer neared the bed. She gazed down at the elaborate serpentine dragon tattoo on her mom's back.

She touched her mother's shoulder. It was cool, not warm.

"Are you okay?" She grabbed her mother's shoulder and shook her.

§

Somebody touched me. I bolted upright. As I spun around, I pulled the sheet around my naked body. My hair hung in my face.

Jennifer recoiled.

"What's wrong?" I asked.

"Uh, sorry to wake you, but Rebecca needs your help."

I rubbed my eyes. "Alright, give me a second."

Jennifer looked around. I assumed she was looking for Tristan.

"Don't worry. He's asleep."

"Oh. Where is he?" Her gaze halted past my shoulder.

I followed her eyes. It wasn't Tristan she was worried about.

Droplets of blood stained my sheets. They were not large, but they were big enough to catch anybody's attention.

My thoughts wandered to last night. Oh, yes. I remembered it well. I pulled my hair around to cover my neck.

Her eyes narrowed.

"What are those?" She pointed to the bloodstains on the bed. Her jaw dropped.

I couldn't look her in the eyes.

"I cut myself," I lied.

"The hell you did."

"I did, Jennifer. I didn't realize that I bled on the sheets."

"Say that in front of Rebecca." Her big brown eyes were wide. "You look really pale."

I changed the subject. "What does Rebecca need my help with that can't wait?"

She buried her hands in her jacket pockets. "I found a man lying on our porch out front. It looks like he was attacked by something. Rebecca's trying to give him first aid, but I doubt he's going to live."

"I'll be right there."

Jennifer turned and left my room, her head hung low. She avoided looking around the room.

I presumed she was leery about seeing Tristan sleeping somewhere she didn't expect him.

Once the door shut, I ran into the bathroom and pulled my hair aside. I stared at my neck in the mirror. Two fang marks stared back at me. The son of a bitch did it. This was the second time I was bitten by a vampire. If I remembered correctly, it took three vampire bites before I would turn into one. Was that fable true? If it was, then it would only take one more time, and I was done.

Jennifer was right. I looked horrible. My hair was disheveled, my eyes tired, and my skin colorless.

Sighing, I hurried back to my room, dressed, and ran down the stairs. I rushed through the baby gate at the bottom and nearly fell over it to get to Rebecca's side.

Rebecca knelt beside the bloody man. Her arms stretched across him—one hand on his thigh, and the other hand on his forehead, obstructing my view of his face.

She had already stripped him down to his underwear, cleaned him, stitched up some of the wounds, and was chanting in a foreign language. His body was lined with herbs and odd medicinal items.

"Jesus," I said. My eyes widened.

I ran to them, stopping on the other side of the man.

Rebecca arched her neck back and bared her teeth. She stared up at me with the whites of her eyes, her pupils rolled back.

"What the fuck?" I screamed.

Her pupils rolled forward. They made contact with mine.

"You're becoming one of them," she snapped.

A shiver ran up my spine. I had never seen her use her witchery. It was creepy.

"No, I'm not. I'm one of the family. Now what the hell is going on?" I knelt down to look the man over.

His head was turned toward her, so I couldn't see his face. But his scent was familiar. It was woodsy, musky, and distinct. I gasped.

Rebecca lowered her head to him.

She rocked back and forth. Her moves were articulate, slow, yet deliberate.

Rebecca reminded me of a voodoo witch. I stared up into her face.

Is that where her ancestry came from? Or was she a modern day witch? A necromancer?

Because last I remembered, Warrant was dead. Or was it him?

His face turned toward me yet he remained unconscious.

My mouth dropped open. It was Warrant. Tears welled up.

Rebecca's eyes narrowed in on mine.

"You know him? And well, I see."

Rebecca's aura put off an eerie yet viable strength in the room. It invaded my senses. I sat back before I lost my balance.

"Yes, I do."

His eyeballs moved rapidly beneath the eyelids.

I worried that when he awoke he would be uncontrollable.

He shouldn't be here. Hell, he shouldn't be alive. He was nearly decapitated the last time I had seen him. And, how he survived, I would like to know.

"He's a wolf," Rebecca said. "I can smell his canine blood. Tristan won't be happy your ex-lover is here."

I looked up at her. She was right.

Now I understood why Tristan left his mark on me. He knew Warrant was in the vicinity. This was his way of letting Warrant know I belonged to him now.

I glanced down at Warrant. "Is he going to be okay?" I asked.

"Hopefully. He's a strong man—a strong wolf—but he needs to heal."

Our eyes met.

"He needs to lie down somewhere, where the kids won't bother him," I said.

"We can lay him down in the workout room," Rebecca said.

It was apparent she didn't trust him to be alone in the office or den.

"Alright," I said, nodding.

"Unless you want to risk laying him in your room." Rebecca raised an eyebrow.

"Uh, no, I don't think that's a good idea. I don't know how Tristan will react to Warrant sleeping in my bed."

"I'm going to see if I can find something that will fit him. He's a little bigger than Robert, so I don't know if we have anything, but I'll look. Can you keep an eye on him?"

"Yes, I can."

Rebecca went upstairs.

I gazed down at his face. It was pale and cool to the touch. Warrant's skin had always been warm. So, that was not a good sign. I worried that he was sick. There was no telling how long he had been in the cold or where he had been. Had he spent the night on our porch, Robert and Tristan would have known. So, he must have arrived after Robert went to work.

I laid my hand upon his chest. His heart beat beneath my palm. His skin was warm. That was a good sign.

My mind drifted to the morning Tristan brought me here. Did Warrant arrive alone? Or did someone bring him? If someone brought him, then it must have been the werewolves or somebody other than the vampires.

My heart almost lurched out of my chest. Most of his wounds were covered, including the bandage that wrapped around his neck. I turned his head to examine that particular wound. Because of the dressing, I couldn't see it.

I grabbed the end of the dressing. Just then Rebecca walked into the room.

Rebecca rushed over and slapped my hand away. "What are you doing?"

"I need to see the wounds." I went for the bandage on his chest this time.

"He needs to heal," Rebecca said, sternly. "Leave him alone."

I peeled it back, revealing large, deep claw marks across his chest.

I gasped. "It was a wolf attack."

Rebecca worked to re-bandage his wounds. "Yes, it was. All you had to do was ask. What are you concerned about?"

"I just—I thought they might have been from something else," I answered.

Rebecca peered up at me. She taped the gauze back onto his skin. "You thought they were from a vampire?"

"Yes." I looked him over.

Jace had originally sent vampires after us. I had gotten away. But Warrant had not. Instead, he had been brutally attacked, almost to the point of decapitation. I wasn't sure if a werewolf could self heal a severe wound like that though.

But who could have reattached his head? My thoughts turned to Jace Templeton. Jace had done some strange things like pitting Wayne, my prior captor, against me in an arena fight. I couldn't rule out the possibility that Jace did this. But why?

A surge of adrenaline pumped through my body. Then I thought about this attack. Wolves had tried to kill him this time. I sat back on my rear. Raw pain struck my heart. They had tried to get to me through Warrant, with both the vampire attack and now the wolf attack.

I was convinced that if Jace did not capture me alive, he would take the closest person I had in order to get to me. At that time, it was Warrant. It had to be Jace. He tried to save Warrant so he could find me.

My heart beat faster. Jace was still after me and he would do anything to get me back. Next it would be my family and Tristan. If Tristan or Robert weren't around, I was going to have to fight to the death to save my family. I had put my family in jeopardy.

Tears brimmed over. I buried my face in my hands.

"It's okay." Rebecca wrapped her arm around my shoulders. "Everything's going to be okay."

"No, it's not. This is a warning, a threat to our family. He's going to come after everyone here next. I shouldn't be here."

Tears streamed down my cheeks.

"Yes, you should be here. But, right now, we need to worry about getting him dressed and moving him. The girls are going to get restless. They'll be down soon, so we need to do something with him."

"Yes, you're right." I rubbed my eyes. "Let's take care of him real quick."

Rebecca moved around to the opposite side of Warrant. As we dressed him in a pair of sweatpants, Rebecca struggled to lift his leg. I did it with ease for I had Tristan's poison inside of me.

"His curse makes you stronger," she said, staring at me.

"Yes, it does."

"How many times have you been bitten?"

"Twice," I answered.

"One more time and you turn into one," she said. She pulled up his pants.

"Yes, I know," I said. I wished she wasn't a damn witch. It made things harder to hide.

I knelt down next to Warrant.

"Hopefully Tristan won't bite you again." She pulled the t-shirt over Warrant's head.

"I hope not either," I agreed.

"You know why he left his mark on you, don't you?"

"Yes, I figured that out." I pulled his arm through one sleeve.

"He wouldn't have bitten you otherwise."

I sighed. "I know." I lifted Warrant's head and shoulders so that she could pull the t-shirt down.

"He wants it known that you're his, and not Warrant's. He knew something was amiss, that somebody was coming back into your life. Somebody that might want something more than a friendship."

I stopped and stared at her. Did that mean that Tristan was going to leave his mark on me again? I hoped not, because if he did, it meant that I would have to live a life opposite of my children and my grandchildren. Living my life at night as a vampire was not an option. The very thought of not being able to spend time with them tore my heart apart.

"Do you want to spend eternity with him?" Her eyes lingered on mine.

I didn't answer her. I wasn't sure. But, I was positive that I was not going to give up my family.

"Think about it before you answer, Brandy. He wants to spend his life with you. Are you willing to give up everything for him?"

I looked away. I enjoyed my life with my family. But if I wanted to commit to Tristan, then I would have to move out soon. A life of immortality with a vampire was not going to work well with my family. My life would never be the same.

We stood.

"I'm going to have Jennifer help you move him. I'm not as strong as you two are," Rebecca said.

"Why don't you just use your witchery, Rebecca? I'd like to see what you can do with it."

A thin smirk arose on her face.

"I would, but I try not to use if I don't have to. I think you and Jennifer can handle it," Rebecca said. She turned toward the stairwell. "Jennifer, can you come down and help us? The girls can come down, too!"

Jennifer came down with the girls trailing behind her. "What's going on? Is he going to be alright?"

"Yes, he is. We just need him moved to the back room," Rebecca said.

Jennifer grabbed him by his shoulders and hoisted him up.

I grabbed his legs and pulled them in tight to my body. We walked him into the exercise room and laid him down on the couch that sat opposite the exercise equipment. That way we could keep an eye on him from the living room.

§

Werewolves were a bit on the unpredictable side when awakening, especially after being wounded. And I sure as hell wouldn't want him to awaken in a grumpy mood around the children. So, I spent most of my time in the exercise room with him.

As I pushed myself harder on the elliptical machine, I glanced up at the mirror. Warrant still lay in the same position, his chest steadily rising and falling.

I looked down at the panel on the elliptical machine. My pace had been steady for fifteen minutes. It was time to pick up the speed.

Warrant groaned. A thud followed.

I peered up at the mirror. He lay on the floor.

"Oh, shit! Warrant!"

I jumped off of the machine and ran toward him.

Warrant's fingers elongated into claws. His muscles pulsated against the cotton material.

I stopped in my tracks. "Rebecca, get the kids out, now!"

"What!" Rebecca yelled from the kitchen.

Chairs scraped against the floor in the kitchen. Papers and crayons fell.

Warrant's shirt ripped.

"Come with me!" Rebecca screamed.

"I can't!" I stared at him, afraid to move.

The children ran through the house to the front door.

"Get the hell out of there!" I yelled.

Robert was right. She was a very stubborn woman. Hard headed, much like myself.

The front door slammed shut. Silence followed.

I looked up at the wall clock. It was almost five-thirty and Robert still wasn't home. Jennifer wasn't home either. She had stayed after school to try out for a dance class. She was due home any time.

The sun gradually hid behind the mountain. Orange rays spliced through the blinds, sending lines of light along the walls.

"Warrant, it's me, Crystal," I said. Fear hung in my voice.

The werewolf emerged from his body, his large muscles ripped and defined. Even if I wanted to get out of here, I was trapped. Whether I ran through the living room to the front door or ran out the back door, I would pass right by him. Any sudden sounds might aggravate his temper.

He growled, sending a vibration throughout the house. Glass shattered from somewhere within. His clothes lay tattered at his feet.

I looked back at the arcadia door. It was getting near dark. Tristan would be waking soon. I only wished it was sooner rather than later.

Outside, the rumble of Rebecca's SUV came to life.

"Warrant, can you hear me?" I wanted to move in closer to comfort him, but I was frozen.

He snapped his head around to stare at me. He had picked up my scent, but that didn't change his demeanor. A growl escaped his mouth. Then, he took a step in my direction.

My heart beat hard in my chest. I couldn't breathe. I stepped back. The wall pressed against my back.

He lowered his head and inched in closer. His nose wrinkled. He must have picked up a vast array of scents. Crouching down, he looked around the room, as if looking for another presence.

"Warrant, do you recognize me?" I asked, nervously.

He stopped.

"It's Crystal."

Warrant reared back on his haunches and leapt at me. His front paws struck the wall, one front leg on either side of me. Drywall crumbled. He stood on his hind legs, his face in mine.

I shrank back into the wall. I threw my arms up to cover my head.

A deep and low growl erupted from him. His eyes narrowed in on me. Then, he pressed his nose into my arms and pried them open.

I struggled to get away, but fell up against his front leg.

"Get away from her, Warrant!" Tristan yelled.

Oh, thank God he was awake. Maybe he could reason with the angry beast.

The werewolf snapped his head around. He growled, baring his teeth.

"Back off!" Tristan stood just outside of Warrant's reach.

Warrant snapped at him.

Every time I tried to glance back at Tristan, Warrant inched his face in closer to mine.

He grumbled. Then, he dropped to the floor, paced, and stared at Tristan.

"Yeah, I know you're upset. Just change so we can talk," Tristan said.

The werewolf grumbled some more, as if cussing Tristan out. If I didn't know any better, I would have sworn he was arguing with Tristan.

Warrant's body trembled. He dropped to the ground, his body transforming back into his human form.

I turned and rushed into Tristan's arms.

"Are you okay?" Tristan asked. His eyes never left Warrant.

"Yeah, I'm fine," I said.

Naked, Warrant stood and faced us. The wounds on his chest were healing. Torn bandages lay on the floor.

"Put those on." Tristan threw a garment at him. "I don't want to see you naked."

Warrant gnashed his teeth together at Tristan, as if still in wolf form. Then, he glanced at me and drew in a deep breath, calming his inner wolf. He put on the black pajama bottoms. Red hearts adorned the pants.

"What the hell happened to you?" Tristan asked. He looked Warrant over.

Ignoring Tristan, Warrant stared down at the pajama bottoms.

"What's this shit? What the fuck did you give me?" Warrant asked.

"What does it look like?" Tristan laughed. "You look rather cute in them."

Warrant stared up at him. "Fuck you. Do you really wear this?"

"No, I don't wear that shit. That happens to be Brandy's, er, Crystal's son's pajamas, not mine."

"Fuck." He stared down at the torn sweatpants. "Where did my jeans go?"

"Tristan, you don't have any jeans I can wear?"

"Really?" Tristan threw his arms out to the sides.

"You're bigger than me. I don't have anything that will fit you. Maybe Robert will. We'll ask him when he gets here. If not, you can stand here naked, but I don't want to particularly see your junk." Tristan raised his eyebrow. "And I'm sure her family doesn't either. Be thankful."

Warrant sat on the couch and rested his head in his hand.

Tristan crossed his arms. "What the hell happened, anyway? And I'm not just talking about now. I thought you were dead."

Warrant looked us over. His gaze averted back to Tristan. "I should be so lucky."

The front door opened. A cool breeze swept in to the house. The wind slammed the door against the wall. It sent a chill up my back. My hair flew up and into my face. Enraged, Robert ran up behind us.

I swept my hair back.

Tristan brushed past me and caught Robert by his shoulders. He held Robert back.

Fury had settled into Robert's eyes. He bared his teeth. A deep growl escaped his lips.

"Don't get in my way, Tristan." He flexed his hands, curling them into fists, his muscles engaging…and then releasing.

Tristan let go of Robert. He held his hands up in a *wait* gesture.

"Sorry, Robert, but if anybody's going to tear this man apart it's going to be me. Then you can have your turn. I promise."

Confusion arose in Robert's face. He cocked his head and glanced from Tristan to Warrant.

Jennifer rushed up behind Robert. She, too, stared at the men. Her face was flushed.

Great, I had my family versus my lover and his friend. This definitely was not a good thing. I grimaced.

"You just go ahead—turn me over to the wolves. See if I don't do the same for you," Warrant said. He leaned forward on his knees and shook his head.

Tristan turned and faced Warrant. "We need to talk."

"Yeah, I was getting ready to tell you the same." Warrant turned his attention to me. "By the way, um, Crystal, is it possible to get some food? I'm starving."

Everyone exchanged glances. Then small footsteps entered the house.

"Is it okay, Mommy? Can we come in now?" Katie asked.

"Robert, is everything alright? Can we come in?" Rebecca asked.

I peeked back at Rebecca. She stood close to the door.

"Are we going to have an issue?" Robert asked. He stared at Warrant.

"No, we're not," Warrant said. He stood and extended his hand to Robert. "I'm Warrant."

"Robert." Robert firmly shook his hand.

Warrant went to release his hand but Robert held on tight. "I don't want any issues, you got it? Otherwise you're not going to like me."

"Answer me!" Rebecca walked up behind the rest of us.

The scent of testosterone lingered in the air. We were going to have a dominance issue, if somebody didn't back down.

"Why don't you and Jennifer take the kids in the kitchen? Dinner sounds really good right now, and I'm sure everybody is hungry. I know I am," I said. That was my hint for her to leave the room.

Rebecca caught on. She shuffled the kids off to the kitchen.

Jennifer didn't move.

"Jennifer?"

Her gaze shifted to me.

"Go help Rebecca," I said, cocking my head.

She wrinkled her nose.

The testosterone pumped up her adrenaline. I knew it, because it pumped up mine, too.

FOR ETERNITY

We sat at the kitchen table and made our plates. Everybody was speechless, except for the children. The girls giggled at one another.

Rebecca folded her hands neatly under her chin and waited for the rest of us to get our hamburgers.

Tisa threw her food around the plate.

Normally, Rebecca would have been all over the situation. Instead she sat, motionless and speechless.

Warrant piled his plate to the hilt. He sat on the opposite side of me, away from Robert.

After Robert's confrontation with Warrant earlier, the men had gone to the den so they could talk in private.

Jennifer, who was getting more attuned to her keen hearing, had caught part of their conversation. As she had walked by the door, her ears had perked up. She stopped, and then looked at me, as if something was wrong. She had a solemn look on her face.

The redness in her eyes stood out at dinner. Her gaze shifted from one man to another. Finally, her eyes rested on Warrant. She had a look of confusion, sorrow, and anger in her eyes.

I wasn't sure what to make of it.

Warrant must have been hungry. Half of his plate was already gone.

Tristan sat before an empty plate. Periodically, he would glance at Jennifer.

The silence and the tension in the air made dinner uncomfortable, at least for me.

Robert pushed his food around the plate. He barely ate anything. Usually, when he came home from work he would gorge on his food like a hungry wolf.

Tisa, who sat next to Rebecca, had her French fries piled neatly on the table top. She was proud of how neatly she stacked it.

"Okay, I guess I'm going to have to be the one to speak up," I said. "What the hell is going on? You were all ready to fight earlier and now you're all somber, like somebody died."

Warrant, Tristan, Robert, and Jennifer stared at me with an odd expression on their face.

I almost regretted having said anything.

"What?" I threw my fork down on the ceramic plate. "Is somebody going to say something, or do I have to badger all of you?"

"We need to talk." Tristan stood and grabbed my arm.

A chair scraped on the floor beside me.

"I'm coming with you," Warrant said.

"Fine," Tristan snapped.

"I'm coming with you too." Jennifer stood up.

"No, you're not, Jennifer. Sit down," Robert ordered. He remained in his seat.

"Why? Because you're going, too?" she asked.

"No, I'm not going. It should only be the three of them." Robert stared up at me, his eyes furrowed under his brow.

"What is going on? I can't seem to read anybody's aura," Rebecca said.

"As well you shouldn't right now." Robert turned to Tristan. "Thank you."

"For what?" Rebecca asked. Her voice rose. "Somebody answer me."

"For blocking you. When they leave, I'll fill you in, but they need to talk to mom alone," Robert answered. His voice was low.

"What about me?" Jennifer asked. She sat back down.

"I'll fill you in, too. Let's just finish eating and get the kids to bed so we can talk."

Katie and Leah's pile of French fries were mounting.

"I think they're done eating," Rebecca snapped.

Tristan and Warrant escorted me to the den.

I sat in one of the wicker chairs opposite them.

The light was dim. A basking glow illuminated the middle of the room.

I pulled my legs up on the chair towards my chest, afraid to find out what they wanted to talk about.

Tristan leaned in toward me, his elbows on his knees. He and Warrant exchanged looks.

Whatever it meant, Warrant nodded.

Tristan swallowed hard. "Brandy, we have an issue."

"Alright," I said.

Warrant hung his head.

"The man we're looking for is Jace Templeton." He sighed. "We have confirmation that he's been trying to trace you and has apparently tracked you here—how, we're not really sure, but he has. We can only presume he has his resources."

"This house is being watched day and night by several vampires and werewolves that he hired to track you." His voice lowered.

Warrant spoke up. "Crystal, they're not going to back off. I just happened to be in the area the other day when they attacked me. This is a result of what happened. They almost killed me before. You saw my neck. Jace had his men bring me back to an abandoned building where they are doing their experiments." He drew in a deep breath.

I was right!

"He put me back together, but I don't know how long I'm going to be able to hold out," Warrant said.

I shook my head. "What do you mean, *hold out?*"

"I'll get back to that."

He took my hand in his.

"Fingerprint tests came back from the break-in here." Tristan rubbed his chin. "They tracked it to a man by the name of David Wineberger. Does that name ring a bell?" He looked at me.

My heart beat accelerated. Oh, hell no.

"He has a man named David that works with him. I don't know his last name though," I said.

"Bald guy, about six foot five, three hundred pounds, muscular. Large-built broad guy?" he asked.

My heart sank.

"Yeah, it's him," I muttered. I wanted to cry.

"I thought so." He glanced at Tristan.

"Well, he's the one who broke in and stole your family's important papers," Tristan said.

Oh hell! Just kill me now and get it over with. All I wanted was for them to leave my family alone. I lay my head on my knees. Tears clouded my view.

"Crystal, he wants you for his experiments. He's dead set on claiming you and he's not going to give up," Warrant said, pointing at me. "Those creatures out there are going to kill your family if we don't do something about it. They will wait and get you when you least expect it. And there's one thing we don't have—time. Tristan and I both agree on a couple of things, unfortunately."

Tristan nodded.

I took a deep breath. "And what is that?"

"We think he wants to make you into one of his hybrids."

My jaw dropped. I straightened up. "What?"

"He wants you to fight in the arena as a hybrid. Do you understand where this is going?"

My heart lurched up into my throat. I found it difficult to breathe. I glanced from him to Tristan.

Tristan sat next to him. He said nothing. Only a grim expression remained on his face.

"We have to get him out in the open, and we don't know where he lives. If you're fighting, I can guarantee he's going to be there and so will his men."

My eyes widened. I was horrified at the prospect of stepping foot in the arena again.

"We need to take him down, and you're our only hope. We're not fond of this, but we think it's necessary."

"You want me to fight?"

"If you don't, he will kill your family."

"Listen…" Tristan said.

I gestured for him to wait. My family's bloodshed became a vivid picture. I leaned forward on my knees. It was one thing to expect him to show up here, but to get back in the underground fighting circuit was another thing.

"Crystal, the more you fight, the more chances we have of killing Jace. We don't have any other options. All we need you for is bait. The rest is up to us," Tristan said. He tapped his fingers on the arm of the chair.

I didn't know what to say. All I could do was stare at him.

"That, and to be quite frank, we may not always be around here to protect you and your family. And then, it's going to be up to you to protect them, not us."

Warrant and Tristan exchanged looks.

Something shimmered in their eyes. Hope? But what did that mean?

"Crystal, we think you'd be stronger and better able to protect your family if you were changed," said Tristan.

"What do you mean?" I asked, blinking.

Tristan rubbed his hands together.

"You'd be much stronger, more powerful, and faster if you were changed into one of us."

My heart about leapt out of my chest.

"Are you kidding me? You want to turn me into a vampire or a werewolf? And what about my family?" My voice rose. "I'll kill them if I'm turned."

I couldn't believe we were discussing this.

Tristan scooted in closer to me. He took my hand in his.

"We can help you with that, both of us, because what we're talking about is not just changing you into a vampire or a werewolf, but both, a hybrid. We think you're strong enough to control it."

Jesus Christ, did that make this any better than what Jace wanted to do to me?

His blue eyes were hypnotic.

"We're concerned that he might want to take you on himself and, if that's the case, then you need a lot more strength, power, speed, and agility to fight him. He's a lot older than you are. He's fast, strong, and defiant. Granted, if you have to fight him, Warrant and I will intercede but we're still concerned about you and your family."

I swallowed hard. "I don't think it's a good idea. I'm scared..."

"So are we," Warrant said. He neared me and then dropped to one knee. He looked at Tristan and then at my hand still in his.

"I know I can speak for Tristan as well as myself. We both care about you. We don't want anything to happen to you."

Tears came to my eyes. I turned away, staring up at the ceiling light. My throat locked up. I didn't want anybody hurt, especially my family.

"You're going to have to fight. That's the only way this vampire is going to come out. This is for your protection and your family, Crystal."

"Can I think about this?"

"We really don't have the time for you to think about it," Warrant said. "He could come out of the woodwork at any time. He could show up in the next few minutes. They already know where you live and they're waiting."

I thought about this. If I did have to fight him, I had no chance against him as a mortal. As a werewolf or a vampire I would have a chance, but to be a hybrid, now that's where my chances were. I was more worried about my family than myself. Even if I ran to hide, he would come after them, even Warrant or Tristan. They were right, but could I lead a halfway normal life? I presumed not.

I pulled my hands from theirs and squeezed them shut in my lap, biting my lip.

"How can I refrain from killing or hurting my family?"

"We'll be there for you. We can help you," replied Warrant. "Like I told you about my disease, it's controllable. It's hard, but I can control myself and I know you can do it."

I brushed my hair behind my ear, and scratched my head.

"I can help you as well," Tristan said. "I can generally feel my hunger before it hits. I can get you away before you hurt anybody here. I'll take you away from them, so you can feed."

Ah, Jesus, I hadn't thought about that. I would go back to killing people. I didn't have the stomach for this. "No, I won't do it."

"Crystal, you need to think about this." Warrant's eyes were pleading. "I can help you during the day. At night, Tristan can help you."

"I just wish I had more time."

"We don't have the time. You need to make a decision, and soon. As it stands now, you must be prepared should you have to fight," Warrant said.

"I'll be killing people, Warrant! You think I can live with myself?!"

"You've already killed people for survival and you live with it now!" He leaned back on his heels.

I recoiled in horror, internalizing his words. He was right—I had killed for survival. I wanted to cry because I knew he was right...and because it finally became clear that I had no other choice. Slowly, deliberately, I nodded.

"You're right," I whispered. "I'll do it."

They seemed a little more comforted than they were before, and, yet, I still sensed uneasiness.

"So...how do we do this?" I asked.

"There's only one way," Tristan said. I was wary, but I knew it had to be done.

"What's that?"

"We're going to have to do it at the same time. We don't want to risk any chances of one breed taking over more than the other. My suggestion is to target the neck, one on each side. We could take turns, but there's still the possibility that one gene may take dominance over the other one and not be as effective. We need both of them to be equally strong. If we do it this way, then they take over the body at the same time."

I exhaled, wishing I had more confidence in this procedure.

"This isn't going to be easy for any of us," Warrant said.

Okay, I definitely wasn't ready for this.

I drew in a deep breath, and looked away. "So, when…"

In a heartbeat, they were both on me, throwing me backwards off of the chair, slamming us all down to the floor. Although I landed with a thud, one of their hands cradled my head so my skull wouldn't crack open on the hardwood floor. They pinned me down, each on half of my body, with a leg in between mine. I tried to fight back but was powerless against them.

I started to scream when one of each of their hands grabbed and pushed my head backwards to angle my neck towards their mouths, forcing mine shut. I hissed through my teeth. The piercing of their fangs slid into my skin. Blood oozed from the bite marks that now scarred my flesh. The tension of my muscles made it that much worse. My muscles strained against their strength and power. I trembled beneath them. I could actually sense the blood draining from my body. It was as if somebody had hooked up a water hose. It sucked the life out of me. I fought to keep my eyes open, to fight the inevitability of death.

As I stared up into the light above me, it looked as though it swayed…and then it dimmed. A thought deep in my brain told me I wasn't going to make it through this. Oh, God—I was going to die! I tried to raise my arms to fend them off, but instead my arms lay limp, next to me.

When I closed my eyes, warm liquid enveloped my back, my neck, my shoulders, and my chest. My breath came in short gasps. As I fought to retain life, their mouths released my body. Lying there, I struggled to open my eyes. I gazed up at the two men who had taken my mortal existence away from me. In their dim outlines above me, they looked like angels, but angels they were not. Blood dripped down their chins. They lowered their wrists to my mouth, lines of blood dripping down their arms and into my lips. Tristan propped me up to suck the blood from their wrists. I recognized the coppery metallic taste Wayne used to feed me. Although I should have been disgusted by it, I welcomed it, savoring every morsel. I took turns on each of their wrists, slowly regaining my energy.

A renewed energy flowed through my body. As I licked Tristan's arm clean, Warrant whispered in my ear.

"Tristan will take care of the rest." He stood and left the room.

Tristan tried to pull his wrist away from my mouth, but I continued to hold on, my mouth seeking his life force. I lapped up the rest of the blood on his forearm. My tongue traveled up his arm to his shoulder. I sought out his neck, his ear, and then his mouth. He responded back, clutching and pulling me in closer to him. I thought our bodies were going to merge into one. He pulled away. Not wanting him to recoil, I tried to move in closer. I halted, then lunged for him again.

"Crystal, I'm so sorry. We figured it would be best that you not know when it was coming. I'm…"

I cut him off with my mouth, our tongues seeking each other's. I drove him backwards onto the floor and ripped his shirt apart with my hands. My fingers had elongated into claws.

He stared back at me, grabbed my wrists, and drove them down next to him. My claws connected with the wooden floor. I curled my hands inward, cutting deep scratches into it. My tongue trailed down his neck. He rolled me onto my back, and pinned me down.

He whispered, "Control, Crystal, control."

I followed his gaze to my claws. My eyes widened in horror. I could have seriously injured or killed him. It wasn't like he was dead already.

Trying to focus strictly on his passion, I clutched onto his hair. His lips moved down my neck. An enlightened sensation ripped through my body, a feeling that was ten times more sensationalized than when we had been together before. Just the flick of his tongue could take me to my sexual height at this moment. Wayne's words suddenly bore into my head, reminding me to refrain from becoming too passionate.

"When you're like me, you have to be careful—try to keep your emotions in check. It's not easy, especially during sex. It's better when you're with somebody like you. You know what you're capable of and what to expect from the other one."

Oh, boy, was this going to be a challenge, because right now I was primed and raring to go. I glanced up at Tristan, who had already torn off my shirt and bra. His hands and mouth sought my breasts; his fingers, tongue, and lips teased me. I pressed his face closer into my rosebud, his tongue savoring every morsel. As my fingers entwined in his hair, any hint of normalcy left them. I moaned and threw my head back. I'd already gotten used to the idea of sex with a vampire, but this was a whole different ballgame. Sex as a vampire was so much more sensual.

I got the sensation he was watching me, and I stopped, realizing I was already reaching my sexual peak just from his tongue on my breast. He didn't smile, and he didn't frown. Was sex like this normal for a creature like me? If this were the case, then it was going to be more like an exploration where I would find my treasure at every turn. Hell, I would spend the rest of my life in bed with him, eager for a chance to find my gold.

"I..."

Tristan's lips were on mine.

I don't know when but at some point, he managed to get us both completely undressed. He lowered himself onto me. Our bodies hit the perfect degree of temperature with his cool skin and my warm body. Our skin sizzled together. We latched onto one another, kissing passionately. His arms went around me and then he was inside me, his chest grazing mine with every thrust. Oh, yes. I wanted to spend the rest of my life in bed with him. Hell, right here on the floor was perfect for me.

Thankfully, everyone had gone to their own bedrooms, and the children had been put to bed early.

We moaned in unison. He seemed to have a more heightened sexual awareness as well, his body stiffening atop mine on more than one occasion. His blue eyes darkened as they met mine. This was paradise. I worked on controlling my passion, but at times thought I was going to lose control.

As our pace quickened and he reached his sexual peak, he stiffened, his head sinking into my shoulder, his fangs digging in to my neck. A low growl escaped my lips, thrusting me into a loss of control. I dug my nails into his skin, my claws fully extending, dragging down his back, cutting him deep. He stiffened again, groaning in excitement, his fangs still buried in me. His blood slowly dripped down his body while the pressure of his fangs deepened. The smell of his blood struck a hunger and a passion deep inside—and that was when the curse took over. I arched my back, the adrenaline pulsating within.

A strange power took over my brain, telling me what to do. My lips peeled back and my fangs descended from my mouth. I bent my head in towards him and penetrated his skin. His body trembled against mine, and then his muscles relaxed as he let go, turning his cheek in towards mine. Blood coated the inside of my mouth as I bore down on him. I wrapped my arms tightly around him. He hissed in my ear, and then he nipped me again. Only this time he bit the neck muscle that controlled the side movement of my head. I let go, gasping as waves of pain shot through me. The muscles in my left cheek vibrated, a twitch now forming in the corner of my lip. My body molded into his, his scent suddenly overpowering my senses. As he licked the blood from my wounds, I melted in his arms, my muscles suddenly weak.

Within seconds, I quickly became exhausted. Even lifting my arms was a chore in itself. I stared beyond him at the ceiling in a hypnotic state. I swore the light above his head was changing colors but I knew better. My lips and mouth were dry, even after feeding off of him. I fought the urge to close my eyes and go to sleep while he lapped up the remnants of my blood.

THE GIFT

I slept for the next two days. During that time, I would periodically wake up growling and snarling, only to instantly fall back asleep again. In the daytime, the distinct scent of Warrant and my children would alert me to their presence when they came to check on me. My sense of hearing heightened, allowing me to distinguish their soft voices from across the house. I detected every little sound, from a drop of water to the ticking of a clock. Except for my grand-daughters, the family was notified of the change that was to come and of what was to be expected. In the meantime, I needed my rest so that I could continue to heal and accept the transformation within.

Their voices interrupted my dreams, reminding me of the others who prowled in the forest, stalking my family. Jennifer was growing more concerned, for she noticed some of them getting closer to the house, coming nearer the side where the girl's room was. I cringed at the thought.

In the night, Tristan would lie next to me when he wasn't hunting for dinner. With him pressed against me, I identified the smell of his victim's blood of which he consumed. I licked at his lips. The predator within me searched for a source of food that wasn't there.

His lips met mine. I relinquished myself to him. The fangs of my beast descended. He pulled away. Just far enough for me to catch a reflection of myself in his eyes. I latched onto him again.

I not only wanted him, but desired the taste of blood. Suddenly, my stomach cramped up with hunger. I hissed through my teeth, bearing the pain that balled up inside.

"You need to feed, Brandy," he moaned.

My insides felt like they were being ripped out.

He rolled atop me, and bared his neck for the taking.

Drawing him in nearer, I clamped down on him, piercing his skin. He hissed through his teeth, the muscles in his body tightening. The first few drops deepened my thirst. I sucked the blood from the wound, pumping more of it faster and harder through his veins. I wrapped my legs around him, afraid he would try to pull away when I needed him the most.

I stroked my hand down his back, the bony claw emerging, and drawing a thin line of blood. He arched from the slight touch. I continued to feed upon him. Wrapping his hands around my hips, he plunged deep inside, releasing me from my feeding. Caressing me, he slowly moved up, cupping the outer curvature of my breasts. I moaned.

He pulled me into him, his fingernails digging into the top of my shoulders. I arched my back to allow him further domination over me, exposing my neck. Oh, I knew what he wanted...what he needed. His fangs sank deep into my neck, and our tension mounted to a higher degree of closure. His hunger sought out my life force.

I held him in my arms, admitting to myself that though the change was frightening for me, it was well worth it. I ran my fingers through his dark hair, slowly twisting it. He lay with his head in between my bare breasts, his eyes closed, inhaling my scent. He stroked my stomach, almost tickling me.

"Is it always going to be like this?" I asked, dreamily.

"Life, or sex?" he whispered.

"Both," I said.

He laughed, his chest vibrating against my stomach. "Sex, yes. Life, not always. We won't be able to make love all the time like we are now. I still have to work."

He raised his head and gazed into my eyes.

"Mm, but we'll make time," I whispered.

"Always." We smiled at each other.

Then there was another cramp within my stomach. I groaned.

He pulled himself up more, his face next to mine. "You're still hungry. You need more food."

The urge to vomit became overwhelming.

"Oh, Tristan, it hurts."

He quickly dressed and left the room. I curled up into a ball, clutching my stomach. As fast as he had left, he was even quicker returning. Warrant accompanied him. They carried several bottles of crimson liquid. Warrant helped Tristan carry the bottles. He shut the door behind him.

Then, they were at my side, helping me to sit up. Still naked, I clung to the blankets, in an attempt to not expose myself to Warrant. Each of the men opened a bottle.

"Can you hold this?"

My fingers trembled as I tried to take the bottle. Instead, he held it to my lips while I drank from it.

"Once you drink a few of these, you'll start getting your strength back," Tristan said.

I gulped down the first water bottle, noticing that it and the others were refilled with blood. They set the other six on the nightstand next to me. The blood pumped hard within, empowering me with a sense of worth. Warrant and Tristan sat on the bed, watching me. Warrant reached out to touch my arm.

Tristan cast him a vicious look.

Warrant retreated. "Sorry, Crystal, Tristan. I was just going to ask how you feel."

Tristan watched me intently, not looking back at Warrant.

Then I smiled for the two of them. "I'm feeling better. The cramping is gone, and that's a good thing."

I licked my lips, eager for another romp in the bed with Tristan. I gazed at the muscles in his chest and shoulders, watching them flex while he moved. Our eyes met, his seeming to inquire about my intentions again when Warrant spoke up.

"Crystal, his men are getting brave. They're going to attack soon. We need to set something up so they stay away from your family. I know you just woke up and need time to recoup, but we don't have much more time."

A red aura appeared around Warrant. The heat pulsated from his body. The blood I consumed had to have done something to my senses.

"Then set something up." I grinned at him.

"Brandy, we need to make sure you're ready," Tristan said. He stroked my arm.

"Oh, I'm ready….and call me Crystal."

I let the blankets drop to the floor while I walked to the bathroom past them, exposing my nakedness. I was unexpectedly full of new energy, new life, and new vitality.

Tristan looked at him. Warrant dropped his gaze.

I shut the door behind me.

"You get everything set up," Tristan said. "I'm going to make sure she is ready."

Even in the bathroom, I could still hear them as plain as day.

Tristan's voice lowered. "And, by the way, don't betray my trust. I didn't when she was with you."

"You know me better than that, Tristan." Warrant's voice was low but clearly he understood.

The mattress shifted. Somebody stood.

"I'll get everything set up, and tomorrow I'll see if she can walk in the daylight."

Again, the mattress shifted. The other man stood.

"Just be careful with her. She's special."

"Oh, I know. You don't have to worry about me." Warrant left the room, quietly shutting the door behind him.

Only Tristan's scent remained in the room.

I stepped into the shower. I stood underneath the water, letting it envelop me. He unzipped his jeans. I grinned. His pants dropped to the bedroom floor.

Tristan was quiet. Yet, I still detected his footsteps and the opening of the bathroom door. I faced the water, turning my back to the shower curtain. He stepped inside the shower with me. As I closed my eyes, his hands were upon my body. I melted into them.

§

I awoke the next morning, searching for the man who'd made love to me almost all night long. I glanced over the blankets. Oh how I wished he could walk in the sunlight. I wanted to spend all day and all night with him. But, it was impossible. I rolled onto my back, gazing at the blanketed window and the narrow beam of sunlight coming through.

Then I threw off my covers, catching a glimpse of my body. I stared down at my strong legs. They seemed slightly more muscular than what they had been when I was human.

As I sat upright on the edge of the bed, I ran my hand over my stomach. It was much more muscular than it had been.

Then I ran my hands over my breasts. An awkward sensuality pulsed through them. My eyelids fluttered. A moan escaped my lips. Then, Tristan groaned. From the confines of his deep sleep, Tristan stirred, his body trembling against the sides of the boarded floor in the closet. I removed my hands from my breasts and he stilled within his sleep. Apparently, if I were frisky, he was going to know. I smiled.

"Touché, lover," I whispered, slightly pinching my nipple.

He stirred again and all I could do was smile. Oh, dare he ever turn me down sexually, I knew my revenge.

I walked to the window behind the shadows of the blanket. I stared down at the stream of light lining my floor. Carefully, I held my open hand out and slowly moved one finger into the light. I was expecting it to hurt, or to burn. But, it did not. I dared to hold my hand out. The warmth of the heat radiated from my hand. I was ready to welcome the awaiting sun.

I dressed in a pair of jeans and a t-shirt, brushed my hair, and opened my door, knowing there was going to be a wolf waiting for me. Warrant leaned against the stair railing, watching me, his arms across his chest.

The scent of bacon and eggs filled the air. My stomach growled.

"Would I piss Tristan off if I told you that you look magnificent?" Warrant asked, looking me over.

A smirk crossed my face. "Probably."

"Well, you do. Absolutely magnificent." His tongue slithered out and over his lips.

"Are you hitting on me?" I moved in front of him.

"No, my lips are just dry."

"Uh, huh."

He grinned.

Warrant turned and pounced over the top of the railing, dropping to a crouch on the bottom floor. He stared back up at me. He waved his hand in the air, prompting me to follow him down. I braced my hands on the top railing, reluctant to try jumping over the railing like he had. I was fearful of falling and breaking my neck, though I knew it probably wouldn't happen. I would most likely land on my feet. Still, I fought the urge.

"Come on, Crystal. You have to get used to it. You have to learn how to use your gift."

As I braced myself for the jump, three balls of fury seemed to fly up the staircase, suddenly stopping next to me on the railing.

"Come on, Grandma, it's fun," Katie said.

She dove from the railing. I gasped in horror, watching her. I wanted to reach out, grab her, and stop her from hurting herself, but instead I watched her little body plummet. She looked like a professional diver, her arms fully extended to her sides, her body lithe, straight, and extraordinarily beautiful. She curled inward as she touched down, completing three inward tucks before rolling out onto the floor. She stood up next to Warrant who also urged me on.

I leapt over the side of the railing with more grace and flexibility than I thought I would have. I also made sure to land in a crouch as Warrant had. There was a renewed strength in my body. I glanced up as Tisa slid down the stair railing, her body rolling bottom over head. She made sure to follow the railing. Tisa vaulted off the end of it and onto the floor, where she stood up. She smiled at me.

Leah leapt on to the railing, her feet on the rail. Then, Rebecca rushed out of the kitchen, her hair standing on end, gripping a towel. She stared up at Leah, her eyes wide. Leah pushed off and slid down the railing. She was more graceful than a snow skier—her arms were braced out to her sides, her knees slightly bent—and then she suddenly catapulted off of the end of the railing. She flipped in midair, landed on her feet on the floor, and jumped around like a playful kitten.

"Well, so much for those baby gates." Warrant laughed.

Rebecca gave the girls a stern look. The girls sulked, and followed their mother into the kitchen.

"Guess that wasn't a good idea," he said. "I think I got them in trouble."

I laughed and headed for the kitchen. The girls plopped down in their seats. I shook my head in amazement. Every day, the girls seemed to find something new to surprise all of us.

"Do you need help, Rebecca?" Warrant asked, approaching her.

Rebecca flipped the bacon over in the pan. "You can put the condiments and dishes on the table."

He opened the cabinets, pulling out dishes. Apparently, he had learned where everything was. I sat down and watched him set the table as Rebecca finished cooking. I glanced at the window. The sunlight illuminated the room.

"You look more comfortable here," I said, glancing from him to Rebecca.

"Yeah, everybody's been wonderful. You have a great family, Crystal."

Rebecca looked at me, a look of curiosity on her face.

"How are you doing?" she asked.

"I'm doing really well."

"So it seems," she said, her eyes meeting mine. "Do you realize that almost every night when I go to bed, I have to cast a spell preventing our minds from merging? I dreamt of making love to Tristan one night and freaked Robert out."

I lowered my head.

Rebecca walked over to the table with two plates in her hands. One had eggs on it, and the other had toast.

"He thought Tristan was in our room until he rolled over and saw that we were alone."

"Sorry, Rebecca. I honestly don't know how that happened." I peered up at her.

"Neither do I, and I don't like it. I should be screaming Robert's name, not Tristan's," she spat.

Warrant looked away. There was a moment of awkward silence. Once Rebecca and Warrant sat down, everybody began grabbing their food. As I piled some eggs on my plate, Warrant spoke up.

"Uh, you need to make sure you can eat regular food first."

"Why?" Fork in hand, I stabbed my eggs. Confusion set in.

"Because you're part vampire. You might not be able to eat human food. I'd try a little bit, wait a while, and make sure that you don't get any cramps. It might actually make you sick to your stomach."

"Oh," I muttered, staring at my plate. The vapors from my food smelled good.

I shoveled it into my mouth, anyway. The hash browns had more pepper than salt. It tasted good.

"And I'm not sure if you know," he began, "but even though you're not a werewolf, you're mind is linking up with—"

"Robert already explained it to me," Rebecca cut him off. "He had the nerve to tell Tristan what happened, so Tristan explained it to him. Robert didn't even understand why it happened."

"It's the pack of the wolves. Crystal just happens to be the most dominant female in the house, and she really will be now. Because you're a witch, your mind seeks magic. Wolves and vampires alike have a sense of magic to them."

Rebecca chewed on her food, and glanced from him to me. I took another bite of mine. The cramps started up again. I doubled over, groaning. Pain shot through my body.

"Here, let me help you," Warrant said.

He was at my side, tearing me away from the table. The room spun wildly around me. He rushed me to the bathroom, and shut the door behind us. I almost buried my head in the toilet. Warrant stood behind me, patting my shoulder as violent waves of nausea and vomit took over.

Though I expelled the human food, I also projected a portion of the blood I had consumed the night before. Once the vomiting stopped, I laid my cheek on the toilet seat. He brushed the hair out of my face. I lay in the bathroom waiting for the nausea to subside. Warrant remained by my side.

After laying me down upon my bed, he peeled off my vomit-covered shirt, rinsed it in the bathroom sink, and threw it in the tub. I laid on my bed, sweating profusely. While Tristan slept, Warrant continued to take care of me. He moistened a washcloth and wiped down my forehead with it. He draped a sheet across my body, covering my bare breasts.

"Well, I guess we know you can't eat human food," he said. "But it looks like you can walk in the sunlight. That's a good thing."

I rolled my eyes.

"Get some rest."

"Shit, is it always going to be like this?" I asked, clutching onto the pillow.

"Every hybrid is different. You have to learn by experience. There's really no other way."

I sighed. He knelt before me, his face inches from mine. He patted my forehead some more with the cloth. I fell asleep.

I awoke sometime later, stumbled out of bed, and dressed myself. All the while, my stomach grumbled at me. The raviolis Rebecca made for the girls permeated the air. It made me even more hungry. My stomach twisted into knots. I fought the urge not to expel anymore food. Holding onto the side of the dresser, I glanced at myself in the mirror, studying the changes in my body. My large, dark eyes stood out more than they had before. My hair was fuller. I touched it. It seemed healthier than it had been before.

Leaning into the mirror, I pulled my lips back, afraid to see the reflection of fangs glaring back at me. Instead, there was something else. My lower and upper canine teeth seemed almost longer and at a more noticeable angle than those of a normal human being. My teeth appeared to be whiter. They still were not long enough to draw attention or cause alarm, should I come into contact with a mortal.

Closing my mouth, I touched my face. There appeared to be a slight slimming of my facial structure. Odd.

I glimpsed something strange in the mirror. Then, I realized how cold my hands were, so I pulled my hand away. I touched my cheek once more.

There it was again. A tiny, thin line of smoke trailed the air next to my face, swirling up and disappearing. I leaned in closer to the glass, touching my other cheek. Another curl of smoke wafted through the air. It started as a thin curl but the longer I let my finger rest against my cheek, it became thicker. I stared at my mirrored image in awe. Fascinating but peculiar.

My mind tried to find reason behind the oddity. Warrant appeared next to me. I quickly dismissed the thought, and turned to face him.

"You're using your nose? That's great. Keep practicing," he said, casually looking me over.

Just then I doubled over, my stomach knotted up again. I clutched it, groaning. I leaned my backside against the wall behind me.

He peered down at me, a thin grin on his face. "Guess what? You need to learn how to hunt."

"Not now," I muttered. "I'm in pain."

"Yeah, you are, so this makes the perfect opportunity."

He grabbed me by my waist and tossed me over his shoulder. My stomach bounced against him. The urge to retch almost overtook me.

I tried to stifle it. I clutched on to the back of his shirt. "Put me down Warrant, I don't feel so good."

"No can do." He leapt over the stair railing.

I closed my eyes, waiting for the room to quit spinning. I trembled against him. His feet hit the bottom floor. He carefully set me down, planting my feet on the ground.

"Asshole, I feel like shit and you had to go and do that." I reached out to hit him. Then, my arm cramped up.

I leaned into him instead. He was the only thing that kept me steady.

"Language, please," Rebecca said from behind me.

I turned to Rebecca.

She recoiled. "You look like shit."

"Language, Rebecca."

She smiled back. "How are you doing?"

"How does it look like I'm doing?" The pain was getting worse. I grimaced.

"What's wrong?" she asked.

"She's hungry," he answered.

"Oh," she said, seeming to understand, then quickly backed off. "I'll leave you two to be."

"Yeah, good idea."

"Oh," I groaned. "I think I'm going to be sick."

"Good, let's go." He pulled me out of the house.

I barely made it out of the door when I had to rush to the side of the patio, dry heaving. I fell on all fours waiting for something to come up, but nothing did. It was probably best that it didn't, not just for the fact I didn't want to get sick again, but because it would have been all over Rebecca's roses. The stench of her roses filled my nostrils, driving me backwards on the porch.

Warrant laughed behind me. He caught me from falling. "I see you found the flowers. They can smell really good when you're feeling good, but when you're sick, it really sucks. It's like going from one extreme to another."

I rested on my butt with my shoulders against his legs, trying to steer away from the rose garden.

"Jesus," I muttered.

He shifted, suddenly on alert. Then I detected it too. We had an intruder. I glanced up at him. He was focused on the forest. I, too, glanced into the woods beyond. The smell was wild, dirty, and catlike. I narrowed my eyes towards something in the trees, something hiding deep within the confines of the camouflage. It was more than thirty yards away, but I distinctly recognized a figure staring back at me. I lowered my head, peering out from under my brow. My nose told me it was not friendly. I shifted my weight, turning my shoulders cautiously towards my enemy. The wind carried its stench to me. Its odor invaded my nostrils. I watched it slowly lower its head, its shoulders arching up and back.

I uttered a low growl. My lip curled back revealing my descending fangs. It moved, its paws getting ready to pounce in my direction. As my pupils contracted, my vision became clearer.

I recognized what it was. My mind drifted back to that day in the woods, the same day I ran into Tristan in the park. I remembered the creature who could have prevented me from coming home sooner.

Before I knew it, I was off and running, my clothes shredding from my body as I transformed into something wild and vicious. Pain etched throughout my muscles and my tendons. They stretched, almost as if they were going to rip apart. I struggled to fight it, but the more I fought it, the more painful it became. A loud and horrendous howl erupted from my throat. A stronger presence stood next to me. I snapped my head around. Warrant had also transformed. I dropped to the ground, racking with convulsions against the rocky earth as the transformation completed.

I rolled over, scrambling to grip the ground with my paws. I glanced back at Warrant, catching a vague reflection of myself in his eyes. My fur was dark with a burnt orange tinge, my eyes golden in color. My jaw was strong and my nose long, my ears perked and tall. I wasn't the biggest wolf, but then, I wasn't the smallest wolf either. I definitely couldn't match Warrant's size. My shoulders were broad but my body narrowed down before broadening again along my hips. I gazed back into the woods, listening for the faintest sound.

I lurched forward, head low, roaring at the mountain lion standing on the other side of the old fallen tree. We lunged over it, and into the forest. The mountain lion slinked back around and struck at us with its claws. It hunkered down on its back legs and leapt at us. We narrowly missed him. We tumbled back down to the ground. The mountain lion slinked in between us, separating Warrant and me. It bared its teeth at us, slinking back and forth like a caged animal, its defenses up and ready for attack again.

She was a beauty, I had to admit. Her long, lean, brown body slithered through the brush, her eyes deep and golden. She growled at me, her teeth gnashed together. There was movement in the brush behind her. She whipped her head around. The three of us turned, our backs to the edge of the forest, striking a common ground.

Off in the ravine, the werewolves came forth. They had been silent until they reached the brush. To my left, the mountain lion growled. Her aroma wafted in my direction. She was still leery of us, but she knew she had to worry more about the werewolves who were coming in the distance. They stopped at the top of the ravine. The mountain lion glanced at us. She turned and ran off.

She left behind a stench of fear as we turned to greet our new visitors.

There were three of them. Three massive, broad bodies looming in towards us. I circled back around, lowering my face as the middle one rose his head, howling. He was tall and lean, his coloring darker than mine. His eyes moved from me to Warrant, then centered in on Warrant. I presumed it was because he was a bigger wolf and was trying to prove who the real alpha was. The other two were slightly smaller and grayish in color, one with a white paw and the other with a bleeding partial tail.

The wolf with the partial tail obviously just had his ass handed to him in a recent fight.

The middle wolf lunged at Warrant. The other two charged me, driving me backwards against the fallen tree. Warrant and the alpha battled it out against the tree next to me, their bodies pounding against it. Branches, leaves, and pine cones fell atop me. I swiveled as one of them snapped at me, his teeth barely missing my face. I swung around again, whipping my tail to strike him in the head. His teeth gnashed together.

The one with the wounded tail came towards me from the rear as I circled back. I struck, aiming for his face. He ducked the attack.

I was stuck in between these two and needed to find a better position. One came at me, his mouth inches from my ear. I dodged him, striking from underneath. I jumped at him, driving him backwards. At the last second, I struck him with my claws, leaving deep scratches in his chest. Blood poured from his wounds.

I slinked around to face another wolf. Warrant was just on the other side of my enemy. Warrant reared up, his face snapping at the alpha straight on. The alpha pulled his head straight back, falling over backwards atop my attacker. Then Warrant was on him, his jaw snapping shut on his throat. The creature mewled. Warrant snapped up the alpha and shook him like a rag doll, whipping his head from side to side. Then he tossed his body against the tree, like a dog would play with a toy.

While Warrant nearly decapitated the alpha, the wolf that laid under him darted off further into the woods, leaving his friend behind. Taking a couple steps after him, the wounded-tailed wolf scooted around in the brush.

I stopped.

Warrant stood frozen, watching him from four feet away, his teeth bared. I peered down at the creature that laid next to me. Its back legs were limp and oddly deformed. I lowered my snout to him, prodding his back legs. It growled, whipping his head around. I clamped down on his neck, drawing blood. Ah, the sweet smell of…blood.

Before I knew it, I transformed back into my human form, naked, my mouth still enclosed around the creature's neck. Fangs dug deep into his throat, I sucked the life out of him. I held him down by the base of his neck and his muzzle as he struggled against me. I relished the taste, that sick, sweet, metallic, coppery taste. He stilled below me, and when I was certain he was dead, I pulled away. With his blood covering me, I raised my head and stared up into the warmth of the sun. I licked my lips. The blood comforted my irritable stomach. Yes, I knew what I must survive on and it wasn't that nasty-tasting human food anymore. I closed my eyes, breathing in the smell of pine and dead carcass.

I was still hunkered down on my knees when Warrant touched me. I turned towards him. His face was in mine. His tongue slithered from between his lips, lapping up the remaining blood on my face…the blood I couldn't get to with my own tongue. I let him clean my face before escorting me home.

We came in through the side door that led to the laundry room, finding some clothes to put on before continuing to my room. I was glad Rebecca and the children were not anywhere in sight, though I was sure they knew we were there. In my room, Warrant and I showered and dressed. Separately, of course.

Later, when the downstairs door opened, I knew it was Jennifer by her scent. Robert would be home soon, and Tristan would awaken not long after sundown. Glancing out the window, I watched the sun disappear behind the mountains. I remembered what Tristan had said to me about wanting to show me all of the remarkable treasures in the night. I looked forward to it.

Smiling, I gazed back at Warrant, who sat on the edge of my bed. My smile faded. I frowned when I realized what would happen if Tristan found him in my room without also being present. My imagination leaned towards the unthinkable. Darkness began to settle in through the window. I detected slight movement inside the closet. Turning to Warrant, I mouthed the words, "Get out," but it was too late.

Warrant stood up, reaching for his shirt. Tristan appeared in the room. The look on Tristan's face made me want to cry. First, he was confused. Then, it turned to hurt. Quickly, he was fueled by jealousy and anger.

"No, Tristan, no! It's not what you think."

Tristan glared at the two us.

Warrant held his hands up in surrender. "Wait, hold on."

Warrant was flung violently, his body smashing into the wall that separated my room from the hidden room. Pieces of wood and remains flew about.

Yelling, I ran to Tristan. "Tristan, no! It's not–"

I was thrown across the room, smashing into the outer wall by the window. My head hit the wall. I had no control over my body. Slats of the wall broke apart. I was lucky he hadn't thrown me out the window. Even though he didn't physically touch me, he used an invisible force to squeeze my throat. I gasped for air, and kicked my legs against the wall. I stared at Warrant, who was also held against the other wall by an unseen force.

"Tristan," he gasped. He clutched at his throat. "It's not..." His voice broke off, gargling.

Warrant fought to make the change, his fingers curling into claws. He tried to strike at the invisible force which held him. Tristan stood in the middle of the room with his arms extended and spaced out towards us, levitating us. His gaze switching from one to the other. His eyes were dark, almost crimson, his fangs descended.

He glared at Warrant. "You said you wouldn't betray me."

"I didn't…and…neither…did…she." Warrant's veins pulsated against his skin.

I focused on Warrant. "Don't…"

Warrant broke the hold. He fell to the floor, and stared up at Tristan.

Tristan raised his hand, levitating Warrant again.

"You son of a bitch, stop it," Warrant said, exasperated, almost four feet in the air.

"Now stop it and put me down. And put her down. You're going to kill her."

Tristan's eyes trailed over to me, the look on his face changed back to confusion. He loosened his grip and levitated me to the bed where he dropped me. But instead of letting Warrant go, he maintained his grip on him. Warrant continued to fight his inner demon.

"I'm not going to let you do it! You're not going to bring out my disease," he snapped.

Once again, the smell of testosterone filled the air.

"Tristan," I said, inching toward the edge of the bed. "Nothing happened." I stood, cautiously approaching him.

Our eyes met. "I swear on my life, nothing happened."

I spoke with tenderness, trying to keep him calm so he wouldn't go any further over the edge.

I moved into him, enveloping him. I kissed him long and hard.

Warrant was still elevated in the air.

Tristan wrapped his left hand around the back of me, gripping my neck hard.

"Really, you can put me down anytime now," Warrant said.

What the hell was it going to take for him to put Warrant down? Oh, yes, I had an idea.

I pulled Tristan into me, and whispered in his ear, "There's no reason to hurt Warrant. I want to spend the rest of my life with you."

Tristan looked at me. His mouth hung open.

I pulled away so I could look into his eyes. "By the way, you'd be proud of me. I hunted today."

I flashed him a thin smile. Though I wasn't happy about what I had to do, I knew Tristan would be proud of me. He would be thankful that I had tapped into my gift and used it.

"And, she made her first kill," Warrant replied.

Continuing to watch us, Warrant sat cross legged in the air. Tristan cast his eyes upon Warrant and then back at me, searching mine.

"Tristan, you know me better than that. I would never betray you, and neither would Warrant. We both care for you. Neither of us would ever hurt you. Hell, how many times have you saved our lives? We owe our lives to you."

The one thing I knew he wouldn't be happy about was how Warrant had helped to clean me up. Though it was mostly on my face and arms, I'm sure Tristan would be upset.

Still, I'm sure he would have understood, considering I couldn't exactly be walking through the forest naked and bloody in broad daylight.

I detected a hint of softness in his face; and then his eyes. They were turning ocean blue again. I smiled at him, his hair-entwined hand pulling me into him. Our mouths met, his arms wrapping around me. The thump to my left told me Warrant had dropped to his rear on the hard floor. The floor creaked beneath his weight.

Tristan pulled back, his eyes intent on mine.

"Okay, now that you two are made up, you need to know that they sent three werewolves today," Warrant explained, standing up.

Tristan spun his head towards Warrant. "Who were they?"

"Pawns. Just lesser cubs. But they wanted her. We really need to be on the watch tonight," he said, crossing his arms against his chest.

"Did you get anything set up yet?" Tristan snapped. He let go of me.

Tristan's frustration was wearing on him. He had a constant look of annoyance.

"I might have something set up, but I'm waiting on confirmation. I'm sure somebody's going to say something to J.T., and he'll be there." Warrant gazed back at us, a troubled look on his face. "That and one of the wolves got away today."

"What?" Tristan got in Warrant's face. "You didn't destroy them all?"

"No, I killed one and so did she. I didn't go after the other one, because I want word to get back to the son of a bitch. I want him to know that she's changed, that she's ready for a fight. If he knows she's changed, he might issue a challenge. And if not, well, I already have a messenger working on getting something to him." Warrant smiled.

Tristan cocked his head, glancing back at me before inquiring. "And that would be…?"

"Her challenge," he replied.

They both turned to me. Tristan's face became shallow.

My jaw dropped open. "What? You issued a challenge from me to him?"

Feeling faint, I promptly sat down. Warrant sat down next to me.

"Look at it this way. We're going to get you back in the circuit. I'm hoping that by advertising you're ready to fight, he's going to come out in the open and show up. If he does, then Tristan and I will take care of him. I'm hoping that it doesn't come down to you fighting. But if it does, this is why we bestowed upon you our gift. You're strong, powerful, and you can hold up to him."

He turned toward me. "And the best thing is, Crystal, you saw your transformation earlier when you changed into the curse. That was only your wolf side. Imagine what you can do when you let both your wolf and your vampire take over. There's more to come."

I swallowed hard. A chill ran up my back. He was right. If that was just the wolf taking over, then I was in for one hell of a ride.

"How did she manage the change?" Tristan asked.

"She did great. Hell, she started the change when she took off running after the mountain lion that was watching us, and she was a big son of a bitch."

"Mountain lion?" Tristan asked.

"Yeah. The mountain lion ran off, when the wolves came over the rise. She knew what they were. Hell, she almost backed us up, but high tailed it out of there instead. Can't say I blame her. She would have been a match for Crystal, though."

"Yeah, I think that's the same mountain lion that my son mentioned got into the backyard one time. She is big." I looked at Tristan.

"And beautiful. She would have been a great catch for you," said Warrant.

A loud bang reverberated through the house, along with the slamming of doors and the shuffling of feet.

THE GIRLS

Robert and I had run outside. Rebecca had followed us out, but he told Rebecca to go back into the house. He was mad, even furious that she would even consider coming outside and helping us. Granted she wanted to help, but she should have thought twice about it before just running outside. If she had been killed, she would have left her children motherless. She stomped back to the house. Her fury treaded across open ground, the grass bending to her anger and remaining there, helpless under her feet. I not only felt her fury through her footsteps, but in the back of my mind, she left me a message, telling me she was there if I needed her. I tried to ignore it, but she wouldn't let me. Her words tore through my brain again. Even as I stood near my family, ready for combat, she screamed it at me. I cocked my head, trying to shake out her thoughts. A hand appeared on my shoulder.

I glanced at Robert. He gave me a questioning look, and when I turned to stare back at my rivals, I caught sight of Rebecca glaring at Robert before walking up the stairs to the porch. As she disappeared into the house, she took one last glance around. She whispered in my head that she was scared. So was I. I prayed that my gift would increase my chances of defeating them.

I turned to face them when Rebecca wormed her way through my brain again. I closed my eyes, worried. Something was wrong in the house, but I didn't know exactly what.

§

Rebecca walked into the house where the girls played in the living room. The lights were bright, so she dimmed them before rounding up the kids. They giggled, screamed, and wiggled in her arms as she took them upstairs to their room. Luckily, they were still young. Had they been older, they would have already tapped into their curse and known what was happening outside. Trying to remain solemn and keep her thoughts under control, she helped them change into their pajamas and brushed their teeth. They talked to her the whole time. Leah and Katie asked their mother over and over if she was okay. Rebecca just smiled and said yes, she was fine. Her smile didn't convince them.

Leah and Katie begrudgingly laid down. Tisa jumped up and down on her bed.

"Listen to me, Tisa. It's bedtime. You need to go to sleep," Rebecca demanded.

Tisa screamed at her mother, sat up, and tried to wriggle out from underneath the covers. Every time Rebecca started to cover her back up, Tisa kicked them off again.

"Dammit, Tisa, it's bedtime. Go to sleep. I don't want to have to use my witchery on you." She swatted her on the butt. Tisa started to cry.

"Tisa, stop it! Go to sleep. It's time for bed." Leah sat up, her eyes meeting Tisa's. Then Leah mouthed the word, *stop*.

Rebecca turned to her, "Leah, you're not her…"

The room became quiet. She peered down at her daughter, who laid still under the covers, smiling at her mom.

Rebecca sighed, glancing between the two before looking at Katie, who laid still with an angelic smile on her face.

"I swear. Tisa, I think you're the devil's child sometimes. You can be an angel and then you can be a little demon."

The kids laughed, a sparkle in their eyes.

Rebecca smiled down at them. "I love you, angels."

They all chanted back at her, "Love you too."

Rebecca kissed them goodnight, her thoughts shifting back to Crystal and the vampire who had approached her family in the front yard. She wanted to be out there defending her family and her home. She felt disgraced, dishonored, and ashamed she wasn't with them, but she also needed to be with her children.

Closing the blinds above Leah's bed, she could vaguely see what was happening outside. The watchers approached her family in the front yard. She thanked God she was putting the kids to bed. Should something happen, they would be asleep, unaware of the horror. She wanted to cry, but pushed back the tears that welled up in her eyes.

"Goodnight, girls," she said, praying this wouldn't be the last time she put her daughters to sleep.

Though she couldn't foretell the future, she did have a sense of things that were to come and a sixth sense of others' feelings and thoughts, particularly those she loved. She had tried to read the girls' thoughts on several occasions, but always had difficulty. She thought if she could communicate with them through her witchery then she might be able to teach them better, but because of their short attention span at their age, she couldn't stay connected with them. They were smart, but their thoughts were jumbled with spurts of miscellaneous uncontrollable brainwaves, making it difficult to keep a connection. She had brief connections with Leah, but it never lasted long. She decided it was best to wait until they were older to try with them again.

Now, the girls on the other hand seemed to be on the same wavelength. They understood each other and comprehended what the other was saying regardless of their age. A prime example was what Rebecca just witnessed with Leah and Tisa. Tisa seemed to understand her sister. Maybe it was because they were children, close to the same age, or maybe it was their genetic gift that brought them closer.

She turned off the bedroom light, watching the nightlight come to life. It gave off a pearl white angel shape on the pastel pink wall. She pondered the image, hoping it wasn't a sign of things to come. She swallowed hard and left the room, leaving the door ajar. The girls wiggled around, giggling as they tried to get comfortable in their beds.

Once in the kitchen, she looked out the window above the sink, her mind focusing in on the fight. She wanted to find a way to help from inside the house.

Robert, Warrant, Tristan, and Jennifer stood nearby, waiting for others to storm into the battlefield, ready to kill.

§

A strong unknown source connected with me, something so strong that it pulled my attention away from the fight. I glanced at the house. One of the vampires separated from the group. As I tried to focus on the vampire I was fighting with, somebody tried to make a mental connection with me. The connection was strange, new–and wrong. As I tried to merge into the connection, my blood pumped through my veins. My adrenaline pushed more power, speed, agility, and hostility through me. I fought with my opponent, regaining the upper hand, and then taking my opponent down.

§

Leah wiggled out from underneath her blankets. She stood up and glanced out the blinds. Leah's mind connected with her mother's. Her mom was focused on something outside, and now Leah knew why. A man was hurting her grandma. Her grandma was in danger. She turned to Katie with tears forming in the corners of her eyes. Their eyes met and Katie silently ran over. She jumped on Leah's bed and looked out the blinds with her sister. She turned her head in Leah's direction, tears dripping down her rosy cheeks. Tisa slipped over the side of her crib. Leah leapt to catch her. A faint thump followed Leah as she bounded to the floor. The girls looked at each other before glancing back at the door.

Leah listened intently, waiting for mom to come through. She and Tisa stood silent, and then realized she wasn't coming. Leah pulled Tisa into bed with them. Katie turned to Tisa, catching Leah's attention. They stared back at Tisa with their small fingers poised over their lips in a shushing gesture. Tisa raised her little finger to her lips too, and then poked her little face in between her sisters, peering out the blinds.

She connected with both of her sisters. They had to help grandma. Something violent and bad was happening below while daddy, auntie, and grandma's two friends stood by.

Leah led the way. They had to follow her actions. Neither Katie nor Tisa disagreed. Leah remembered how her mommy had opened the blinds by grabbing onto the string, so she grabbed and pulled, raising the blinds diagonally about a foot. It didn't open like when mommy did it, but it was close enough for her. The blinds looked like an awkward smile, and she giggled at the sight. Then she remembered how mommy always opens the window—by spinning the dial. Her fingers grabbed onto it and tried to spin it but it didn't do anything. She tried again but the dial still would not move. She and Katie looked at each other. Then she grabbed Katie's hand and positioned it on the dial, illustrating how to open it. Katie smiled and spun it with one hand, the dial completely unlocking beneath her grip. Leah shot her a frustrated look. She knew Katie was stronger, and had figured she could open it, so it shouldn't have surprised her. But it wasn't fair that the younger sister was stronger than the bigger sister. After a struggle, they succeeded in opening the window. A gust of cool air came through. They shivered. The girls wrapped their arms around their bodies. Then Leah realized they were going to get cold. She and Katie quickly put on their shoes, socks, and jackets, and then helped Tisa with hers.

Once they were finished, they put their thumbs up, like their mommy and daddy always did when they were ready. Leah climbed out the window, and then turned to pull Tisa through. Katie pushed Tisa's butt through. Tisa giggled. Leah and Katie shushed her again. They walked down the porch awning. Tisa stumbled and tripped, losing her balance. She rolled down the awning. A flash of fast movement scrambled by Katie and Leah. The girls gasped and jumped for their sister. Katie tripped and stumbled after her. Katie and Tisa fell into the bushes below. Leah launched herself after the other two. As Leah prepared to take the soft but bristled landing, a man lunged at Leah. He was pale, thin, and scary looking. His front teeth were long and sharp. His long balding hair was greasy, knotted, and tangled. When he moved, his hair pulled away from his face, revealing black, glassy eyes.

She yelped and, before she could hit the bushes, he knocked her off course. She fell to the grassy meadow. Her small body struck the ground hard. She lay there, the breath knocked out of her. Katie and Tisa jumped at him from the bushes, their obnoxious speed taking control. They drove him backward onto the ground. Then Katie and Tisa grabbed Leah, prepared to run in the other direction. A horrendous looking woman launched herself after them, fangs bore, snarling like a wild animal. She too looked thin and fragile, her dirty blonde hair strewn about her face. Her eyes were small and dark. Her pale skin made them stand out more. Her tattered dress hung limply around her body as she sprung at them.

Their only option was to fly upwards to their bedroom window, hauling their older sister in tow. Tisa was practically flying as she hung on to Leah's other arm. Powerful little Katie held tight and hurled all of them upwards. The man lurched at them again. He came within inches of Tisa. She flailed behind her sisters. She remembered how her mom had tried to teach her to ride a big tricycle with her feet. She kicked her feet outward and opposite each other, making contact with his face, pummeling him with her speedy heels. She wasn't about to let anybody near her older sisters if she could help it. The bedroom window was still open. Katie ran through it, pulling her sisters inside with her.

They fell on the bed, and tried to catch their breath. Something moved behind them. They turned to look at the window they had just come through. The male vampire crawled up the awning to the window. He reached for the open window. They screamed in horror.

§

High-pitch shrills caught everybody's attention. While I fought one of the vampires, Robert, Warrant, Jennifer, and Tristan ran towards the house.

§

Leah and her sisters bolted out of the room. They zoomed down the stairs, past their mother. Rebecca hadn't even made it out of the kitchen to find out what was happening. At the bottom of the stairs, they turned to their left, darted through the living room, and out the back door. They screamed for mom and grandma. Rebecca ran out of the kitchen after them, screaming at the top of her lungs for her children to come back. She stopped mid-flight in the middle of the backyard, the block wall closing itself in on her. She yelled. Her cries filled the night. She dropped to the ground, not knowing in which direction to run.

§

I felt her pain at the same time my oversized fangs ripped through my gums. The vampire threw a punch. I caught his arm, and pulled him in tight. I bore down on him, driving my fangs deep into his neck. With one clawed hand, I reached up and tore his head from his body. I stood up, his head still in my hand, and faced the vampires who had scared my family.

Several of them backed down, yet others stepped forward. Rebecca's mind connected with mine. Her concern for the girls filled my head. Something was wrong, and I was unable to discern what it was. It hurt deep down inside. Frustrated, a short but powerful howl escaped my lips. The other vampires who had stepped forward now became wary of me. For what they had seen was merely the vampire, not the werewolf. I threw the severed head at them. They backed off.

My inner being tried to come forth. My clothes ripped, my muscles expanding into oversized wolf limbs. Anger overwhelmed me. The heat from it pushed my blood harder. Another howl erupted as I underwent the transformation. The vampires hissed and took a step forward. Then something to my left rushed at the vampires. What I initially thought was a large, silver ball of light split into three separate balls. They slammed the vampires to the ground. I recoiled in horror, knowing exactly who and what they were.

My grandchildren left a trail of reckless bodies on the ground. I tore through the grass after them, trying to track them as they ran through the forest. Their tiny bodies were high on adrenaline and fear so it wasn't easy keeping up with them. Their speed was unbelievable. Balls of light tore through brush and debris, destroying everything in their wake. I stepped it up a notch and found myself hightailing it. Animals scuffled about in the trees. I caught a glimpse of the three balls merging into one again. The brilliant sphere lit up the forest like the Fourth of July, illuminating everything nearby, including the mountain lion that scampered off.

The scent of Robert and Warrant bounded up behind me. Then, I sensed danger nearby. Although I worried about Rebecca, I knew she was safe with Tristan. In wolf form, we continued to run through the forest after the children but my mind lingered on the thought of those creatures outside our home.

Lowering my head, I tore through the brush after the children. Robert came to a sliding halt, burying his paws into the earth. Brush and pine cones flew through the air. Cautiously, he turned his head, and then howled—a long, deep, sorrowful howl. Warrant and I, too, came to a blinding halt. Searching our surroundings, I inhaled a deathly scent. We wrinkled our noses. A branch broke. We spun around.

Jace, David, and Woodrow jumped down from the top of the tree. The three of us jumped. Then, we stood our ground. We growled at them. Those assholes! They held my grandchildren.

"Now, now, I wouldn't do that if I were you," Jace said. He held Katie in his arms. He ran a finger down her cheek. "They are pretty impressive, and pretty special, aren't they? Especially this one." He lowered his nose to her cheek and drew in a deep breath. "She would make a nice dessert, but she's not the one that I want," he said, glaring at us.

Robert met his gaze, fangs still bared.

David and Woodrow stood by his side, holding Leah and Tisa respectively. Tisa scrambled and fought David, her fingernails leaving scratch marks all over his arms. With her human teeth, she snapped at him. She undoubtedly had her father's curse in her. He merely stood there holding her, as if it defiled him just to touch her. Woodrow, on the other hand, stood with Leah wrapped in his arms, inhaling her scent repeatedly.

She sat calmly, but the expression on her face exposed her fear. She clearly kept an eye on him.

I wanted to kill them all, but they held the girls and I feared Jace would use them in retaliation. Then he stepped forward again, his finger jutting down at me.

"I want you," he said, his brilliant teeth gleaming in the darkness. The silence of the night brought an eerie closure upon us.

His words came out slowly. "Such a shame they turned you into a wolf. I had much better plans for you. Much better. But that's still not going to stop me. Friday night, I want you at the Pit. You want to challenge me? Fine, I'll give you something to think about, something to fight for. This one's coming with me for collateral. You'll get her later." His dark arms curled tighter around Katie.

She held her hands out to us. Tears erupted from her eyes.

My heart broke. I felt her aches…her pain…her broken heart.

"Take this one. She's annoying me," David snapped. He sent Tisa airborne towards Robert.

As I watched her fly through the air, my heart plummeted. In wolf form, Robert ran to her. I was glad, even as she was still in danger, that her little mind seemed to focus on her daddy.

"Daddy!"

Robert changed into his human form, miraculously catching her in his arms. She wrapped around his neck, cuddling against him. Robert moved her around to his back while she clung to him.

I turned to Woodrow. He held Leah. I was leery he was going to do the same thing with her. Instead, he set her down on the ground.

"Go on, now, go to your grandma."

She took off running to me, her arms outspread. She stumbled in the brush. Then she bolted up on her feet, and ran. When I lowered my head, she climbed onto my back, burying her hands in my scruff.

Tears ran down Robert's cheeks. "Hey, just let my daughter go. My mom will be there Friday. You don't have to worry about that," Robert said.

I struggled not to show my weakness to Jace, but he already knew it. Tears leaked from the corners of my eyes. Katie cried. She opened her arms wide. I wanted to run and grab her, but I feared Jace would harm her.

"Sorry, Robert. I need to make sure that she's going to be there," and just like that, Jace turned and walked away with David and Woodrow behind him.

I whimpered. I worried about what Jace would do to Katie. Would he use her in one of his freak experiments?

We started to run after them. Then, there was movement in the brush beyond the trees surrounding us. Warrant stood next to me. He hunkered down, his nostrils flaring. Robert stiffened up next to me.

"It's not Jace. It's feline," he said, staring into the distance.

Feline? What the hell? Then it came to me. Oh, shit, it was the mountain lion. She was getting brave, approaching a group of vampires.

"Mom, take Tisa home, please?" Robert pulled Tisa off of him and sat her on my back in front of Leah.

"Warrant?"

Warrant looked at him.

"You got my back?"

Warrant nodded.

Reluctantly, I left him, heading home. I worried about leaving them, but decided it was best. The children didn't need to see them fight, and I'm sure that's what it was going to come to once they caught up to Jace and his men.

Occasionally, I peeked in the distance behind me, watching the forest enclose the darkness. I started off walking, but once I was getting closer to home, I trotted, carefully working up to a run. The girls had a good grip on my scruff and were able to lie atop me, burying their faces in my fur. I did my best to avoid the rough terrain. A couple of times I had to stop so they could reposition themselves.

I was concerned that the vampires were still near our home, but when I got closer, only Tristan and Rebecca stood out front. Nearing the edge of the forest, I slowed down, careful to not surprise Rebecca and scare her. I glanced around, seeing no sign of vampires or their remnants other than a couple of puddles of blood. I stopped short, and sniffed about. The girls climbed off of my back. They ran for Tristan and Rebecca. A curious look arose on Rebecca's face. She carefully studied me while Tristan followed her.

"Where's Katie?" she asked, her voice trembling in her throat.

Tristan touched my head. Then he turned to Rebecca.

"Robert and Warrant are going after her," he relayed.

I remained in my wolf form, for I didn't want to reveal my naked body to the family.

Rebecca snapped her head around. "Where is she?"

She grabbed Tristan, her fists curling up in his shirt as she maneuvered around in front of him, her face coming within inches of his.

"We don't want to worry you." He spoke softly, his eyes finally meeting hers.

The two girls curled around their mother.

"Goddammit, I can't read your mind! Where is my daughter?" she screamed.

Her outburst scared the girls. They screamed. Then tears erupted.

"Tistan, up. Mommy's scaring me," Tisa said. She wrapped her arms around his leg.

The children climbed up him, using their feet and legs, like a monkey. They finally pulled themselves into his arms. Small droplets of tears rested on their cheeks. Rebecca started to grab Tisa from Tristan's embrace but Tisa pulled back.

"You're scaring me," she mumbled, burying her face in his arms.

"Oh, honey, it's okay. I'm just worried. Tristan, where is Katie? Damn you, look at me!"

Tristan finally glared into her eyes. "Rebecca, I'm trying to keep you from harm—you and your family. If you knew where she was, you'd be out there looking for her too, so I'm not going to tell you. You'll only endanger yourself."

Leah and Tisa rested their heads on his chest.

I walked up and nuzzled against Rebecca's leg. She glanced down at me, tears pouring from her eyes.

In the darkness beyond the forest, something shrieked. An unknown animalistic sound echoed in the night. Rebecca recoiled into Tristan's arms, something she would have never done regardless of the circumstances. He maneuvered Tisa around to his back as Robert had done. With Tisa clinging to him, he pulled Rebecca into him.

"We should get inside," he said, walking her towards the house.

Her mouth hung open. "What was that?"

"I don't know. Now, let's go inside." He wrapped his arm around her shoulders and escorted her into the house.

A horrendous scream echoed throughout the forest.

I wondered if I should go back out to look for Robert and Warrant. Something was dying in the forest, and I couldn't detect what it was. A lump formed in my throat. Then Tristan's hand was upon me, grabbing me by my fur.

"Crystal, get in the house. Now!"

I faced him. Rebecca and Leah stood in the doorway. His expression was hard, almost stone-like. I stared back into the forest, trying to determine where my devotion lay, when he grabbed my snout, his eyes inches from mine.

"You could get yourself killed. Robert and Warrant will take care of it. Now get inside. Katie will be fine."

Tisa poked her head over his shoulder. "Come on, Grandma, inside."

She peered down at me, a smile crossing her face. He removed his hand. Tisa climbed off of his back. Her fingers touched my muzzle. She soothed my nerves. My heart beat slowed. I went inside the house.

Upstairs, I changed into my human form and dressed. Tristan appeared in my room. He laid his hand on my shoulder. I leaned against him.

"I'll fight him, and I'll kill him," I whispered, tears streaming down my face.

"We should probably go downstairs. Your daughter-in-law needs you," he said. He slightly pushed me away from him. He wiped my tears away.

Then Jennifer popped into my head. "Oh my God, where's Jennifer?" My eyes were wide with horror.

"She had gone to her room."

"Oh my God, I—"

"She's okay, but she's scared too."

With that, I pushed past him and ran downstairs. Jennifer laid lumped up next to Rebecca on the couch, her hair wet, her face red.

"I think they got her, Mom. I can feel it," she said, her arm wrapped around Rebecca's shoulders. I noticed something different in her eyes.

"Jennifer?" I stepped closer to the two of them. She gazed back at me. Her skin was moist. I eyed her suspiciously, watching her stroke Rebecca's hair.

"Yes," she replied.

Something was off, but I didn't know what, and I didn't know what to ask her. The door opened. Rebecca and Jennifer jumped off the couch. Out of the darkness and into the light stepped Robert and only Robert. I couldn't swallow.

"Honey?" Rebecca asked.

Rebecca fell to her knees, breaking down, her head on the floor. I glanced back at Jennifer, who smiled strangely.

"What is up with you?" I asked her, appalled at her reaction to the situation.

"Nothing, Mom."

Her gaze trailed over to Tristan, who stared at her. I turned towards Robert, who walked into the house, shutting and locking the door behind him. He approached his wife who laid on the floor crying like a banshee. An odd noise toward the back of the house caught our attention. Jennifer hurried to the back door.

I went after her as she proceeded through the back door. In the darkness, stood the outline of a figure but I was unable to make it out. Tristan and I followed Jennifer onto the back porch. It lowered its head and set something to the ground. I peered out into the darkness. The mountain lion backed up. My heart raced. Then, I sensed something familiar in the object—or so I thought. It rested on the ground. I couldn't breathe.

Jennifer stepped onto the grass. I reached out to grab her arm. She shook me off and hunkered down. The mountain lion slinked over to her, and lowered her head under Jennifer's hand.

"You're a good girl, aren't you?" Jennifer said. The feline's face neared hers.

Rebecca and Robert ran up behind us. Rebecca gasped.

I cranked my head to the right to see the present the feline had brought us stand up. Katie stood before us, her head covered by the jacket hood. Goosebumps broke out all over my body. My hair stood on end. Rebecca stepped off the patio. The feline stood only a few feet away from her, cautiously watching Rebecca approach the figure. I worried she was hurt. Jennifer remained knelt down next to the feline, her hand brushing along the hair on its body. It nestled against Jennifer. Rebecca started to rush towards the other figure.

"Don't run. You'll scare her," said Jennifer. The feline's hairs bristled.

Rebecca knelt down next to Katie. She pushed the hood back. She had a few scratches on her face, but nothing serious. Rebecca picked her up and held her against her body. She ran kisses all over Katie's face, as the two of them clutched onto each other. Tears flowed from their eyes. She cautiously walked past the feline, eyeing her.

Jennifer seemed to pick up on it. She smiled.

"It's okay Rebecca. As long as you don't make any sudden movements, you'll be fine."

Rebecca brought Katie to me and anxiously unzipped and removed her jacket, to examine her body for any wounds or marks that needed medical aid. She handed me the jacket, pulling up her shirt and pants to examine her.

"Baby, are you okay?" Tears streamed down Rebecca's face. Katie held her hand out to her mom, wiping away the tears.

"I'm okay, Mommy. She took me away from the bad man."

Rebecca pulled her back into her arms, clutching onto her for dear life.

"Jesus, thank you, God," she exclaimed. She rushed inside the house.

I turned the jacket around in my hands, looking it over. There were a few tear marks where the mountain lion had bitten into it to carry her away, but she'd been gentle enough to not even break through the entire coat. I looked at Jennifer. The mountain lion licked her face. I recoiled in horror. It was sure to latch onto her.

"How the hell…" I stopped.

Jennifer pulled back. "Thank you, sweetie. You've been good to us. You can go now."

Jennifer stood. The mountain lion lowered her head and backed off. It appeared to smile before it jumped the block wall.

I turned to Jennifer. "What–"

"Go in, Mom," she muttered, pushing me into the house.

FIGHT

I listened to Jennifer's story as she explained what had happened. Apparently, after we'd left to track the girls, she too had left, leaving Tristan to watch over Rebecca. Jennifer was the last person Jace and his men would be concerned about, and she took advantage of that. She'd grabbed some meat from the freezer and left through the backyard, knowing nobody would circle around to come looking for her. In the woods behind the house, she went to her favorite sitting place, where she had on many occasions seen the mountain lion.

Whenever she would see the lion, she would sit and watch it, careful not to tempt fate. But since her first meeting with the mountain lion, she'd begun to initiate the transformation into her wolf. She playfully jumped around, prompting the lion to come near her, communicate with her, and play with her, even though they were natural enemies. They'd begun a friendship—an odd and deadly friendship.

Tonight, she had baited the meat on a nearby log, changing into her wolf form and waiting for her friend. She knew she would come, for this was a weekly ritual for her and the lion. Within a brief amount of time, the lion showed up, ate, and hunkered low. The lion caught sight of the werewolf Jennifer had changed into. The mountain lion had not displayed any aggression toward Jennifer, so she knew she could count on her to keep her temper under control. She approached the mountain lion with a plan.

She had arrived too late to find the girls. Jace and his cohorts already had them. So she stayed back, watching. When her family and Warrant arrived, trying to get the children, the lion was the first to make a move. She waited until Jace and his men had left with Katie.

Jennifer had become worried Katie would get hurt and urged the lion to stay behind, but the lion didn't.

Instead, she became the aggressor, as the men neared her hiding spot. She lunged, driving Jace backwards into a ravine. He lost his hold on Katie and dropped her. Though his men detected something in the woods near them, they had excused the smell as that of an animal in fear, leaving it to be.

The fear they had smelt was probably Jennifer's. When Katie fell from Jace's grip, Jennifer lunged at the child. She grabbed at the loose hood and ran off with her in the distance. Their footsteps were close behind her. A large bald man was fast on her tracks, nearing her. The lion appeared, snarling at him.

The man lunged at Jennifer, caught her by her feet, and threw her to the ground. The lion catapulted past them. Jennifer turned and snapped at him, releasing Katie. Katie scrambled to get up. Then the lion grabbed the child by the loose hood and took off. As Jennifer struggled to stand, the vampire attacked again.

His hands found her throat. She clawed and snapped at his face. Then another wolf attacked. He threw the vampire to the ground, allowing her to escape. She turned and ran off, several hundred feet behind the lion. She expected the lion to be near her home when she got there, but it was not. So Jennifer sneaked in through the side door to the laundry room, which allowed her to steal into the bathroom, past Rebecca. Noticing the blood on her body, she took a shower and waited for the mountain lion to bring Katie. There was something distinct about this mountain lion, something different that she hadn't smelled before. She couldn't place it. But she did know tonight that she could count on her. As long as the lion was properly fed she wouldn't harm Katie. Had she not been, then Jennifer would have worried.

When she was asked about the shrieking in the forest, Jennifer could only claim the lion had made some of the noise throughout the fight, but not enough to overtake the forest. She, too, had heard the sounds, but by then she was almost out of the woods.

I turned to Robert, who sat on the couch, glancing periodically out the window.

"Where's Warrant?" Tristan asked him.

"I don't know. I lost him at some point. He took off after one of the vampires. I assumed he was after the one that attacked Jennifer."

"And the other two?"

Tristan eyed Robert curiously.

"They took off. Once I realized they didn't have Katie anymore, I turned my attention to looking for her. I caught a glimpse of her jacket somewhere in the distance traveling away from me, so I assumed somebody else had her. I thought it was Warrant, but I was wrong." He lowered his head, biting at his knuckles.

"Are you okay?" asked Rebecca.

"Yeah," he said. "Let's get the girls to bed. I'm a little concerned about Warrant, should he show up. I don't want the kids to see him if he's been attacked."

Jennifer and I gave the kids kisses and hugs. Then mom and dad started to walk them upstairs.

"Daddy, hold on," Leah said, pulling at his hand.

"What, hon?" He let go of her and watched her approach Tristan, who now sat on the recliner. She climbed onto his lap.

"And what do you want?" he asked. She touched his face.

"Thank you," she said, wrapping her arms around him.

He wrinkled his nose and tried to turn away. Her scent was mouth-watering. So, I presumed he was trying to keep her scent from filling his nostrils. I smiled at him.

"I think they like you," I said.

"Yeah, that's nice," he said. "What are you thanking me for?"

Leah pulled away and gazed into his eyes. "For helping daddy."

"Oh." He smiled.

She climbed off. Then, Tisa and Katie climbed on him, and hugged him. Katie lingered a little longer than Tisa had, placing her hands on his face.

"You need to be careful," he said, shaking his finger at her. "All of you do. You're strong little girls, but those men were bad. They would have hurt you."

Then Katie leaned in and gave him a kiss on his cheek. She left him stunned and looking away. They jumped off of his lap.

The back door opened. Tristan stood. Warrant stumbled in. His eyes were wide and wild-like.

"Jesus, are you alright?" Tristan asked.

Warrant was disheveled. His gaze shifted frantically around the room. "Where are the kids?"

"Going up the stairs to bed, right now," Jennifer answered.

"Good, we need to talk."

"Are you alright?" I asked. Camouflage clothes replaced the jeans and t-shirt he had worn. They were tattered, torn, and seemed extraordinarily short and tight on him.

"Yeah, I'm fine."

"Where'd you get those clothes?" Jennifer asked. She looked him over.

"From the hunter they killed." He sat down on the floor hard, not seeming to want to move.

I turned to Jennifer. "Would you mind getting him some water?"

"Yeah." She left the room.

We sat back down, watching him. He wasn't himself. His eyes were shifty, and they didn't settle on anything for long. He tapped his fingers repeatedly on his legs. Confusion, paranoia, and anxiety replaced his calm and laid back demeanor. His behavior seemed odd.

"Was that what we heard in the forest?" I asked.

Jennifer returned with a bottle of water.

"I don't know," he said, taking the water from her. He guzzled it down within seconds. "Thanks."

§

We made it through the night without incident. I awoke sometime in the dark and heard strange noises coming from Warrant downstairs. I sent Tristan to check on him. Tristan was becoming increasingly concerned about him. Something just didn't seem right, but we couldn't pinpoint it. If Tristan had detected something, he didn't say.

§

The next night, Warrant, Tristan, and I left the family alone with Robert and Jennifer to protect our home. I was leery about it, but Warrant had a hunch nothing would go awry. He was sure Jace would wait until Friday night for his battle. Tristan, on the other hand, was not so sure, so he insisted on taking the car. He was worried that we would get jumped in the forest.

We piled into my car with Warrant at the wheel. Although Tristan didn't want to travel by vehicle, he welcomed the comfort instead of battling the rocky terrain. He sat back, his head leaning against the headrest.

"Warrant, can you put some music on, please?" I asked.

He flipped on the stereo, and the CD blared out hard music. He went to grab the knob when Tristan pointed his finger at the dial, turning it down himself.

"You're slow," Tristan replied, grinning from ear to ear.

"Fuck you," Warrant said. "You want to see who's really slow, let's pull over."

He grinned back at Tristan.

"Not tonight, but maybe another night. Crystal's going to be late."

I jammed out to the music while they bickered back and forth.

Warrant drove us out of Flagstaff and down to Prescott, about a forty-five minute drive southwest. We rode down the highway and then took a right several miles west to a bar that was hidden behind a shopping center. I was glad the cities in northern Arizona closed down earlier than the central metropolitan areas. Anything happening up here was less likely to be noticed.

We pulled up in front of the country western bar. Several cars and trucks were parked outside. It seemed like an abnormally busy Wednesday night. But, it didn't matter, I was pumped and raring to go. My workout and the music had helped to set me in the mood.

I jumped out of the SUV, threw a couple of jabs in the air, and shuffled around. The guys glanced at me.

Amped up, I strutted past them toward the bar. It was nice to have them with me. Whether, I could kick ass or not, they would have my back should anything happen. Just when I walked in the door, a large black man to my left, kicked back in his chair, and threw his feet on the table. I did a double take, half expecting it to be Jace. I was ready for him to attack.

"What? You think I'm going to bite?" The man bared his top fangs at me. "Well, I might."

I bared my fangs, and hissed. Mine were abnormally larger than his—actually, than those of any other vampire I had met so far. That was one advantage I had since I was half werewolf.

He recoiled, then sat up, taking off his dark glasses. Warrant and Tristan stood by my side. They glared at him.

"Fuck me," he commented. His friends stared at me.

"You're one of them," his friend said, pointing at me.

I shifted my gaze. My pupils dilated to focus in on him.

He sat back and crossed his arms. "Nice to meet you...,"

"Crystal," I answered. Modern county music blared over the speakers.

"Ah, I know who you are," he said, smiling. "Welcome. I so look forward to seeing you fight tonight." He threw his arms up in an elaborate welcome while I continued forward. A hand slammed down on the table.

I turned and stared back at the men at his table, when one of them yelled out, "Can we get some good music on? And, not this country bullshit!" The word *bull* was long and drawn out.

The bartender, a tall and large Native American, leaned over the bar. His features were hard and scarred from fighting too many battles through the years. His long hair was pulled into a tight ponytail that hung down his back.

"No problem. We don't discriminate around here. But if we put on your music, then we listen to my music, too." He turned his attention to the crowd in the bar.

"Does anyone oppose?"

The crowd shook their heads, glancing back at him. The bartender waved his hands in the air, questioning the man at the table. I could tell the black man thought long and hard about it.

"Aw, fuck it. Do it, but I want to hear my music first. And none of that whistling bird shit either." He made a gesture with his hand as if trying to dismiss the thought. With a scowl on his face, he sat back, and laid his arms across his chest.

The corner of my lip curled up. The bartender turned to another man at the end of the counter.

"Lloyd, get some good music on. A little bit of everything. No discriminating either." Lloyd, an older Native American, reached over and hit the jukebox with his fist.

When the sound of heavy hip hop came on, I stifled a grin. The bartender wrinkled his nose at it. He surely wasn't going to say anything, but he would put up with it just so he could hear his music.

I neared the bar when a man to my right slammed his glass down.

"Can I get a drink, man?" he spat, his voice slurred.

The bartender leaned on the counter, his arms out wide. "Don't spit on my bar."

"I didn't spit on your bar."

"You spit on my bar. Now don't argue with me. If you're going to argue with me and you're going to spit on my bar, then you're not going to get a drink. You want a drink or not?" He arched his eyebrow at the man.

"I'm not arguing with you," he spat again.

I stood before the bartender. The older gentleman argued with him. I wished he would shut up. The bartender grabbed him by his head, and slammed it on the bar sideways.

He helped him down. "Are you done, old man? I really don't want to hurt you."

He turned his head to avoid looking at the patrons in the bar. His fangs protruded from his gums. He rolled his eyes and sighed. Maybe he didn't want to hurt him, but the man was testing his patience and his virtue. I glanced about. The tension escalated in the room. Several vampires looked around, revealing their fangs. Those who were mortal looked away. They didn't want to gain any attention from a vampire. One lone wolf sat on the other side of the offender, licking his chops.

"Yeah, you know we don't discriminate around here. We like dark meat, white meat, red meat, even yellow meat," the wolf said, staring up at the bartender. "It's all good stuff."

He looked at me and then back at the bartender. Before I could speak up, Warrant came around the left of me. "Hey, can we get some service?"

"Sure," the bartender answered. He turned toward Warrant, letting go of the customer's head. He grabbed a bottle of beer and slammed it down in front of the customer, who sulked in his seat. He turned toward Warrant. "I actually prefer draft."

"It's on the house. Be thankful and don't fuck up again." The bartender turned to us. The man left the counter, sucking on his bottle. The lone wolf followed him to a table.

"Yeah, what do you want?" he asked, eyeing me. "Aye, I know you—yeah, you're Crystal. Everybody's looking forward to seeing you fight tonight. It's been a while. What have you been up to?"

"Life," I said.

"Yeah, I know how that goes," he replied, glancing at Tristan who stood behind me. "Who're these two?"

"My managers."

He nodded. "Good idea—a wolf and a vampire. I like that. Keeps you on the up and up."

Warrant leaned on the counter. "We're looking for Tom."

"You're looking at him. I'm the owner, manager, accountant, and whatever-the-fuck-else you need for The Fighting Bull. You just talk to me."

We all eyed him. Tom looked us over too, and then added, "Your opponent's here but I think she's still getting ready. Fight starts whenever you're both ready. Are you prepared?" He cocked his head like a puppy dog, his ponytail flipping to the side.

"Yeah, I'm prepared," I said. "Where's it at?"

He leaned his elbow on the bar, pointing to his left. "Down the bar. See the sign for the restrooms? Down that hallway, last door to your left. Once you're in there, go to your right. The hallway will take you to the arena. Just wait inside the door. Oh, and by the way, you and your opponent come out the same door. Sorry, I don't have separate doors for you two."

Great, I thought. My luck, I'll get somebody with a vendetta. Tristan and Warrant followed me down the hallway and into the hall to the right. I was thankful this arena didn't seem that eerie compared to some of the other ones I'd been in. It just seemed gloomy and dirty. Stopping by the door, I peered back at Tristan and Warrant.

The pungent smell drifted up my nose. "It stinks."

Tristan wrinkled his nose. "Yes, it does. It smells of wolf. Wet and mangy wolf."

"You know, your girlfriend here is a wolf. You disrespecting her that way, Tristan? I didn't think you were that type of man," Warrant said, smiling.

"No, she's not mangy and wet." Tristan glared back.

I half listened to their humorous bickering while looking around.

"Does she smell like wet wolf after a shower?"

"No, she doesn't. Her shampoo masks the smell of wolf." He stopped briefly and then stammered, "…at least most of it."

I shot him a dirty look. "What does that mean?"

"It means I'll put up with your odd smells," he said, his lip curling up into a thin smile.

I turned my attention back to my pending battle and peered through the glass wall. "Who am I fighting?"

"Uh, I believe Kristen."

"Hmm! Why isn't anyone coming in here yet?"

I stared into the stands on the opposite side of the arena, looking for somebody, anybody.

"I'm going to find out what's taking so long," I said.

I started down the hallway, Tristan and Warrant on my heels. I went out the door, the music still bellowing out the speakers. Right when I reached the entryway to the bar, Tristan and Warrant shouted.

"Crystal, look out!"

But it was too late. A body swung down from the top floor railing. The woman's feet connected with my face. I flew backwards, knocking down both Tristan and Warrant. I should have seen that one coming. I hadn't let my senses take over like I should have. Dammit all to hell. I stood staring at the long-haired blonde woman who hung from the railing slats. She looked like a mountain climber, the way she propped her right foot back up on the edge of the framing. She wore khaki shorts, a black muscle shirt, and tennis shoes. Her hair was pulled back from her face with a bandana she wore over the top of her hair. Her eyes were dark and large as she stared back at me, expressionless.

"You must be Kristen," I snapped.

"And you must be Crystal," she spat. "Your reputation has preceded you."

I walked up to the framing, afraid she was going to try another sneaky blow, but instead she climbed up the framing, then up and over the stair railing. I walked out into the bar.

The patrons started backing off when I came through. Chairs scraped across the floor. The fight was just beginning and everybody was getting out of the way. I stared up at her, watching her climb onto the second floor, and peer over the railing.

"Come and get me, Crystal," she exclaimed. "That is if you want me bad enough!" She smiled. Her fangs glistened.

I grinned at her. Oh, I was going to come and get her, and I was going to rip her fangs from her mouth while I was at it. I found my footing and pushed off hard from the wooden floor, lunging at her as I came up and over the top of the railing. She jumped and her feet connected with my chest, heaving me across the bar. I struck the wall some forty feet in the air. I smashed into a couple of picture frames that broke beneath the weight, some of the glass sticking in my back. People ran from beneath me as I toppled to the floor. I landed with a heavy thud, on my face. That was twice now. There was not going to be a third.

Kristen turned to a customer. "Yeah, some champion she is. She can't even defend herself."

Then her feet appeared in my face, the weight of her foot stomping down in the middle of my back. Above me, I caught a glimpse of her flexing her arms like a bodybuilder.

Bitch. That was it—she was mine. I grabbed her other leg and wrenched it out from underneath her. She crashed down onto her back while I stood, one leg still in my hand, her other leg free. I slammed my body weight down on her captured leg, completely bending it towards her body like a pair of scissors. She screamed, a loud pop from her hip sounding in my ear. Tears of pain welled up in her eyes. I forced a look of sorrow on my face.

I thought about her earlier sneak attack and irritating comment. , and then said, "Oh, some competitor you are. You can't even stand on your own two feet."

I forced my weight down harder on her, my arm still wrapped around her upper thigh. The bones gave way beneath my power. She shrieked. Her voice pierced my ears.

"Oh, while you're at it, why don't you shut the fuck up," I said, sitting on her chest.

I pounded my fist into her face multiple times, breaking her jaw. The crunch of bone and teeth churned my stomach, but gratified the beasts inside of me. I stood up, grabbed her by her hair, and wrenched her above me, flinging her head over heels. She slammed into the second floor wall. She crashed into the railing. As the broken pieces fell to the floor below, one of the railing posts embedded itself into her chest, piercing her heart.

I turned towards the spectators, for the beasts inside were still agitated, the fight having ended too quickly. They wanted more. Then a long blonde haired man stood up. He lunged for me. And, I was ready. His hair whipped behind him. He was fast, so I had to be faster. I lunged, striking him in mid air, driving him back and into the wall behind him. I clutched onto him, my face buried in his throat, my fingers already transformed into claws. Burying one of my hands— claws and all—into his face, I forced his head out of the way. I pulled his shoulder, dislocating the joint. The pop of the ball from his joint echoed loudly in my ear, leaving his arm to dangle loosely at his side. As I pierced his neck with my fangs, I wrapped my legs around his torso.

His head rolled limply on his neck, now barely attached to his own body. I pulled away. His lifeless form fell to the ground. The impact of the fall dislocated the head completely, so that it rolled under a nearby a table.

I turned and stared at the crowd, waiting for somebody else to come forth. Instead, most of the patrons scooted their chairs and tables back. Some of the vampires hissed through their teeth, but they didn't dare meet my eyes. Tristan and Warrant hurried me out of the door as the bartender stared on.

The adrenaline continued to push its way through my system while the beasts inside wanted more. Warrant and Tristan each held my shoulder and pushed me towards the car. I squirmed from underneath their grip, lunging away.

Warrant grabbed me and slammed me into the side of the SUV. "Control it, Crystal. You need to control it."

The SUV gave way, the indention neatly wrapping around my body. The wolf and vampire in me pushed to get out. They wanted to hurt somebody, to kill again. Then Tristan shoved my head against the car.

"You have got to control it! Otherwise it's going to control you."

I fought to manage my inner beasts, to calm down my heartbeat. The smell of my victims blood wafted up my nose. Tristan leaned into me. They maintained their hold on me. Closing my eyes, I retracted my fangs and slowed down my heartbeat. I trembled against Tristan and Warrant, the coolness of the night upon my skin.

"Good, Crystal, good," said Tristan, leaning into me. "I can feel you relaxing now."

Voices filled the air, followed by people coming out of the bar. A woman cried, saying she wished she hadn't seen such a fight.

She should feel lucky she got out alive, I thought.

"Come on," Tristan said. "Let's get her in the car."

"We need to get the blood off of her. The smell is making her hunger worse," Warrant said.

They shoved me in to the back of the SUV and climbed in, trying to avoid the patrons attention. Warrant reached out and pulled the hatch shut behind me. The light stayed on until Warrant reached up and hit it with his fist, breaking it.

By then, Tristan had already lowered the back seat. Warrant climbed through to the driver's seat. Tristan's face was on mine, his tongue lapping up the blood on my body. I lay across the floor with my eyes closed, humming. Although I could still smell the blood, my nerves were calming down. I focused on his fluid movement which also helped to calm me down, despite the cries and voices outside the bar.

§

A short time later, we arrived at an old broken down gym within Prescott for the next fight. Because it was old and falling apart, it was known among the teenagers as a party place, so cars were forbidden from parking in the lot. Those who drove to the gym parked around the corner in an older shopping center or down the road near campgrounds in the forest. We parked near the campgrounds and walked up to the gym, the scent of vampires and wolves lingering in the air. I was thankful Tristan and Warrant had cleaned the blood from my skin. At least I didn't look like I had murdered someone.

I glanced around the old building as we walked by. Though the windows were mostly boarded up, sections of the boards were broken. Wood slats were missing from the side of the house, and debris clung to nails that were left on without wood to hold. In front of a door with a big No Trespassing sign stood a young man. His perfectly—styled brown hair went with his boyish charm. He looked like the All Star athlete of his school, and I'm sure everybody else thought the same thing. I looked him over, distinguishing his inner wolf. He smiled back at me, his athletic build taking up most of the doorway. We stood to the side, watching everybody pay their way into the gym. I glanced at the crowd. It was a young age group. I glanced back at Warrant, sneering at him.

"Sorry. I was trying to get you a decent fighter and, well, I had this teenage boy who was interested in taking you on." He smirked.

"Thanks, I appreciate it. But I would have appreciated not having to kill a teenage kid either," I said.

Focusing on the crowd, I sighed. Several teenagers eyed me suspiciously. I presumed they didn't know who I was. They probably thought the three of us were parents coming to check on their kids or that we were undercover cops. We didn't exactly blend in. I approached the boyish charm kid who took the money and let them in the door one by one.

"Excuse me. I'm one of the fighters, Crystal. Where do you want me to enter?"

He looked me over, his eyes briefly stopping on my breasts before meeting my eyes. Then a devilish smirk spread across his face.

"You're Crystal? Wow, you look great for an old lady," he said, gnashing his teeth together. Catching himself, he replied, "Sorry, I meant you look great for a lady of your age. Absolutely phenomenal."

I rolled my eyes, aware that Tristan was peering at him over my shoulder.

"And your name is…?"

"I'm Tony. Nice to meet you." He offered his hand, and I accepted it. His grip was strong.

"Well, Tony, I'd like you to meet my mate, Tristan," I said, grinning.

Tony hesitantly put his hand out for Tristan to shake. I glanced back at Tristan.

He firmly shook Tony's hand and grinned back at him. A slight change appeared in Tony's face. I shook my head. Tristan leaned in to Tony's ear.

"She's my lady. Don't fuck up again, and keep your eyes to yourself."

I hid a smile, peering inside the gym.

"No problem," he said, lowering his head to me. "Sorry, ma'am. You and your men can go inside."

We walked in past the crowd, and the smell of mortals drifted into my nostrils. I tried to ignore it.

I pushed my way into the gym. The arena was not separated from the bleachers. Everything was completely open to everybody. We exchanged looks.

"There's no separation," I said, watching the youngsters walk through. Not one person in the gym was older than twenty.

I didn't like the idea of fighting amongst a bunch of teenage kids with no separation between the fighters and the audience. My inner beasts might continue the rampage into the audience once the competitor was killed. I didn't want to kill a bunch of teenagers.

"Sorry, Crystal, I didn't know," Warrant said, also looking around. "I've never been here before."

The look on Tristan's face was grim. "You keep control, and you'll be alright. We'll be right here if you need us. We'll stand against this wall."

I turned around, gazing at the large crowd. The arena encompassed a smaller square with bleachers on three sides. The wooden walls and bleachers were deteriorating. One light shone dimly on the arena floor.

After standing there for several minutes, the door shut quietly behind us. A chill shot up my spine. I turned to focus on the fight, leaving Tristan and Warrant's side.

Tony approached me. He laid his hand on my shoulder. Tristan shifted.

Tony leaned down in my ear. "Well, looks like we're ready."

"Great," I said. "Where's my opponent?" I looked around the gym, spotting double doors beyond the bleachers.

Tony backed off. He held his hands out to the sides. "You're looking at him."

I turned back to him, my mouth hanging open. I turned towards Warrant, a look of surprise on his face. Tristan glared at him, his mouth straightening into a thin line.

Tony eyed Tristan. "Sorry, man, somebody should have told you. And unfortunately, I can't keep my hands or my eyes to myself. Otherwise, I wouldn't be able to fight."

Then I heard Tristan in the back of my head: *If you don't kill him, I'm going to fuck him up.* Tristan shoved his hands in his pockets.

The cocky little bastard, I thought of the kid.

Tony struck me, an open-handed slap across the face. The burn melted deep inside my bones. Tristan and Warrant shifted forward behind me, their arms folded across their chests, on guard. As the crowd cheered Tony on, I clenched my teeth together, the beasts within me rising. Tony open-slapped me across my other cheek. The heat rose within my body.

I closed my eyes.

The heat from his breath was in mine. "Wow, you going to fight back or what? I thought you were some badass. Such a shame I have to mess up that pretty face."

Then his hands were on me, grabbing at both of my shoulders. I opened my eyes, threw my forearms up and out, stepping forward with my right leg in between his legs. I snapped my arms back down and delivered a chop with both hands to the sides of his neck, pulling him into me. My left knee came up, striking him in the bladder. He doubled over. I kicked out again with the same leg and connected with the inside of his knee, driving it out from under him. He grabbed me around the waist while my arm encircled his head. He pulled me off of the mat and straight into the air, dropping me backwards to the ground.

Fuck, I'm no damn wrestler. I struck the mat, scrambling to my feet. He ran at me like a football player. I lurched into the air, and then drove my foot down in the middle of his back. I shoved him face first into the mat. He bolted to his feet when I dropped full force on him.

He was up in the air, driving his leg up and forward in front of him, at an angle. His foot connected with my face before mine struck his. We fell to the floor. The pain pulsated through the muscles in my legs.

With my leg throbbing, I let the beasts take over a little. They helped me to push onward, straight at him. He rolled over onto his back, and that's when I aimed straight for his sternum. To my dismay, he rolled out of the way, and I connected with the ground. On my attempt, he rolled towards me, grabbing my farthest leg. I fell over backwards onto the ground. Then he was on me, his body enveloping mine. His arms wrapped around my legs, struggling to gain control of me, when his face moved up to mine.

"What a fine predicament we're in, aren't we?" he whispered in my ear.

"Fuck you." I glared back.

His hands moved up my body. "You think your mate is pissed?" He grinned down at me.

I was so looking forward to knocking his teeth out.

"Yeah, I'm sure he's writhing with hatred right now. Now, get your fucking hands off of me."

While he tried to pin my arms down, I maneuvered my legs out from underneath him. I wrapped them around his waist, locked my ankles together, and clamped down.

I pressed harder with my thighs, locking him until his eyes rolled back. Then I bitch slapped him, open-handed, across the face. At first he smiled down at me, but then I backhanded him. His face slowly turned pink. He reached down with his hands to grab at my throat. I snuck a fist straight up into his face, striking him square in the mouth. One of his fangs pierced my knuckle, but I thought nothing of it. I struck again. His right hand found my throat where he pressed his thumb into my soft spot. The second punch caught him again in the mouth. I maneuvered my left arm past his right arm and struck, clocking him in the nose and breaking his hold on my neck.

Eyes wide, his face descended, dropping closer to me. I reached out and struck him with a right hook to the side of the neck, sending convulsions throughout his body. I hit him again. His muscles gave way. I struck his nerve in the left arm with a half fist. He fought to regain control. Then I drove my right fist into a nerve in his neck. He squirmed atop me, his scream piercing the air. I clamped down harder with my legs, confining him. His ribs cracked and popped while he grabbed at my thighs, trying to release the hold.

"Bitch," he muttered.

I grabbed him by his hair and drove his head down towards me, sinking my fangs deep into his cheek. He fought, trying to brace himself and push up from the ground. Clenching my teeth tighter, I maintained my hold on him.

Tony's ribcage gave in, caving in on his heart. With his body lying over me, I clung to him, violently shaking my head like a wild animal. Flipping over, I unwrapped myself. Shaking my head with all the power I had, I threw him to the side and let go. He flew up and over everybody on the bleachers, striking the wall. Blood sprayed the room; splashing all over the floor, walls, bleachers, and the audience. They sat immobile, staring at me.

I glanced about the audience, and then slowly backed up. It was then I realized I had transformed into my wolf while I was flipping him over. The audience remained quiet, watching me. Tristan touched my scruff, urging me to come with him. We fled the building. I changed into my human form before jumping into the back of the SUV.

As I entered the house, Robert peeked out from his bedroom. Once we disappeared into my room, he closed his door. Beyond the walls, I detected Rebecca's fear growing. Her home was turning into a house of horrors and she had no control over it.

"So, when will we hear anything?" I asked. I slid out of my sweatpants and panties.

"I don't know. If we don't hear anything soon, Warrant will have to check into it." He threw his t-shirt on the floor.

Naked, I stepped into the bathroom and shut the door behind me.

§

The next night, I fought in Sedona two times, annihilating my competitors. One fight was close to a tourist attraction called Slide Rock. From atop the red crag, I threw my competitor onto the rocky water slide turning the pearl waves into a crimson waterfall.

§

Tristan and I laid in bed next to each other after the fight, our hair still wet from the shower.

"Tomorrow night's the big fight. Are you ready for it?" he asked.

"I am." I drew a thin line down his bare chest with my finger.

"You looked great tonight," he said. "You weren't as sloppy as you were in your first one last night."

"Oh, thanks." I kissed him on the nose.

He smiled. "Make sure to work out really good tomorrow. Jace is much older than you, so he's much stronger than you—although I beg to differ now that you've changed."

I curled up next to him, propping my leg on his hip. "I'll give him a run for his money."

"Yeah, but you need to be careful. I don't know what kind of antics he has in store for you. I'm still a little leery about this fight. Keep your eyes and ears open. And don't let your beasts control you. You control your beasts. You've gotten better, but I think I might have Warrant work with you on that tomorrow."

"Well, I know a way you can help me work on my beast," I said, rolling atop him and pushing him onto his back.

I sat up, straddling him, my black negligee shifting ever so lightly across his stomach.

"Is that all you think about lately?" he asked, his hands sliding up my arms, his hands silky smooth. "Not that I don't mind, but..."

I leaned down and kissed him. From downstairs, Warrant growled in his sleep. Tristan broke the kiss. He turned his head, and listened to Warrant.

"Ignore him," I whispered, nipping at his ear.

"I can't." He turned his face to me. "Do me a favor, Crystal?"

"What?" I said, kissing his face.

"Be on guard with him. I know he's been a good friend of mine for a long time, but something's wrong. He's not the same man I've known."

"I don't think..."

He cut me off. "I know he would never intentionally hurt you or anybody else in this house, but be on guard, please. Something's wrong and I can't pinpoint it. I have my suspicions, but I can't say for sure."

"What do you mean?"

"Ever since that one night when he was nearly killed, he hasn't been the same. I catch him once in a while acting strangely."

"How?"

"I can't explain, it's just...something." He met my eyes. "Please be careful."

"I will," I replied, realizing his concern was genuine.

THE PIT

Tristan and Warrant made sure that Robert was with us so we would have the backup we needed. Jennifer had tried to come, too. But the men were persistent that she remain with Rebecca and the children. Our main goal was to keep her and the girls safe from harm. Rebecca needed Jennifer. We didn't know if Jace was going to send somebody to the house while we were gone, and that uncertainty put the fear of the Devil in Rebecca.

We decided it was best to leave the vehicle at home. Since the fight was in the Pit, Warrant and Tristan advised against the use of motor terrain vehicles. The vampires and werewolves didn't like too many vehicles near the Pit. It would only draw more attention to them and what they might be doing. There was going to be people from all over to watch the best of the best fight, whether mortal or immortal. They also warned me that there were creatures of every caliber and to be aware of my surroundings at all times, whether the three of them were with me or not.

About five miles southeast of the highway we knew we had arrived when we smelled the smoke. It was a sickening smell of rubber, charred human remains, and metal. The beasts inside me stirred, the smell awakening their senses. Warrant and Robert changed into their human forms. I handed them the clothes I held for them. I turned away while they dressed.

Tristan grabbed me by my face and kissed me, his mouth lingering momentarily before he broke the hold.

"Don't forget what I told you," he said.

His eyes churned in the darkness. I wasn't quite sure what his gaze meant but I feared the worst. I nodded. Then my son approached me, hugged me, and kissed me on the forehead.

"I love you, Mom."

I stared up at him. I also saw something there I feared.

"I love you, too."

He wrapped his arms around me again and held on tight. Then he turned and walked away, his gaze moving towards Tristan.

I glanced briefly at Warrant. His eyes cast an eerie glow in the darkness. Tristan was right—something was wrong with Warrant, but I could not determine what it was. He embraced me, his lips lingering at my ear.

"Just remember that we all love you, regardless of what happens tonight." He pulled back with his hands still on my shoulders. His fingers left an impression within the form fitting shirt I wore.

Through his hands I could feel the tension and the heat built up within him. Something was terribly wrong with him.

He leaned in and gave me a passionate kiss.

Tristan started after him when Robert's hand fell on his shoulder.

"It's not worth it, Tristan," he said.

Tristan glared back at him.

"Really, it's not worth it."

Voices and other strange noises grew louder as we walked up the hill. The smell of smoke was getting stronger. Fire popped and crackled in the forest as we rounded the hillside. There was a massive crowd below, walking and talking with each other. If I'd had to guess how many people were here, it would have been hundreds, maybe even thousands. We followed the curvature of the hill down and around the Pit. The orange swirl of the fire escalated well over the top of the Pit, the night illuminated with its life. We moved around the creatures and made our way down below to the Pit.

We stopped at the top of the Pit. I gazed down below. The Pit had to have been well over 100 feet deep and 30 yards wide all around. Within the Pit, there were two torched vehicles spread apart from each other on opposite sides. Both vehicles were still on fire. The flames from the vehicles stood twenty-foot high. Within each vehicle, the smell of charred human remains escaped. I wrinkled my nose.

"Jesus Almighty," I muttered.

"Jesus ain't here to save you, child," a voice said behind me.

I turned to see a couple of black women. They examined me, their eyes dark and menacing. They backed off.

"Ignore them," Tristan said.

I turned back to peer into the Pit. Nature had built ledges into the hilltop of the Pit. Several packs of wolves lined the ledges to await the fight. The woods stood behind the hilltop to the northwest and northeast, gradually surrounding it but thinning into dirt to the south, where we stood.

Tristan and Warrant were right. There were wolves and vampires of all types who stood by for the announcement of the fight. Among them were several other creatures I couldn't identify. They could have passed for either vampire or wolf, but when I looked at them carefully, they did not. I carried on about my business and passed them by. I didn't care to meet their eyes.

Then a voice echoed throughout the Pit. It was loud and expanded up and into the stillness of the night. The crowd quieted and slowly turned their attention to the Pit. I looked in, unable to locate a physical body belonging to the voice. Then I saw Jace. He stood opposite me on the ledge above and to the center of the fire almost thirty yards ahead. His eyes centered on mine. My hatred for him made my blood boil.

When I jumped into the Pit, my feet hit dirt and I slid halfway down the side. He lunged in across from me, smoother and more graceful than I had. I didn't care if I was graceful at the moment. Hell, I didn't care if I was sloppy. I just wanted him….dead. My inner beasts swaggered on the edge of my body and waited for the right opportunity to emerge. His feet hit the earth and settled into a challenging stance. His dark clothes blended in with his dark skin.

Once at the bottom of the pit, the heat from the blaze ignited the warmth of my skin. I inhaled the scent of the fire and along with it the smell of death. Jace came at me fast and hard as he lunged forward, much unlike a vampire and more like a wild animal. His hands and feet shoved off the ground, pushing him harder along the earth. I lurched into the air above him. Then, he jumped at me. He was quicker than I'd expected, and his hands clamped down hard on me. Jace grabbed at me, using his hands to climb up my body. When he pulled me down far enough, we came face to face with one another.

He snapped at me. I recoiled. His fangs barely missed me. He drove me back into the pit wall. Dirt and rocks dislodged above me, tumbling down upon us. Jace grabbed me by my throat and pulled me in close. Then, he hurled me past the twenty-foot high fire into the dirt wall opposite us. Smoke wafted up into my face. I glanced down at my pants. They were on fire. I buried my leg in the dirt wall while clinging to a protruding rock, in hopes of putting the fire out. He was coming at me, flying through the air, his leg extended in front of him.

"Shit," I muttered.

I let go of the rock that held me in place and tumbled down the side of the pit. I dug my heels into the ground, barely catching myself from hitting the burning car. Then, I caught sight of Jace. I jumped forward in front of it. He came down full force towards me.

I called unto my beasts as I tumbled forward, head over heels. His heavy boots vibrated on the ground. Coming up on my knees, I turned and glared at him, baring my fangs, my fists extended in front of me. He sneered, his lower lip curled up over his fangs. And then he ran at me. I jumped up and threw a snap kick, connecting with his chest. It was enough to stop him, but not enough to hurl him back.

I fought to control my beasts as they came forward. I landed on the ground. He kicked me square in the chest, knocking me off my feet. My face caught the side of a rock. Blood trickled from the gash in my cheek. I struggled to get back up. Jace's foot slammed down hard on my chest, sliding down to my throat. I grabbed onto his boot, heel and toe, and pushed against the full weight of his body.

Jace disappeared. My eyes rolled backwards. An unknown assailant threw Jace against the dirt wall. I stared up at the moonless sky; its darkness permeated the Pit. I bolted to my feet and turned to see a figure in the darkness. Jace bore down upon Warrant.

"I saved you, and you fight me!" Jace screamed, his face inches from Warrant's.

He slammed Warrant against the dirt wall and then threw him across the Pit. He started after Warrant.

I yelled at him, "Hey, let's finish this!"

Jace glared at Warrant, and then at me. "Somebody get that motherfucker out of here!"

He pointed at Warrant.

The sound of rock and dirt filled my ears. When I looked back in Warrant's direction, two figures were upon him. It was David and Woodrow. I glanced back up at Tristan and Robert, who stood on the edge of the pit, their faces grim. They were ready to jump in here at a moment's notice. Dirt crept out from under their feet while they stood ready for attack.

I turned just as Jace grabbed and pulled me into him. "You want me, bitch? Let's go."

His eyes fumed, a fury deep within. I snapped at him, but my teeth caught nothing but air. He sneered. He pulled me completely off of my feet, and then hurled me across the Pit again. I slammed into rocky terrain, anger rising within me. The curse coursed through my body, alerting my beasts to take over. I tumbled to the ground.

They took the pain away when I struck rock. It didn't hurt and it didn't sting. I felt defiant, strong, and confident. I stood. Something was different, something I hadn't felt before. I glanced at the side view mirror of the car next to me, noticing the changes that took place in my body.

I stood before Jace, my muscles massive. My fingers elongated into long and sharp claws. The bone within my face grew into the wolf snout, setting my eyes deeper into my face. The hue of my eyes had changed to a yellowish-golden color. Tattered and torn, the clothes from my body hung in places where the wolf had taken over. The mass of muscle had torn my pants from the knee down.. The sleeves had torn from my shoulders all the way down my arms. Rips across my shirt streaked my bosom and my back. Cold air seeped in through the shredded clothing. I stared into the mirror. The wolf had not taken over my skin, the vampire had. The werewolf hair was absent.

I turned my attention back to him, glaring at him.

He smiled. "Oh, that's good. I knew you'd make a good hybrid, but to know that your lovers changed you themselves, that's good. It'll be even better when I kill you myself."

He bared his teeth at me.

I ran at him, jumped up, and kicked him in the chest. He flew back, hit the dirt wall behind him, tumbled, and then came up even more pissed than before. I snarled at him and lunged again. This time I connected with his face. He snapped back to the ground and struck his head on a rock. I came down to the earth upon my knees. I drew in the scent of his blood. He stood.

The beasts in me hungered for his meat. Anger rose in his face. Jace's eyes darkened. His jaw tightened. Then, he kicked at me. I slid underneath, caught his leg, and drove my foot deep into his groin. He locked up and started to double over, a wild sound escaping his throat. I continued to hold onto his leg while I delivered another kick, this time to his abdomen. A kick to his face jerked him forward.

I let go of his leg and spun backwards to my right to deliver a spinning rear kick to his face, my heel connecting with his mouth. A tooth snapped in his mouth. I spun out. My left fist and elbow connected with his sternum as I came face-to-face with him. My right fist came straight up with an uppercut under his chin and drove his head back. Then, I extended my fingers, drove my claws through the bottom of his head, and shoved them in harder, impaling him. I grabbed onto him before he could stagger back, lurched with him above the fire and dropped him into it.

Turning my back to the fire, I fell back down to the floor of the Pit, glancing at the spectators above. His shrill cries sounded throughout the forest. Somebody attacked me from behind and drove me into the dirt wall beyond the car. I spun around.

It was Warrant, whom I held dear to my heart. Startled and astonished by the attack, I surrendered, afraid that I could not fight him back. I curled up into a ball and tumbled to the earth a few feet from the car. Warrant came at me again. The beasts fought for survival but found it difficult to battle him as well. He pulled me to my feet, my body limp beneath his grip. Robert and Tristan wrenched him away from me. I stood and stared at the fight that ensued. Robert and Tristan buried Warrant beneath their fists. He fought back. Soon, he weakened.

My heart hurt, my stomach churned. I fell to the ground, unable to do anything. I watched in horror while my son and my mate broke every bone in Warrant's body. He continued to fight until the end, and then was thrown atop the other vehicle, into the fire.

§

I later learned that Jace had made Warrant into a hybrid the night his head was nearly taken off. Though the wolf in him was strong, he fought to take control back over his own body.

Warrant had fought his own battle. He could no longer fight the other monster. That creature had tried to reveal itself and to overcome the wolf—to destroy it. Tonight, Warrant let it take partial control and allowed it to destroy him for he would not live with the curse Jace had put upon him.

I had yet to learn the unknown creature deep inside my body…the other creature Warrant bestowed upon me. It hid, lurking, waiting for that right opportunity to emerge—to escape and reveal to me what it was.

Sometime during the night David and Woodrow had disappeared, and fights ensued between the other creatures, the natural enemies of one another. I held my tears for Warrant back the best I could as Tristan and Robert escorted me away from the Pit.

Once home, I laid in bed and cried in Tristan's arms. He had been right—he had known something was wrong with Warrant—but because the wolf's scent was stronger, he could not detect the creature beneath. He knew that I still cared for Warrant, so he held me. He held me and stroked my hair.

"I'm sorry, Crystal," he whispered. "I really am. Warrant was a good man. He was proud of what you did tonight. And, he was thankful for your help."

Tears of blood left a trail on my face and coated his chest.

CLOSURE

"Mom, I need to talk to you. It's important," Robert said.

Robert took me into the den. Moonlight wafted in through the blinds, illuminating sections of the room at a time. We sat down in the wicker chairs opposite each other.

Still dressed in his Deputy uniform, Robert sighed. "We got all of your paperwork from Vital Records, your marriage license and your birth certificate. Rebecca and I are still waiting on our paperwork for ourselves and the kids."

"Oh, okay. Thank you, hon."

He removed the papers from the inside pocket of his jacket and unfolded them. Leaning forward, he handed me my birth certificate. I skimmed through it as he unfolded two more documents.

"Mom, there's two marriage licenses here."

I glanced up at him from behind the papers. "Two? Why are there two?"

Robert peered up at me, his brows creased. "You know, I'd always thought Chris was my dad. At least, that's what you used to always tell me."

"What are you talking about?" I was confused now.

"Well, the birth certificates we originally had here in the house didn't have dad's name listed on them, but these ones do. By chance, do you ever remember anybody else before Chris?" He cocked his head, watching me, his eyes droopy.

I figured he was just tired, but I could have been wrong.

"No, I don't. Hell, I barely remember anything before I was stuck in that damn cell."

"That man that was killed in the bar with you that night—that wasn't my father."

"What?" I rubbed my forehead. This was bullshit. I needed to remember everything. I couldn't deal with this anymore.

"He wasn't Jennifer's dad either. He was your second husband. You were married before him."

"You know I never really looked at the birth certificates until your disappearance, and that was when I noticed dad's name wasn't on the document. I never thought much about it until now," he said, gloomily.

"Jesus," I sighed, leaning back in the chair.

"Yeah, and Chris was your second husband. I asked around. Everybody says dad left us early, not long after Jennifer was born. Apparently, he decided we weren't good enough for him." He raised his eyes to me, searching mine.

I leaned forward, touching his shoulder. "I'm sorry, Robert. I wish I could remember. I feel horrible."

"That's okay. It's not your fault." He reached up and took my hand. He held it gently in his.

"You've been through a lot. We don't have any hard feelings. Jennifer and I understand."

"Thank you, honey. That means a lot to me." I squeezed his hand back, tears welling in my eyes.

We looked up at each other.

"Yeah, I guess Chris was kind of an ass. Apparently, he cheated on you a couple of times." He eyed me curiously, as if waiting for a reaction.

"Yeah, well, that's one of the few things I remember."

"It's funny—we always seem to remember the bad times more than we remember the good."

"Yeah, it sucks."

A faint smile crossed his face. His grip tightened. "A few people said he deserved what he got."

"Well, I wish I could remember so I could say the same." I laughed. Then I looked down at the floor, swallowing hard.

"You know, I made it my mission to find you, dead or alive. I wasn't going to stop until then."

Our eyes met.

Tears welled in his eyes. "I guess that's the main reason I became a cop."

I sniffled, fighting the urge to cry.

"Thanks. You're a good son." I enclosed my other hand around our joined hands.

"Jennifer's been a mess ever since you disappeared." Droplets ran down his cheeks. "She's been through a lot, too. She needs you right now."

"I know. And I hope I can make it up to both of you."

"I tried to take care of her the best that I could," he replied.

"I'm sure you did. Thank you," I whispered back. I leaned forward, kissed him on the forehead, and embraced him.

"I love you, Mom."

"I love you, too."

Silent cries trembled within him. That was all it took. I began to weep, reveling in the fact I had a family again, whether it be with or without their father. We cried and held onto each other for a moment. When he finally broke the hold, he wiped the tears from his face.

"I'm going to do whatever it takes to not lose you again." He shook his finger at me, smiling.

"Yes, sir." I sat back in my chair.

"And if Tristan ever does anything to hurt you, I'll kill him—for good."

The look on his face was stern, almost ice cold.

"He's a good man," I said.

Robert nodded. "Yeah, he is. Regardless of his past, he's been good to you. Good to all of us. I wasn't sure about him at first."

I smiled. Robert reopened the marriage licenses.

He stood up, looking at the papers again. "I wonder, if you heard a name, do you think it might release some memory—anything at all?"

"Well, I guess I can try…"

"Wayne Joseph Devereaux?" He looked down at me, quizzically, hoping for a reaction.

"No, that doesn't sound…"

I thought back in time, remembering only one Wayne in my life. That man was a werewolf, but he had also been my captor. Could he have possibly been my children's father? I couldn't swallow. I stared up at my son, praying that he was not. If he was, then I had to know why he held me captive.

"Mom, do you know him?" Robert knelt down in front of me. "Are you okay?"

Chills ran up my spine. My life would have been much simpler had Chris been the father, but now it was confirmed he was not. I cringed at the thought it had been Wayne. With the thought of him being their father, I suddenly remembered the pictures I had found in my lingerie drawer. I immediately ran up the stairs to my room. Robert called after me. On my dresser were the two pictures. I grabbed them, recognizing both men in the photos. The husband I recognized was Chris—my second husband, my children's stepfather. The other man was a young Wayne…my captor. His eyes were distinctly familiar. *He* was my first husband—my children's father.

Also From
Cryptic Bones Publishing

Bad Elements:
The Hybrid

THE THIRD INSTALLMENT IN THE DARK AND
TWISTED BAD ELEMENTS SERIES, CRYSTAL
DRAGON!

FOLLOW CRYSTAL ON HER
HORRIFYING DISCOVERY OF THE TRUTH
BEHIND HER CAPTIVITY!

COMING SOON

Also From
Cryptic Bones Publishing

THE SHADOW OF EVIL

WHEN GOOD BEFRIENDS
THE SHADOW OF EVIL,

WHERE WILL YOUR FAITH LIE?
WITH GOD OR THE DEVIL HIMSELF?

COMING SOON

ABOUT THE AUTHOR

LYNN MULLICAN was born and raised in Phoenix, Arizona, where she currently resides with her husband and three children. She has woven her fascination with the paranormal into written works including short stories, dramatic plays, poetry, and full length novels. In *Bad Elements: Blood for Blood*, she incorporates years of knowledge in self defense and martial arts. Lynn began writing in her childhood, and to this day, her family has continued to support her dream, and has inspired several different ideas for current and upcoming new stories.